# The Curious Case of the Whispering Corpse

# The Curious Case of the Whispering Corpse

## Lady Astley, Monster Hunter

### BOOK 1

Rebecca Gage

**Publisher's Cataloging-in-Publication data**
Gage, Rebecca, author
Lady Astley, Monster Hunter : The Curious Case of the Whispering Corpse / Rebecca Gage.

ISBN: 979-8-9880888-1-3 (paperback)
ISBN: 979-8-9880888-0-6 (digital)

1. Fantasy—History—Fiction. 2. Steampunk—Fiction. 3. England—Social life and customs—19th century—Fiction. I. Gage, Rebecca. II. Lady Astley, Monster Hunter: The Curious Case of the Whispering Corpse.

Printed in the United States of America

10 9 8 7 6 5 4 3 2 1

Cover design: L1graphics
Design: Suzanne Uchytil

*The first one is for me*

# Trigger Warnings

This book contains mild language and some depictions of fantasy violence, murder, and sensuality.

# Chapter 1

The corpse lay sprawled on the gaslit cobblestones. No Tesla lamps hummed above the narrow opening to the Whitechapel alley. Lady Charlotte Astley pulled her cape tighter as though it could protect her from the miasma of misery pervading this London slum. Moulding detritus from water-stained crates slicked the stones under her feet and the fetid odor of humanity assaulted her senses. But the most noticeable characteristic of her surroundings was the deafening silence. Even the rats were absent. No corpse ever had that effect—unless it was a supernatural one.

Despite the obvious impropriety of Charlotte already standing so near to a murdered body in this part of town, she stepped closer, leaning over the deceased.

"Why does 'e look so much...deader than usual?"

Charlotte turned and gave the speaker, a bearded, dark-haired policeman, a flat stare. "Because he *is*. I don't mean to be rude,

Mr. Singh, but I require silence. This man"—she gestured to the corpse—"is trying to tell us something."

"Righ'. Clues an' the like." He nodded so vigorously his blue custodian helmet nearly toppled off his head.

"No," she said, kneeling, her skirts rustling against the pavement. "Literally." She leaned down, bringing her ear closer to the barely moving lips of the dead man.

Behind her, Mr. Singh's shoes ground against the stones as he, too, leaned over the body—though Charlotte suspected it was merely to gawk.

Cold air exited the corpse's lungs and brushed Charlotte's ear, sending goose pimples down her neck.

"Holy," the body whispered. "Holy, holy."

A chill pulsed through her blood.

"Tha's a new one," Singh murmured, retreating and making the sign of the cross. Charlotte couldn't blame him for his unease. The sight of a soulless body—ashen, the whites of the eyes completely swallowing the iris and pupil—could cause anyone to quail. Unfortunately, it was a sight she was rapidly becoming familiar with. Only two months as the Royal Monster Hunter to Her Majesty Queen Victoria, and this was already the third soul-sucked casualty on Charlotte's watch.

She glanced at the victim again. The man's oriental brocade fabric was slowly absorbing the shallow puddle he was resting in. A small collection of pins were clustered along his lapel: a minuscule sun embedded with cheap paste-diamonds, a poorly made green horseshoe, a leaping fox, and a few large holes from where other pins had been ripped. Small spatters of ink stained his fingers, which could be significant, but Charlotte herself often spilled ink when writing letters. Tiny vampire fangs protruded over his lower lip. The man's dark curls and sculpted face would have made him the darling of many a debutante this Season. During his vampiric afterlife, his brown skin would have looked as if it had been dusted with an opalescent sheen, but now it was grey, dull, and lifeless. He looked young, but with vampires it was hard to tell. Whatever his age, the outcome would be the same—without a soul, the body would expire within a few days. She shook her head and sighed. *What a waste of afterlife.*

Soulless bodies may have been familiar to her, but they'd never whispered that particular word. Nervous excitement wound her up like the springs of a jack-in-the-box, as it always did when she was one step closer to solving a puzzle.

Charlotte stood, brushed off as much dirt as possible, then pulled out her telescriber. This particular model, a birthday present she had purchased for herself, was reminiscent of a palm-sized type-writer with tiny brass alphanumeric buttons and an enclosed ribbon of paper. Capable of receiving and sending messages as well as notes, the device was quickly becoming an indispensable investigative tool.

She pressed the keys and added the word "holy" to her small collection of words from soulless victims. With tonight's addition, there were three: "Ink," from a shifter in Kensington, and from a French vampire expatriate, and "cloud" from a Northumberland gytrash who had been visiting his cousins. Every human body the soul-eater had consumed ended up an empty husk. However, when the creature consumed supernatural souls, its victims each murmured one word over and over like a dented gramophone record—at least until the bodies themselves expired. The victims could never be revived and the bodies decomposed shortly after. Prior to her appointment, the victims had been disposed of quietly and quickly, without official death reports. With this sudden influx of white-eyed corpses, and due to Charlotte's vigilant watch, hasty burials had been impossible.

Charlotte's lips pressed into a tight line as she fingered the tele-scriber's tiny buttons. To this vampire, what did *holy* mean? Scanning the scenery for anything that might be considered holy, her eyes fell on the gothic steeple of St. Mary's Church barely visible in the distance. Did *holy* describe the location? Did the word lead to the next victim? Or was it just a reflection of the man's last thought before he was killed?

She shifted her weight. For that matter, where had the soul-eater, whatever it was, come from? Why would it emerge now, practically a decade after the Origination? Why not appear ten years ago when all the other supernaturals had?

How could she stop it before it consumed another victim?

"Is it a new supernatural, miss?" Mr. Singh's gravelly voice cut through the foggy alley. "It's not another Origination. Can' be." Fear laced his words. "Tha' was a one-time event." The man sounded like he was trying to convince himself, his deep olive skin turning ashen.

Charlotte's heart chilled as her own dark memories of the Origination rose to the surface of her mind. She swallowed them back and punched descriptions of the victim and crime scene into her telescriber, suppressing a shudder. Then she put the device back in her satchel.

"No." She hoped he didn't notice the catch in her throat. "The creature most likely appeared when all the others did. It has probably been hiding." But why?

Shuffling boots scraped the pavement, breaking the silence. A small huddle of people gathered on the cobblestones at the opening of the alley. Her heart stuttered. Crowds of any size could be unpredictable.

"It's not another Origination," she said, a little louder. Blazing suns, it would be catastrophic if she were wrong. She'd be sacked for certain, not to mention she'd have to witness the fear and chaos and countless deaths that would ensue.

"Back inside, please." Mr. Singh hardly raised his voice, but it echoed off the brick walls of Whitechapel Road. He waved his arms wide, attempting to herd the bystanders into their buildings. A few faces peering from windows dipped back behind curtains and walls—dead bodies in the streets were nothing new in these parts, supernatural or not, and curiosity about them faded quickly. The people on the street shuffled toward their buildings, but some lingered in warped door frames, almost as if afraid of being swallowed by the dark of their own homes.

Charlotte glanced back down at the whispering body. Was someone waiting for *him* to come home? She swallowed again, dismayed by yet another loss of an innocent person. She imagined the heart-wrenching scene when the police located his family and gave them the horrible news.

"Lady Astley," said a refined but nasally voice behind her, cutting into her thoughts. "How is it you are always to be found next to a dead supernatural? Do you usually frequent vampire attacks?"

Charlotte closed her eyes and drew a fortifying breath. *Not him. Give me a rampaging alpha on the full moon or an army of redcaps to fight. Anything but him.*

She smoothed her outer corset, plastered a smile on her face, then turned. "Baron St. Bridgeman." *Blazing suns, that was a mouthful.* "Where else would you expect to find someone of my caliber?" She lifted her chin a fraction. "I am, after all, the best." The blatant pride would have caused her mother to blanch—heaven rest her soul—but she couldn't help it. No other monster hunter in London had reached her numbers. Plus, no other monster hunter had her unwavering morals. Many arrested supernaturals indiscriminately, a practice which Charlotte was striving to eradicate. Thanks to a healthy dose of charm and some minor bribery, she was now always the first monster hunter to get notified of important supernatural occurrences; if she didn't keep that edge, human and supernatural tensions would bubble over, and then there'd be more than enough bodies to keep everyone busy.

St. Bridgeman's lips curled into something more snarl than smile. His mustache, clearly grown to make him look older than his twenty-five years, drooped over the corners of his mouth, hiding some of his sneer's effectiveness. Though the length of his mustache needed consideration, St. Bridgeman was nothing if not irritatingly precise. The tiny pinstripes marched the length of his suit, and his glacier-blue eyes peered from beneath short, even sandy-colored eyebrows. In his hand was the leather-bound notebook he consistently carried with him.

"Though with monster-hunting being a relatively new profession, it is hard to accurately assess success," Charlotte continued, smoothing her gloves. "And I hate to be a stickler, but this is not a vampire attack. You'll notice that while this body's pallor does mimic vampire assaults, there are no puncture wounds along any of the arterial points on the body. Nor are the pupils dilated from the vampiric allurement charm. Plus, vampires are not cannibalistic."

"Ahh, tha' makes sense," Mr. Singh said in awed understanding, earning him a scowl from St. Bridgeman.

Charlotte adjusted the goggles resting on the brim of her silk top hat. "If you'd prefer to work with the amateurs, Baron, they'll be here in an hour—possibly sooner, judging by your early arrival."

St. Bridgeman's eyes narrowed.

"No? Then you can remain here while I continue my professional investigation." Charlotte flashed him her most winning smile. The stiffening of his posture told her she had hit her mark, as usual. Baron St. Bridgeman was not necessarily a dangerous man, but the ideology he represented discomfited her. The best way to deal with prejudiced fools was to keep them off balance, and she took pride in doing just that.

St. Bridgeman's reputation and connections may have been popular among the upper crust, but here on the street, it was savvy that mattered, something Charlotte had in spades. Even so, a small twinge of guilt nettled inside her as Aunt Hespa's words came back to her. *No one likes arrogant, demanding, ruthless people.*

It was the last description that really rankled Charlotte. One *had* to be relentless, possibly even ruthless, in pursuit of the truth.

When St. Bridgeman still didn't respond, she said, "To what do we owe the pleasure? Am I to take it your stance on supernaturals has changed and you are here because you truly care about this man's death?"

Mr. Singh coughed loudly into his hand, a vain attempt to cover a smile. St. Bridgeman's eyes shot daggers at the policeman. The poor man sobered promptly, and he took a few discreet steps backward.

"This—dead creature is evidence," St. Bridgeman said, a little too loudly, as if trying to be convincing.

"Of a murder? Obviously." Charlotte folded her arms and grimaced. "This was not a natural death."

"It is evidence of supernaturals' inherently dangerous nature." St. Bridgeman's mouth tightened, and he glared at the body on the ground as if it were horse droppings he'd narrowly avoided stepping in. "I'm here to garner civilian support for my bill. This vampire will bolster my point."

The muscles in Charlotte's neck twitched. His bill was going to be presented in the House of Lords in two weeks. He was trying to prove that supernaturals were dangerous and must be tracked. It was common knowledge St. Bridgeman had been working on this bill with an almost angelic zeal, aiming for the identification, registration, tracking, and, in her opinion, prejudiced segregation of all supernaturals. Charlotte certainly did not share this fanaticism, and, surprisingly, neither did his mother, Baroness St. Bridgeman—a crusader in her own right, if the gossip was to be believed.

"I beg your pardon, but do you mean to hold a political rally in Whitechapel? At this time of night? Odd choice and not particularly respectful of the deceased." Charlotte gestured to the whispering body then raised her arm to include the surrounding ramshackle buildings. She could not even begin to divine the inner workings of St. Bridgeman's brain.

"You misunderstand me, Lady Astley," he said, his jaw clenched. "Information about the soul-eater's victims would lend more than enough credence to my platform. There have been enough human victims to prove this." He flipped open his book and ran a finger along the length of the page. "Six victims in total—"

"Ten."

St. Bridgeman blinked.

"The police have confirmed the Mayfair death to be the work of the soul-eater, and with this poor man, the total is ten. Supernaturals are still human and should be treated as such. But please, continue."

"The fact that there are so many deaths by this soul-eater only helps prove my point: supernaturals are dangerous."

Charlotte knit her gloved fingers together. "I've merely proven your prejudice."

"How can you not be pleased with his death? You're a monster hunter. You're a traitor to your profession and to humanity."

Heat flared through her. "This man was *not* a monster."

St. Bridgeman sneered. "It is unnatural—a hunter who sympathizes with her prey."

Charlotte's muscles tightened from her jaw to her toes. She'd been called unnatural before, along with many other things—it was simply nastier coming from this man's mouth.

Mr. Singh's eyes widened and his lips pinched shut, pulling his dark wiry mustache down. Somehow, seeing his reaction to St. Bridgeman's vitriol calmed her just enough that she could control what she said next.

She cleared her throat. "I don't like to repeat myself so please be attentive." St. Bridgeman opened his mouth but Charlotte held up a hand. "I find and bring supernatural *criminals* to justice. It is one's choices that make a monster or a man."

St. Bridgeman's already sour look darkened. Charlotte suspected he was sorely tempted to roll his eyes. She found herself fantasizing about being called to a crime scene where *he* was the lifeless body.

Onlookers were gathering again, perhaps drawn by the raised voices.

"I report to the Pack, the Coven, and the Crown, who have all asked for my specific skill set in dealing with rogue supernatural members of London. If doing my duty is being a hypocrite, then I am proud to be one." Charlotte projected this last bit more for the bystanders. If accruing "civilian support" for his bill was St. Bridgeman's intent, then Charlotte wanted all sides equally represented.

The wary-looking Mr. Singh leaned forward, clearing his throat before his usually chipper voice stammered. "Sh-she *is* a fine detective, sir."

St. Bridgeman whirled, and the man shrank back again.

"Couldn't have put it better myself." Charlotte beamed at the constable, who puffed his chest out ever so slightly. "Mr. Singh, if there are potential witnesses around I'd like to speak with them. Could you please make sure they don't all disappear back inside?"

Mr. Singh nodded brusquely and spun on his heel, the pride in his job apparent even from his retreating frame.

A muscle ticked on the side of St. Bridgeman's face. For a moment, Charlotte lamented the loss of what could have been attractive looks if there had been a drastic difference in his personality.

"There's one thing about your bill that you've overlooked, your lordship," Charlotte said. "Any dangerous supernaturals are *already* being tracked—by me and the other hunters." In spite of her words, though, her stomach soured. With these soul-eater attacks increasing and public opinions of supernaturals weighing heavily on the side of fear...Blazes. He might actually get that idiotic bill passed.

St. Bridgman stepped closer, and for the first time that night, she felt a modicum of fear in his presence. His voice was low, threatening. "For now. You may want to reevaluate your ability to catch this monster before you lose your standing."

The ground fell away as his meaning sank in. Did he have the power to take away her position? Perhaps. If the other members of his ridiculous Council for Humanity club joined forces, they could create some serious problems for her, and all of London could suffer the consequences.

The pit in her stomach hardened into resolve. *Blast this man to the sun and back.* Her nostrils flared as she took steadying breaths.

"I would think the more pertinent point is that if I fail to apprehend this monster, more people will die." She clutched her skirts so her fists wouldn't fly at his face. "I must apologize for my poor taste in allowing myself to be lured into a political discussion at the scene of a murder. I'd like to now focus on the purpose of tonight: catching the creature who ripped this man's soul from his body. So if you'll excuse me"—she stepped around St. Bridgeman and his tomato-red face, "I need to speak with these people. One of them might actually have seen something."

Charlotte squared her shoulders and followed after Mr. Singh, pointedly ignoring St. Bridgeman and his ridiculously overgrown mustache. Her heart fell as she heard St. Bridgeman's footsteps clipping along behind hers. It was going to be a very long night.

# Chapter 2

Following Mr. Singh to the end of the alley wasn't difficult, though it was uncomfortable. The cracks in the poorly placed cobblestones could have seriously injured an ankle if they hadn't been filled with rubbish and layers of mud. From the sounds St. Bridgeman was making behind her, he wasn't enjoying the sight or stench either. Lines of wash criss-crossed above them, resembling a cobweb so pitiful its owner had abandoned it rather than finish.

Even in the short forty-foot walk, Charlotte caught a few pairs of pale-yellow eyes reflecting the moonlight as they peered at her through windows. So there were supernaturals living here. She made a mental note to circle back and talk to that community in this area. They might be more willing than anyone else to speak to her.

Voices from what sounded like a large group of people echoed along the walls and she picked up her pace. She ducked beneath a clothesline laden with laundry that looked as if washing had done nothing.

Ahead of her, Mr. Singh's helmet bobbed above a growing gathering of Whitechapel residents. Snatches of his voice rose to the surface of the clamor, only to be pulled under again by the flood of voices.

"You've got to do something," someone shouted.

"We're not safe," another voice shrilled from the back of the group.

Charlotte steadied herself and, after pressing a hand against her dark brown hair, strode into the fray and stopped beside the harassed policeman.

A quick glance behind her revealed that St. Bridgeman had already pulled out his leather notebook, clearly intent on staying. Just marvelous.

Charlotte pressed her lips together in a tight smile. "Mr. Singh." Her voice cut through the tide of noises. "What seems to be the problem?"

The policeman's now-sweaty face relaxed in relief. Before he could answer, a woman with a pointy chin and sharp eyes pointed at Charlotte. "What are you going to do about the vampire?"

Charlotte nodded, grateful for the easy question. "We'll remove the body as soon as we can, most likely within the next twelve hours at the most." The police would presumably relocate the body in two or three, but it was best to set expectations low and reap better opinions along the way.

The woman shook her head, now jabbing her finger toward the church steeple and alley. "No. The one that ate the dead one."

Charlotte bit back a sigh and closed her eyes, hoping to find more patience. Sometimes having logic and common sense was a terrible burden. There were so many things wrong with that woman's sentence. *They are simply scared. They are simply scared.*

She pressed her fingers together and kept her voice level. "It wasn't a vampire. It is a creature we do not have a name for yet." A lie, but saying "soul-eater" wouldn't help the situation.

"What?" The woman gasped and took a step backward as if Charlotte had struck her. "A new one?"

Charlotte paused, her breath tight in her throat. Last week two people had been trampled and nearly killed at a pro-human rally in the park because someone had thought a woman's Italian greyhound was a werewolf. While there were no pets in sight now, the unease and suspicion in this neighborhood was as pungent as kerosene and just as volatile as what she'd seen at that rally.

A man with a knit cap and thick brown overcoat spoke up. "How can there be a new supernatural?"

Another voice ricocheted against the bricks. "It's another Origination!"

Loud fear rippled through the crowd.

"It's not another Origination," Charlotte shouted, hoping the words were as true as she wanted them to be.

She glanced at St. Bridgeman. The look of satisfaction on his face was as ugly as his mustache. His raised nasally voice scraped against the cinder blocks. "Supernaturals are dangerous!"

Many humans in the crowd nodded, and the few identifiable supernaturals peered around anxiously as the mood shifted. One woman with olive skin, dark curly hair, and even darker eyes held Charlotte's gaze. The woman bit her lips nervously, small fang indentations making the poor woman's agitation more pronounced. She pulled her ragged shawl tighter and shifted her weight back and forth as she eyed her neighbors.

Before Charlotte could think of what to say to calm them, St. Bridgeman continued. "The supernatural population is violent and uncontrollable." His words acted like a call to arms, and the crowd—at least the human part—edged closer to him. St. Bridgeman moved through them stepping onto a crate.

Charlotte's mouth went dry. The walls of Whitechapel seemed to press inward.

"These creatures need to be identified." St. Bridgeman's eyes swept across the throng. "The monster responsible for this vampire death has been killing for the last three years."

Charlotte almost choked. "Years? You mean months."

St. Bridgeman held up his notebook. "I have proof."

Charlotte thought for a moment, then crossed her arms. "If you have proof of three years' worth of murders at the hands of this creature, Baron, then why have you done nothing about it? Why haven't you come forward and presented your findings to the police to help with the investigation?"

St. Bridgeman spluttered momentarily before quieting as a murmur ran through the crowd. The crate creaked and shuddered, giving way slightly beneath him, and he faltered, but still pressed on.

"I had to be sure it was the same creature, and this," —he gestured wildly to the vampire corpse down the alley—"is proof."
The crate caved in. St. Bridgeman stumbled down, righted himself, and nearly slipped on some damp newspapers. In an attempt to regain his composure, St. Bridgeman motioned to his notebook once more before pointing at Charlotte. "You see," he barked. "Even this so-called monster hunter is leading you on. She's trying to distract you from the true problem of the growing deluge of supernaturals!" He waggled the notebook at Charlotte, then, tucking it back into his pocket, sent her a glare that dared her to argue with him.

Her chest tightened with anger and more than a little fear. He was hiding information in that notebook, information that she and the police needed. She was certain. He may be wrong about the supernaturals, but Charlotte knew St. Bridgeman at least *thought* he had proof.

"I want to protect humans from monsters," St. Bridgeman said, turning in a circle. He stabbed a finger at the group. "If it's not the bloodsuckers it will be the mongrels."

Charlotte eyed the murmuring crowd. She needed to stop this nonsense before St. Bridgeman gained too much of a foothold. Hang on, was that a pitchfork in the background? Where had that come from? She snorted. *If we add some torches, I'll have a medieval witch hunt on my hands.*

"*Here's* one of them!"

A thud, followed by a grunt made Charlotte whirl around. Someone had thrown a man onto the stones, and the crowd was parting, forming a small circle around him. The man pulled himself onto his knees, then held his hands up placatingly, his eyes reflecting the yellow lamplight. A werewolf.

"Luther!" A woman and two children shoved their way to the edge of the growing circle, terror pressing the woman's features into tight lines.

The man's eyes pled with Charlotte. Someone spit and it landed on his back.

Anger prickled. Charlotte raced into the opening, grabbing the werewolf's work-worn hands and pulled him to his feet. Enough was enough.

"What about *them?*" Charlotte shouted at the crowd, gesturing to who she assumed was the man's family. The children were clutching their mother's skirt. "Who will protect *them?*"

The crowd was stunned into silence for a moment, and Charlotte plowed on. "The creature *was* at first killing only humans, but now it is hunting supernaturals. *No one* is safe." She knew she was playing a dangerous game, possibly inciting panic, but she would rather the fear be directed towards the soul-eater than each other. She circled, making eye contact with everyone she could, even those peering from their windows. The group fidgeted and glanced at each other. She saw more fear than anger in their eyes now, but they weren't scared beyond what she hoped would allow a sliver of reason.

"Supernaturals are people—" she started.

"Humans don't eat other people," St. Bridgeman retorted, each word slicing through the street.

"Well, erm, tha's not always the case," Mr. Singh said. "There was this one case in Bethnal green—"

"One o' them killed my brother," someone said, ignoring the policeman.

"And my sister," another cried from the back.

"My parents were killed by vampires." Charlotte made sure her words carried, not fighting the timbre of grief in her voice. "We have *all* lost someone—humans and supernaturals. Now it's time to look beyond the past and see our neighbors." She pulled the werewolf closer, then released him into the arms of his wife and children, who quickly and quietly led him away. "Our friends."

The crowd, though obviously frightened, was silent, and Mr. Singh started to disperse them, encouraging them to return home. Before they could go far, though, a guttural moan cut through the alley, and everyone froze.

Shuffling feet crept toward the gathering. Trembling whispers sliced through the silence, and fear rippled through the crowd like static electricity before an explosion.

The moaning and shuffling continued.

"Everyone back inside," Charlotte said, but the crowd only moved a few steps backward, their eyes searching wildly for the source of the moans. With a flip of her wrist, Charlotte unlatched her Tesla ray gun and it hummed, charging to full power. "Mr. Singh, make sure they get inside."

Mr. Singh hardly needed to do anything—the people couldn't scurry towards their homes fast enough.

A large, shambling shadow cut across the alleyway, revealing the creature's progress. Shuffle, thud, moan. Whatever it was, it was slow, but it was almost here.

The thought crossed her mind that this could be the soul-eater, but that didn't feel right. If *this* was the soul-eater, how had something so slow managed to kill so many powerful supernaturals?

Charlotte glanced around and behind her. More than a dozen stupidly curious people lingered near their doorways. The baron had retreated behind a pile of crates, but he was watching intently. Blast.

"St. Bridgeman, get inside," Charlotte shouted. "Mr. Singh, keep the area clear. We don't want anyone getting hurt. I'll see if it can be reasoned with."

Mr. Singh nodded his assent.

Charlotte stepped forward. Suddenly St. Bridgeman was at her heels. A sudden burst of courage?

Shuffle, thud, moan.

The thing reached the corner. Charlotte leveled the ray, squeezing the trigger, ready to fire. Then immediately lowered it.

A rotund figure in a well-cut suit rounded the corner, stepping into the streetlamp's yellow light. Thinning mouse-colored hair curled around his large ears, and his egg-shaped body tottered on unsteady legs. His flushed face sported two uneven fangs.

The vampire staggered farther into the alley and closer to Charlotte. He vamp-misted, his corporeal form transforming into a dark cloud, and lifted a few inches off the ground. The mist hopped, and the vampire solidified again. The process repeated itself every few steps.

Charlotte rose from her crouch. "He's drunk."

He must have been visiting the blood-harlots on the docks. What was blazing wrong with the monthly supply distributed by the Royal Clinic? And why did it have to be *now* that he came stumbling home? Though, judging by his fine clothes, he was as lost as he was drunk.

The vampire misted, bobbed again, then thudded down fully solid. As he walked, his bulbous nose and shiny pate gave him away long before his bristly mustache did.

Charlotte closed her eyes and put a hand to her forehead. "Lionel, not again."

Lionel Pillingsworth, one of the Coven's most bacchanalian vampires stumbled on the uneven cobblestones. He couldn't even mist properly, though that didn't stop him from trying. He misted again, and this time Charlotte was close enough to hear the hiccup from the half-vaporous vamp. With a thud, Lionel landed back on his feet.

The crowd forming again behind Mr. Singh murmured, and a few people moved to get a closer look. The policeman spread his arms wide in an attempt to block them.

"Bloodsucker," one of them hissed.

"Watch out for them biters!"

"This is exactly what we're trying to prevent," St. Bridgeman shouted, his eyes flashing with excitement at this opportunity. "The Council for Humanity seeks to keep creatures like this out of our streets and out of London. You need to know who your neighbors are. You," he pointed at the gathering crowd, "might be next."

"You're right, Baron," Charlotte piped up. "Let's get to know our neighbors." She stepped closer to the vampire, putting an arm around his shoulder. "Allow me to introduce Mr. Lionel Pillingsworth. He'd no sooner hurt a fly."

Lionel chose that moment to give a huge yawn, showing his uneven but elongated teeth. Charlotte wanted to put her head in her hands. *You're not helping, Lionel.*

"Did you see those fangs? He'll bite us all!" Baron St. Bridgeman said, his face reddening in anger beneath his light brown hair. "This *thing* should not be roaming freely. Supernaturals should be tagged like the animals they are."

"I know how it looks," Charlotte said, turning to face each member of the crowd, "but you've got it all wrong. He's not dangerous."

"Of course he is," St. Bridgeman said, his nasal tones echoing through the alley. "I'll show you all."

Some of the crowd were now brandishing makeshift weapons and dark expressions. Blazing suns, this was going to be bad. One woman was holding a broom with a sharpened handle. St Bridgeman grabbed it and strode towards Lionel.

The vampire, unable to stand upright anymore, lurched forward, his mouth open wide. In the process of stumbling, he crossed the distance between himself and St. Bridgeman, grabbing the baron's arm for support.

St. Bridgeman yelped, his eyes wide with surprise, screaming and stumbling backward, and thrust the wooden broom's sharpened end forward. He missed Lionel's heart, but the weapon snagged onto the vampire's arm, ripping through fabric and flesh.

Lionel fell onto his knees, then clutched at his wound and whimpered in pain.

"That's enough!" Charlotte shouted, then fired her Tesla ray into the sky.

The mob and St. Bridgeman jumped back as the blast of blue energy lit the alley.

"Back inside, or I'll have every last one of you arrested for disturbing the peace and inhibiting a police investigation." As the Royal Monster Hunter, she didn't actually have the power to arrest anyone for disturbing the peace—her authority was limited to violent supernaturals—but the crowd didn't know that.

The crowd obeyed, albeit reluctantly. The looks many of them sent Charlotte and Lionel before retreating into the buildings weren't pleasant.

Charlotte shoved past St. Bridgeman, wrapped an arm around Lionel, then stood, grunting as the vampire transferred some of his weight onto her.

"Mr. Singh," she groaned.

The policeman jogged forward, only slighting flinching away from St. Bridgeman's fiery stare.

"Please inform Chief Inspector Dawson of what has transpired, and that I will be informing Lord Wilmott of tonight's incidents. He will perhaps be able to shed some light on the soul-eater's victim. And make sure that body makes it to the morgue in one piece. I want a better look at it."

The edges of St. Bridgeman's eyes tightened. "Please send my best to Lord Wilmott." He smoothed his cravat, as if he were at a society fete. "If I'm not mistaken, he should be at the end of his at-home confinement."

Despite her best efforts, St. Bridgeman's remark hit a chink in her armor, and Charlotte bristled. "I beg your pardon, you mumbled the last part. If you mean his *unlawful* house arrest, then yes. Tomorrow he is once again considered a citizen of the crown."

St. Bridgeman merely inclined his head. "The house arrest lessens a vampire's temptation to bite." He gestured to the unsteady vampire. "And it *is* lawful."

Charlotte grunted as she hefted Lionel higher. "The law is wrong and you know it." Newborn vampires were the only ones in danger of biting, and that was only if they were not immediately fed. This fact was addressed at every vampiric transformation but of course St. Bridgeman had never attended any.

The baron frowned and backed away, as if the mere suggestion itself were contagious. "And you profess to serve the crown."

Charlotte raised her chin, but before she could retort, Lionel nearly toppled over. The irony of struggling to stand under Lionel's weight while trying to stand up for the truth was not lost on Charlotte. She hefted the vampire again and stumbled in the other direction before righting them both.

"Am I at sea?" Lionel said, slurring his words together.

Officer Singh cleared his throat. "M'lady, Chief Inspector Dawson said 'e'll be 'ere shortly. We be able to identify the victim soon."

"Mr. Singh." Charlotte gestured the policeman closer. "Please stay with the victim until the Chief Inspector arrives."

An uneasy but determined look settled in the policeman's eyes, and he ducked through the shadows back towards the corpse.

That man deserved a promotion.

Charlotte glanced at St. Bridgeman, who was looking thoughtfully after the policeman. Charlotte wouldn't be needed in the upcoming police proceedings, and she wanted to report the victim's death to the Coven straightaway. Plus, she realized she was too tired to keep arguing. So she dipped her head in a shallow, awkward bow to St. Bridgeman and turned away. He didn't return the gesture.

She half-dragged Lionel to the nearest gas lamp, propped him against the post—which he promptly slid down until he was resting on his side on the dirty street—then hailed an autocab for them both. She wasn't letting Lionel out of her sight until they were safely away from Whitechapel.

She pulled out a handkerchief and dabbed at the trickle of sweat creeping down her neck. As she waited, the lamp's sickly glow was enough to illuminate the street's general filth along with a broadside tacked onto a nearby wall. The poster's illustration depicted a vampire and werewolf, both with features so exaggerated even a penny dreadful would refuse to print it. The pair were positioned looming over an unconscious human woman. *You could be next*, screamed bold letters.

Charlotte stormed over to the poster. In smaller print were the words "Paid for by the Council for Humanity."

"What rubbish," she muttered. London's supernatural population was, for the most part, law-abiding citizens. St. Bridgeman would condemn all of them simply for existing. In any case, before the Origination, the jails had already been full of law-breakers.

Charlotte tore the offending sign from the wall and ripped it to shreds, wishing she could burn the slander and warm her hands over the flames.

A small gust lifted the tiny scraps of paper, which drifted towards Lionel. He held out his uninjured arm. "It's snowing!"

Charlotte pressed one hand on her hip and the other against her forehead. "You ruined my point as well as any possible dramatic exit."

"S-so-sorry," he hiccuped. "Wasn't my intention…"

"Lionel, please shut up."

What could she do about St. Bridgeman? He wasn't a child that she could scold and send to his room for a lengthy timeout. He was dangerous. He had status, connections, wealth, and, worst of all, determination.

An idea began to form, but it would involve speaking to Aunt Hespa, and involving her in any more of Charlotte's life was something she deeply wanted to avoid. She chewed her lip and pushed the thought aside for later.

The whirring of gears and the clacking of wheels over the cobblestones announced the arrival of the autocab several moments before it pulled into the light of the streetlamp. Steam hissed from the compression chambers as it chuffed to a stop.

Charlotte made a point to step on the shredded paper on her way to Lionel. By the time she managed to situate Lionel and herself in the cab, she was perspiring more than was considered ladylike. She wished she could stretch out, but the vampire was taking up enough room for both of them.

"Lord Wilmott's, fifty Berkeley Square," Charlotte told the driver, puffing for air. He touched his cap and pulled into the road with a splutter and chug.

The night was late—or perhaps the morning was early; she didn't know or care either way. But she did know that Lord Cosmo Wilmott, second-in-command of the London Vampire Coven, wouldn't mind a visit from her, whatever the hour. After all, he no longer needed sleep.

# Chapter 3

Light blazed from the windows, flooding Berkeley Square, welcoming Charlotte in a warm embrace. Cosmo had inundated the house with any kind of light from any source: natural gas, wax candle, Tesla electricity, and so on. He probably had those new handheld Tesla torches shining in every corner. It was a miracle Cosmo hadn't lit the place on fire. Though he had never said as much, Charlotte suspected the thing Cosmo missed the most from his past life was sunshine.

Charlotte glanced over at the inebriated Lionel, cursing him under her breath. He was an annoyance—albeit a not-altogether-unlikable one. Right now, one of his fangs was fully extended and the other so retracted so as to be nearly unnoticeable.

The autocab came to a stop and Lionel refolded his arms and muttered something about, "rough seas ahead."

Charlotte smiled ruefully. That statement was particularly true for Lionel's future relationship with the Coven regarding his drunken behavior. Tonight, after she took care of Lionel, she would try to recruit Cosmo to helping with the soul-eater case.

"We're here, Lionel."

The vampire snored, his overcoat draped across his face.

"Lionel." Charlotte gave the man a shove. He snorted awake, his coat falling to the cab's floor, and the lights of Wilmott house hit him full in the face. He screwed his eyes shut, lifting his arms and helplessly clawing his fingers against the air.

"The sun," he hissed. He tried unsuccessfully to hide under the autocab's seat, then tried to mist. His outline blurred and he rose an inch from the seat, but a hiccup sent him back down with a thump, again a very solid, very hungover form. He groaned and held a hand to his head.

Charlotte rolled her eyes. "It's only Lord Wilmott's. You'd be ash by now if it really was the sun. Honestly, Lionel. You really ought to be more careful keeping track of daylight hours."

Lionel gave a feeble nod, his jowls emphasizing his agreement.

Charlotte stepped down from the autocab, the frame jostling as Lionel shifted toward the open door. Charlotte opened her reticule and handed the driver her card. "Shall I have Lord Wilmott send you the vampiric incident paperwork?" she asked Lionel.

"Don't s'pose you could f-fill them out for me?"

Charlotte glared and Lionel flinched. "On second thought, I—I'd be so appreciative if you would have them s-sent, Lady Astley." He looked so pathetic with one fang shorter than the other and his curly grey hair sticking out every which way.

"Of course, but I'm going to recommend the Coven keep a closer watch on you. This is the third time I've caught you. And you were nearly stabbed."

A little of the red drained from Lionel's face. "I *was*, wasn't I?" he gasped. The wound wasn't bleeding—most vampire wounds didn't—and probably would have been fairly severe on a human. However, with one or two good day's rest, the wound would heal itself. Lionel turned to look at his arm, the sudden movement nearly causing him to tip over. He groaned and his hands flew to his head.

"It's a flesh wound, really, but it could have been much worse," Charlotte said.

The vampire nodded.

"I'm going to send you home now, Lionel."

He nodded again.

"And, Lionel—"

The portly vampire looked up, his chin still hanging over his cravat.

"I never want to see you again." She managed a thin-lipped smile, barely more than a grimace. "Do you understand?"

Lionel's features beamed with gratitude. "Of course. Very right you are."

"Farewell, Lionel." Charlotte told the driver the vampire's address—she had it memorized by now—and heard a faint "goodbye, Lady Astley" drift from the cab as the vehicle trundled out of sight.

Charlotte dusted her hands. One vampire down, one to go.

She turned to Wilmott's townhouse, quickly ascended the steps and rang the bell. She bounced on the balls of her feet in anticipation.

"Lady Astley," the butler said after opening the door. "I'll let Lord Wilmott know you are here."

Charlotte smiled at the droll visage of Cosmo's butler, whose hound-dog jowls and pinched nose contrasted to his frizzy near-electrocuted halo of white hair around his head.

"Thank you, Tiller. Please inform him it's about an ongoing investigation." Charlotte entered the spacious entryway. She removed her top hat with its netted veil as well as her gloves and handed them all to Tiller, who bowed and then strode off to find Cosmo.

Charlotte also placed her Tesla ray gun and holster on the side table—she wouldn't need it in here. Her hand patted her chestnut-brown hair, which was twisted into a bun and held in place by long wooden hairpins.

Her boots clacked on the black and white tiles as she took in the entry. It was completely different since her last visit only three days ago. Then it had been a deep red with Japanese elements with a second wallpaper trimming the upper wall. Her fingers traced the new vibrant-green embossed wallpaper. Large white daisies bloomed from the walls on every side. Some peeked from behind two framed rustic oil paintings, one depicting a field and the second a still-life image of fruit on a platter.

*He's redecorated again. The things that poor man does to entertain himself.*

Something tickled Charlotte's nose and she sneezed. What was that smell? She inhaled deeply, catching an acidic scent wafting from the upper levels. Charlotte smiled. Whatever it was, it was probably relatively safe. Cosmo was likely experimenting with some of the leftover wallpaper paste. Last time he'd caused only a minor explosion, singeing off the hair on his hand. And one eyebrow.

Charlotte moved deeper into the hallway. Now the familiar earthy and herbal smells of the Wilmott house enveloped her. Charlotte sighed and rubbed the back of her neck, attempting to work out a knot lodged between her spine and shoulder. In some ways, this house was more home to her than her own house—alive, warm, and full of inviting memories, despite its owner having been dead for the last ten years. Well, undead.

She *should* go home. She should be responsible and go back to her near monster-proof stronghold, but what fortress of a house could compare to Cosmo's familiar abode? Charlotte felt her usual anticipation at pouring over a case with Cosmo building inside her stomach like electrically charged butterflies.

Her mind reviewed the scene of the crime, trying to pick out little details she'd noticed. Whenever Cosmo was on house arrest, he always appreciated hearing about the mundane minutiae of the world. The flash of eyes in the alleys, the dank odor from rotting debris, even the warmish fetor from a crowded street. All of these would be fascinating to Cosmo—he never tired of her stories, even before he'd turned vampire. His attention to details was one of his most endearing traits.

Charlotte also tried to recall all her quips with St. Bridgeman so she and Cosmo could share a laugh at his ridiculousness.

She pressed hard into the knot in her neck and released her breath as she felt the muscle relax. She settled into an armchair in the great hall, resting her head against the daisy wallpaper. Thankfully, there was only one monster here, and he was on her side. *At least if I can get him to focus that long.*

Suddenly, the lights flared, blasting her face with their full strength. Then, just as quickly, they all extinguished. Completely. Stars danced before her eyes, then darkness.

Something to her right moaned.

Brilliant. She was under attack, and now she was blind.

And she had left her weapon on the side table. *Amateur move, Charlotte!*

How had something gotten inside without Cosmo noticing?

She fumbled in the direction of the entryway. The table jabbed into her hip, but she ignored the pain, fumbling for her ray gun. Her arm knocked the calling tray to the floor.

Something began to glow a pale and lichen green, illuminating a humanlike silhouette. Charlotte's eyes struggled to focus as she kept feeling for her ray gun. Blood roared in her ears. The green light grew in size and intensity, though it continued to flicker. The moaning pitched higher to a keening.

A banshee, this far south?

Charlotte pulled out her wooden hairpins, grasping one in each hand as she crouched low. *Steady girl. Wait until it shows itself.*

The pale green glow pulsed, and a figure of a waifish young woman took shape, her hair flowing out from her head as if she were underwater. Definitely a banshee.

Charlotte dropped the hairpins. They wouldn't be useful in this fight. If the keening continued much longer, though, Charlotte's mind would be entranced, and then the banshee would consume her body. Her eyesight still hadn't completely recovered—she'd have to wait until the banshee was closer for Charlotte to attack.

Something was off, though. The banshee was growing larger, but it didn't actually appear to be coming closer. Uncertainty turned her stomach like a rancid eel pie. Were her eyes tricking her?

The wailing increased, grating on Charlotte's bones like nails on a chalkboard. *Sort it out later, muttonhead!*

Wait. Was that banshee floating…out of a field of flowers?

By the time Charlotte's brain had processed the oddity her reflexes had already kicked in. She pulled two concealed throwing knives from her sleeves and released them in one fluid motion, then rolled to the left. She heard a thud and the banshee's keening continued. Her knives were sticking out of the fruit painting.

*I missed? Impossible.* Charlotte turned and lunged to the right, reaching for her Tesla ray which was perched on the edge of the side table. As her fingers wrapped around the grip, something snatched her shoulder from behind. Charlotte took a step backward in the direction of her attacker and pivoted, her finger riding the hair's edge of the trigger. *I just need a clear shot.*

"Charlotte, it's only m—"

The ray gun gave an electric whine and fired. Surprise flooded Cosmo Wilmott's face.

"No!" Charlotte dropped the weapon.

Cosmo burst into inky blackness and the narrow blue beam went right through him, hitting the banshee. Unfazed, the moaning apparition continued to float. However, behind it, the picture of the meadow burst into crackling flames, and charred ashes drifted to the ground. Her two throwing knives, now melted, dripped onto the floor.

Charlotte growled. She never missed. *What supernaturalcy was this?*

The black mist hovering where Cosmo had been began to reform into a more human shape.

It rapidly condensed, and a now-solid Lord Cosmo Wilmott turned to look back at the banshee and wall. He pushed his dark brown overgrown mop of hair out of his face and grinned. "Magnificent shot."

While Charlotte tried to catch her breath and come up with a scathing reproach, Cosmo walked around her to the corner of the hall, where a device the size of a large phonograph was sitting on the floor. How had she not noticed that before?

A soft clicking emanated from the device, and a beam of light blazed from the machine onto the banshee. No, not *onto* the banshee, she realized in growing interest. It *was* the banshee. Blazing suns. Had that machine captured a banshee?

Cosmo knelt on the floor and fumbled with the side of the device. Suddenly, the beam of light and wailing disappeared and the room was once again dark and quiet, except for the smouldering remains of what had been Charlotte's knives and the painting in Cosmo's entryway.

Her mouth dropped open. She hadn't noticed the soft clicking coming from near her feet during the wailing; she'd been so focused on the possible monster attack. Amazement and curiosity flooded her mind. Then annoyance.

Cosmo raised the the light level in his hallway gas lamps as well as a few Tesla lamps, then gestured grandly to the device. "How do you like it?" His green eyes glittered with mischief and the familiar zing of attraction hit Charlotte. *No, nothing but platonic feelings here. All vampires have differing levels of attractive glamor, and Cosmo is no different. Mental fortitude, old girl.*

"Cosmo!" Charlotte glowered as she stood and brushed falling cinders off her skirts. At least she'd worn her sapphire-blue ensemble and not the mauve—the ash would have completely ruined that dress.

"It's a kinetograph. Just came from that fellow Edison's lab in America."

"I could have *disintegrated* you!"

"Not unless you've invented a solar ray gun."

"Don't tempt me." Her lower lip stuck out. "Those were my favorite throwing knives." She knew it was childish, but those two *had* been the best balanced of her supply.

Tiller, as calm as chamomile tea, emerged from the kitchen with a small bucket of water and began dousing the remnants of the picture frame. When the water hit the molten remains of the knives, they sizzled and filled the hallway with an acrid haze.

Cosmo waved a hand airily. "I am sorry about those, but I'll replace them, Charlotte."

"Yes, you will. They were expensive." It had taken her the removal of three redcaps, two hobgoblins, and a rather nasty lindworm to justify buying them.

"A small price to pay to see the look on your face when you heard the banshee." His sharp canines flashed in the light.

"Perhaps, m'lord,"—Tiller paused to cough—"you should consider the ferocity and efficiency of Lady Astley's defensive strategies before you project a monster over your great-great-grandmother's paintings."

Guilt washed over Charlotte. "That was an heirloom?"

Cosmo clapped his hands. "Marvelous. Never did like that painting anyway."

Tiller merely sniffed, then stomped on some still-smoldering ashes.

Charlotte scooped up her hairpins, plopped herself down into a nearby chair, and twisted her auburn hair into a hasty bun. "You should be more careful, Cos," Charlotte said. "You're not immortal, you know."

Vampires were new enough to the world that it was still unclear exactly what their lifespans were. However, Charlotte had staked enough violent ones to know that they weren't invulnerable.

"Tiller, I'm no longer receiving callers tonight," Cosmo said.

"Very good, sir." The butler nodded sedately, then disappeared down the hall with the bucket and half a disintegrated picture frame in hand.

Charlotte cleared her throat. Now onto the soul-eater, if she could just beat Cosmo to the punch. "Cos—"

"What do you think of my device?"

"It's quite fascinating," Charlotte conceded. Normally she would guide the conversation to whatever pressing matter needed discussing, but she was tired. Plus, Cosmo would need to triumph over his kinetograph; he so rarely got out.

By law, vampires were allowed only five nocturnal excursions every two weeks, and only for a few hours at that. It hadn't been long since the Royal Albert Sanguine Donor Clinic had been established, but although much of the government had been working to ensure that all its citizens— supernatural and human—were adequately cared for, the public was still distrustful of anything that fed on blood.

Charlotte shifted in her seat, trying to listen to Cosmo chatter on about his machine, but she was again feeling rattled from both of today's incidents. With St. Bridgeman working hard, the public's fear was hardening into anger. While emotions ran high in the general population, Charlotte's own concern about a possible uprising grew stronger. The government was still at a loss about how to approach the relationship between humans and supernaturals. Thankfully, there had been members of the elite who were turned during the Origination; otherwise, the supernaturals' plight would have been much worse.

To counter the public's fear, the government had taken the stance of supernaturals and humans having more of a symbiotic relationship than one of predator and prey. Of course, people such as the blood-harlots by the docks had been in business nearly since the Origination and no matter the public's stance or supernatural views. The soul-eater attacks, though, were unquestionably predatorial, which made the creature not just a physical threat to unfortunate individuals walking through dark alleys, but also a political threat to all supernaturals.

Cosmo's voice still speaking of the kinetograph finally broke through Charlotte's thoughts. "It's a clever combination of two devices from several brilliant minds: Marie Curie, Edward Muybridge, and Thomas Edison. And of course, Alaric Watts."

Charlotte nodded and smiled. She'd have loved to squirrel herself away with the kinetograph, tinkering to her mind's content—and Cosmo probably would have let her—but the events of the day weighed too heavily on her mind.

As she and Cosmo sat in the entryway, the staff armed with cleaning supplies bustled into the hallway and noise reverberated in the space. Charlotte glanced at the blackened patch on the wall that was now all that remained of the disintegrated heirloom painting.

Cosmo must have finally noticed her state of mind, because he sobered and motioned for her to follow him from the entryway and into the parlour. He seated himself in a large, well-worn burgundy chair near a much newer and more fashionable settee. Cosmo had redecorated this room with a pale yellow and rich green flocked damask wallpaper, a large Asian-inspired framed mirror, and small pictures of painted wildflowers scattered across the wall. He'd refurbished the settee into a bright daffodil yellow fabric. Charlotte settled into the fraying floral and striped wingback chair across from him, the cushioning fitting her form perfectly. The chair, clashed horribly with the decor, but no matter what Cosmo did to the rest of his house, this chair—her chair—always remained the same.

"I'd love to hear what is happening in the outside world," Cosmo said, giving her a smile.

Charlotte adjusted her skirts, the rustle of fabric hiding her breath of relief that she could now talk with him about her day. "I'm here on two items of business, actually. The first being that Lionel had another unfortunate incident that, this time, almost ended in his being staked."

Cosmo started. "By you?"

"No," she scoffed, dusting cinders from her skirts. "St. Bridgeman. Luckily, he missed."

"May high noon take Lionel, St. Bridgeman and all his councils," Cosmo muttered, running his hand from his temple to the nape of his neck.

"The second reason I came—"

He frowned and gave a small pout. "You mean you did not come to partake of my scintillating company?" He was doing a poor job of hiding that mischievous twinkle and smirk.

Almost against her will, Charlotte grinned. An evening with Cosmo was the antidote to her troubles. "The *third* reason I came is because there has been another—"

"Oh, another murder." He perched on the edge of his seat, waggling his eyebrows. "How macabre, Charlotte, even for you."

"I hoped you could help identify—"

"No, I don't know the man. Just what was on Coven information sheets. He must be newly changed. Poor fellow."

"How many—"

"Newborns? Three this month: Oliver Draper, Johnathan Mason, and Violet Brewster. All were adjusting well to their afterlife."

"So who could have—"

"You don't know?" Cosmo's eyes widened. "Then it must be the *soul-eater*." He said the last word with a spooky, wavering voice and waggled his fingers at her.

"Stop finishing my sentences, Cos, or I will stake you with my hairpin." She took a breath. "Yes, it probably is, would you consider help—"

Cosmo clapped his hands together. "Do werewolves howl at the moon?"

Charlotte scowled. Normally she was adept at blocking vampiric mind-reading, but it was rather late and it had been a trying day, to say the least. She unclenched her fists.

His eyes caught her stress and flicked from her hands to her face. "Tsk, tsk. Threatening my afterlife already? You've only just arrived." His eyes crinkled at the corners, and he held up his finger. "You're not truly vexed—you're hungry."

Charlotte opened her mouth to deny it and politely decline offers of food, but her stomach chose that moment to growl. Loudly. *Traitorous organ.* She sniffed, then nodded, ignoring Cosmo's smug look.

He rang for food. Charlotte's nerves settled at the knowledge that she would soon be eating some very fine fare indeed—the victuals from the Wilmott kitchen never did disappoint. Soon the staff were bustling into the parlour and setting up a small feast upon the sideboard, dishes and silverware clinking softly.

She caught Cosmo's gaze. "So you'll help?" It was more a statement of fact than anything.

Cosmo waved his hand, settling deeper into his chair. "My dear, Charlotte, why ask when you already know?"

Charlotte licked her lips, perching on the edge of her own chair. "We still don't know what the soul-eater actually is."

Charlotte paused, waiting to see if Cosmo would behave or if he would launch a joke or wander along a tangent. Satisfied with his silence, if not his irrepressible smirk, she felt confident in choosing a few delectables from the sideboard. The kitchen had a wide assortment of offerings: cucumber and dill sandwiches, grilled salmon, chopped eggs, scones with clotted cream, candied ginger, and an assortment of shiny glacé fruits. Her mouth watered at the smells wafting from the side table. She tried not to pout that raspberry scones were not on the menu this time, and instead settled on some finger sandwiches and disappointingly plain scones.

While she ate, she told Cosmo everything that had happened, including the whispered clues, the increase in body count, the near mob-like crowd, and St. Bridgeman's involvement.

"I intensely despise that man," Charlotte concluded, dabbing at her mouth with a serviette.

"He's not *that* bad," Cosmo said, waving away Charlotte's sentiments.

"Not that—not that bad?" How could she possibly be hearing this? "Cosmo, he is insufferable and intolerant and prejudiced…and the list goes on."

"I agree that he is not particularly talented at making and keeping friends—"

"An understated fact," Charlotte scoffed.

"—however, as infuriating as he is, I cannot fault him for fighting for something he believes in, however misguided. I may joke at the man's expense, but it is nothing more than jests."

Charlotte moved to the edge of her seat again. "Well, then I'll have to fault him for both of us." She pointedly turned her back on Cosmo as she picked pieces of fruit off of the serving board onto a plate.

She heard him sigh behind her, signaling a sort of white flag between the two of them. He would let the matter lie.

Aunt Hespa had told Charlotte repeatedly that she was too judgmental, and Charlotte tried to withhold that judgement for most of society. But in the case of St. Bridgeman, she felt her inhibitions should not be curbed.

At this time, she couldn't accept Cosmo's white flag. At least not yet. As she replaced the tongs on the meat tray, she spoke over her shoulder. "Cos, if his bill passes…" Her voice was tight in her throat.

Cosmo and Charlotte had argued for long hours about what would happen if the bill passed. Cosmo, along with the rest of the supernatural population, would be restricted in their daily choices—where to eat, shop, and even live. Charlotte's mind raced as nightmare images of a segregated London society flooded her mind.

"I don't want his bill to pass, but I do not want to paint him with the same broad strokes as he and his council do with others. There is already enough hate without adding to it."

"But Cos—"

Now it was Cosmo who shifted in his seat, slouched, and stared somewhere into the distance—classic signs he was on the verge of an epic brood. She coughed into her hand, determined to pull him back from the abyss.

"I believe this soul-eater is a new classification of supernatural." Charlotte gulped down one sandwich, then took another before continuing. "Shifters, werefolk, specters, and vamps have been its victims. This one was a tall male with dark, straight hair and swarthy features."

"Oliver." Cosmo clenched the armrest. Charlotte wasn't surprised he had been able to name the victim so quickly. One of his administrative duties was organizing and integrating newborn vampires—no one knew the Coven better than he did.

Cosmo's voice was subdued. "He was the latest to volunteer to be turned. His wife died in the Origination, but his daughter was bitten and survived the change. He said he couldn't stand being alone—he risked his life so he could be with her." His brow darkened.

Tiller offered Cosmo some tea, but Cosmo waved it away. Though Cosmo never partook of human food in his home, Tiller always offered.

"You're sure it couldn't have been one of the Pack?" Cosmo's tone was heavy with skepticism. Charlotte knew where his train of thought was going. It would be so much easier if it were a rogue werewolf rather than a new supernatural species.

Charlotte shook her head, chewing on her scone, which was actually delicious in spite of its lack of raspberries. If the murderer had been one of the London Pack, her telescriber would have been spitting out messages from the police nonstop. Dealings between the Coven and Pack had been on stable grounds for years, though the relations sometimes frayed at the edges. Thank heavens nothing horrible had happened between them since the Upheavals—the gang-like war between the two supernatural species had destroyed some of the more impoverished pockets of London. Together, the Origination and the following Upheavals had almost obliterated the great city.

Any of the supernatural-related mysteries Charlotte had investigated exuded at least a small element of complexity, but this was the first time she felt completely stumped and frighteningly helpless. That *thing* was out there, and no one knew when or where—or who— it would attack next.

The Origination and the following Upheavals had been more than enough of conflict to last London for the rest of its days.

"But what *is* it?" Cosmo thumped the armrest.

"I wish I knew." Charlotte stood and paced the length of the room. She tapped her chin, her mind grasping at any half-formed possibility that might help. Out of reflex, she reached for her telescriber so she could organize her thoughts, like a notebook. Blast. Tiller had taken her satchel.

Charlotte moved to call for Tiller, then froze. *Like a notebook—St. Bridgeman's notebook.*

"Is there anything I can do?"

Charlotte turned and saw Cosmo leaning forward.

A truly impish idea surfaced. Charlotte tilted her head. "Can you possibly secure me an invitation to the St. Bridgemans' dinner party next week?"

He blinked. "You want to attend a fete? Do you think it wise that England's foremost monster hunter be in the same room as Baron St. Bridgeman, especially so soon after your most recent encounter?"

"Yes, I ran into St. Bridgeman." She dropped back into her chair. "And yes, I need to speak to him. He has proven both annoying and elusive whenever I've tried to approach him about something. Perhaps the man would be easier to deal with in his own home—maybe even more pleasant, though I doubt it." She raised a hand to cover a yawn. "Think you can do it?"

Cosmo raised an eyebrow.

"Yes, yes, I know. *Of course* you can do it." Now that her stomach was full, her body weighed her down like river mud. She glanced at her pocket watch, which was dangling from her outer corset. Blazes, it was nearly two in the morning. "I've got to get some sleep and figure out exactly how to catch this infernal creature and stop it before it consumes all of London. Or most of it, anyway." Charlotte stifled another yawn. "Please excuse me, it's tired and I'm late." Something about that sentence didn't sound right, but she didn't care.

Cosmo let out a rumbling laugh. "Actually, my dear, you're right on time."

Charlotte's eyebrows went up and she blinked wearily. Cosmo's eccentricities had doubled since he turned vampire.

"I might have some other form of help to offer with this case," he said. "I wanted to surprise you for your birthday next week, but it seems you might need it sooner than later. Bring it in, Tiller."

A jolt of curiosity energized her tired bones and she perked up immediately. Tiller carried in the strangest looking but most fascinating device, Charlotte had seen since the world's fair in Paris. The object looked like simple goggles, but she knew better than to expect *simple* from Cosmo.

"What is it, Cos?"

Cosmo's chest puffed out, his green eyes sparkling. For a moment, Charlotte saw through the vampire's innate glamor meant to attract humans and only saw her enthusiastic childhood friend. "It's a supernatural electromagnetic spectographer."

"A what?"

Tiller placed the tray with the goggles on the side table, then exited into the hall. Charlotte quickly crossed to the device.

"It's a machine that finds the supernatural signature of each creature and then leadth you to them exthpeditiouthly—" Cosmo growled. The pair of deadly sharp teeth now extended well over his lower lip. "Blasthed fangth."

Charlotte hid a smile behind her hands. His fangs always extended whenever something was particularly exciting to him.

"It bringth my thirtht to the forefront. Thank you, Tiller."

Tiller had returned with two items: a handkerchief for the spittle, and a decanter of what could have been port—if it hadn't ben so thick.

Cosmo took the proffered glass and sipped, then winced.

"Tiller, what vintage is thith. Tatheth like the Themeth at low tide. A good *vin de thang* should be like a day in the thun."

"Apologies, m'lord," Tiller said.

"Thith ith the fifty-nine, ithn't it? Throw out all the bottleth exthept one. Thave it. We'll give it to Thaint Bridgeman if he ever turnth. Ath a congratulationth."

Tiller nodded, taking the bottle with him.

Cosmo took smaller sips, flinching each time. As he drank, Charlotte noticed his fangs shrinking. She turned her attention to the device to allow Cosmo time to recover.

The details were exquisite. Tiny screws held minuscule gears on the modified goggles commonly used for airship travel. But instead of the standard blue lenses, the glass within the frame was black as night. Several gears on the side and two small dials begged to be fiddled with. Charlotte turned the largest one on the side of the frame and something clicked. The goggles hummed to life, the lenses glowing like moonlit shadows.

"Perhaps they will help in your search for the soul-eater," Cosmo said, his fangs now fully retracted.

"How so?" Unable to resist any longer, she picked the goggles off the tray, slid the strap over her head, and placed the lenses over her eyes. The room plunged into a strange illuminated darkness, everything standing out in stark contrast, similar to a photographic negative. Reaching a finger to the temple of the goggles, Charlotte pulled on one of the tiny levers. The goggles gave another small click, the humming dropped to a lower pitch, and her vision washed to a deep purple. These goggles were a marvel, but they seemed to be utterly useless.

Charlotte turned toward Cosmo, and her hands flew to her mouth, stifling a yelp.

Cosmo was glowing. Brightly.

"Cosmo, you're…lavender."

He smiled, and his fangs glowed brighter than anything else. His skin let off a rather lovely lilac radiance. "Yes, you can see! And it's such a fashionable purple." He tugged on his vest and an afterimage glimmered where his arms had been, trailing color.

It was lovely. *He* was lovely. With or without the goggles.

Charlotte blinked that thought away. It had merely been the shock of the discovery and the excitement of science. That was all. She cleared her throat and took a step backward. "How does it work?"

"You know of the pioneering efforts of the Curies?"

"Who doesn't?"

"What you may not know is that they also discovered that the air around a radioactive element gives off electricity. Supernaturals give off a different sort of electricity—charged elements that this spectrometer can detect. If you change the lens like so"—he leaned forward and tapped the side—"the device tracks a different sort of radiation." He clicked the goggles again and the world turned an ethereal indigo. "Purple is for vampires, the blue is for specters, and the maroon is for werefolk."

"And what of the light turquoise layer underneath?"

"Turquoise?"

She squinted, leaning closer, examining the thin layer beneath the brighter purple one. The color glowed faintly, but it was there.

Cosmo shrugged, and the turquoise and purple glows moulded to his movements.

"Astounding," Charlotte murmured. Her mental gears shifted to cold and comfortable analysis, the cogs of her brain gathering speed. Questions piled atop each other. Ideas for experiments and uses for the goggles swirled through her imagination. Sleep would have to wait.

"Cos, would you mind performing some of your vampiric talents? Then we can really see what these things can do."

Cosmo's smile nearly blinded her. "I thought you'd never ask."

# Chapter 4

An explosion of vibrant purple granules blasted from the spot where Cosmo had been standing. Each vampiric molecule burst outward like a magenta comet, trails of purple pointing to a pulsing amethyst center. Minuscule sea-green motes formed a filament-thin layer beneath the purple. Charlotte pulled the goggles away from her eyes and peered over the rims. The dark vampire-mist looked as it always had, its rich, velvety tendrils wafting around a human-sized cloud.

"Cos, would you mind moving to that corner, near Tiller?" Charlotte said, pointing to the opposite corner.

The dark mist hovered to the white-haired butler, the tendrils swirling around each other. Charlotte replaced the goggles, and the mist again burst into shades of purple with the tiny pale turquoise specks encased inside.

"Fascinating," she breathed. Her fingers tingled as they typed her thoughts furiously into the telescriber. None of these granules were this visible to the naked eye. Vampires in mist form were always little more than clouds of shadow, writhing smoky tendrils as amorphous as steam twisting out of a teacup. But this almost seemed like some sort of…intricately complex pattern.

She pushed the goggles back onto the bridge of her nose, making a mental note to tighten the strap later. "Once again, if you please. And, if possible, try to prolong your materialization." Poised and ready to take notes, she burned with excitement.

It was just past three in the morning, but so far they had conducted strength, agility, vampiric misting tests—the results were riveting. They had ascertained that while moving, vampires left a lavender trail of light that lingered for three seconds, and the length of said trail depended entirely on the speed at which the vamp moved.

"Last time, then we move on to another test," Cosmo said. Again corporeal, he took a long swallow of the *vin de sang* Tiller had placed on the table. Vampires constantly using their powers and pushing their limits were exceptionally thirsty, something Charlotte wished more people—humans and vampires—were aware of. "After all these tests, if I mist any more, I may not be able to pull myself together."

Charlotte tucked a stray tendril of hair behind her ear. "Oh, pish. The likelihood of you dissolving entirely is as probable as…St. Bridgeman trimming that ghastly mustache."

"As Lionel getting sober."

"As me fighting in a wedding dress." She chuckled at the thought.

Cosmo was quiet for a moment, and she looked up from her notes just in time to see a slight tightening around his eyes before he turned and set his drink on the table, the purple glow with the teal outline around him already fading. "And we are finished," he said, turning back to her with a grin. "Time for a new test."

"But I'm not done."

"Be prepared and such." His voice bounced merrily and he rocked on his toes. Charlotte narrowed her eyes, doubting how much his supposed fatigue had been real and how much was merely professed.

He wiped his mouth. "Thank you for the drink, Tiller." Cosmo tugged at his suit and readjusted his cravat. "Please also instruct the ladies of the staff to batten down the proverbial hatches, so to speak."

Tiller bowed, then left the room, the door closing softly behind him.

Charlotte pulled off the goggles and rested them on the table. She narrowed her eyes. "What kind of storm is coming?"

Cosmo made a theatrical sweeping gesture. "Why me, of course."

Charlotte rubbed her temples. "Do you mean to affect an entire household with some vampiric ability? Cosmo Alexander Wilmott, you are not a storm. You're not even a drizzle."

"I—w-what—me?" he spluttered.

Charlotte tried to look serious, but seeing him unhinged was too much fun.

"Tiller!"

Almost before Cosmo could finish the call, the long-faced man was at his side. "Yes, sir?"

Cosmo jumped. "My good man, I've told you to stop doing that. We really have to put a bell on you."

"Very good, sir. I've notified the staff about the hatches. I've also notified Mrs. Graviston in case you require her services?"

"It's like you can read my mind. Yes, in fact, we will be in need of a chaperone."

Tiller sniffed, then exited the room.

"A chaperone?" Charlotte rolled her eyes. "Worried about your reputation?"

Cosmo's chin lifted higher and he peered down his nose. "An eligible bachelor must guard his virtue at all times," he said, sweeping a wide arc as he placed the back of his hand dramatically to his forehead. "He wouldn't want anything to sully his image." Then he winked at her.

Charlotte opened her mouth, about to launch into exactly what she thought about chaperones and gender-specific double standards, when Tiller reentered the room. Following in his wake was was a short, matronly maid whose dour, pinched face would make gargoyles look positively saintly. Something in Charlotte quailed. Now *that* was a chaperone.

"Mrs. Graviston, sir."

A laugh threatened to burst out of Charlotte. It was a thoroughly fitting name for the woman.

"Thank you, Tiller. Would you please have cook prepare some raspberry scones and tea? Bring them in when they are ready."

"Very good, sir." Once again, Tiller bowed before leaving the room. Charlotte wondered if his back ever got sore.

Mrs. Graviston took a seat on a hard wooden bench in the corner.

"What test *are* we running?"

Cosmo ran a hand through his wavy hair and smoothed his jacket. "One of a more…alluring variety. Hence the need for a chaperone." He turned back to Charlotte, one brow arced.

"Oh, Cos, really. I doubt the soul-eater will try to seduce me."

Cosmo held out his hand and motioned for Charlotte to join him by the window. "Only because it hasn't met you yet."

"You're such a tease." A rush of heat bloomed in her cheeks and she smiled. She stood and lightly took his hand. Flirtatious banter was a familiar playing field for both her and Cosmo, even though society was wont to frown on such conversations. *People often preach against things they've never tried,* Charlotte thought.

She and Cosmo moved to the window farther away from Mrs. Graviston, and faced each other. Charlotte released Cosmo's hand but he remained close. She spied over the top of his shoulder and saw the elderly woman shift in her chair and yawn. Charlotte watched with amusement as Mrs. Graviston's eyes grew heavy and closed. *Not much of a chaperone then after all.*

"With your permission," Cosmo said. A quiet intensity flashed behind his eyes, his demeanor growing playfully serious. If such contradictions could exist in one place, they did in Cosmo.

Slowly, Charlotte nodded and closed her eyes, mentally releasing the wall she'd built for herself over the years to prevent any mind-reading supernaturals from accessing her thoughts. It was a strange feeling, letting her guard down. She never would have done this with any other vampire, but she trusted Cosmo with her life.

Something in Charlotte's stomach fluttered, like feathered bat wings. *None of your nonsense, heart. What's the matter with you?* The experiment hadn't even started yet. Had it?

She filled her lungs with fresh air, releasing it steadily to calm her mind. *Think, Charlotte. Focus on the task at hand.* She had experienced vampires' allurement charms before, so this should be nothing new. There had been the time a young vampire, barely more than fifteen, had clearly been putting his heart and soul into vamping her, but he'd barely caused Charlotte's heart to pick up pace, let alone to swoon.

The more experienced and forceful vampires were scarier. Once one had cornered her at a dinner party, trying to seduce and then bite her—without her permission. Her thinking had clouded but she'd still been aware enough to see that his fangs had extended fully—a sign of intent to drain—but when he'd tried to sink his teeth into her jugular, she had gained enough control to stake him with one of her hairpins. A rash decision on her part, especially considering the location. He'd exploded into ash covering the plate of dessert she'd been holding. She'd washed vampire soot out of her hair for weeks. That allurement had been particularly forceful, almost controlling. Only her training had saved her.

But *this*…

A gentle wash of warmth infused the room, like silk sliding against her skin. She felt Cosmo move towards her and pull the goggles down off her forehead, placing them over her eyes. When she opened them, her vision filled with Cosmo's strong chest, which glowed a soft periwinkle. He was now close enough that Charlotte had to tilt her head up slightly to see his face.

"You know, ever since we were young, even before I turned, I knew you were something special." His voice, deeper and smoother than she'd ever heard before, scraped layers off her self-restraint.

Her ribs fought against the tightness of her corset as her heart swelled and her breath quickened. When had he gotten so good at this? She tried to lighten the mood. "Even after our experiments in your parents' lake?" Blast, why was her throat so dry?

Cosmo chuckled. "You mean the one where I submerged myself for an hour to see why vampires still breathed without a need for air?"

"Yes." She could barely get the word out.

He paused for a moment, his periwinkle aura intensifying to an iris purple. "Yes, even after that. But do you know when I realized just how spectacular you were?"

She shook her head. Why was everything so blasted hot?

"When you socked James Hardlow. Three times, if memory serves, giving him that shiner."

Charlotte's cheeks burned, both at his proximity and at the memory, and she broke his steady gaze to drop her eyes to the floor. "He deserved each one. He shouldn't have said those things about people I care for…about…"

"About…" She could sense more than see Cosmo raising his eyebrows expectantly.

Her traitorous blush was heating everything from the base of her neck to her ears. She fumbled over her words. "About you…and my other friends."

"Yes, your other friends you cared so much for. What were their names again?" Cosmo smiled.

Charlotte swallowed. "There was…erm…"

"As I recall," Cosmo said, tilting his head to the side. "You only engaged in fisticuffs after he'd insulted me. You didn't seem to mind his comments regarding your other friends." A tangle of dark hair fell across his forehead, derailing Charlotte's thoughts completely.

"My friends? Yes, I think,"—she swallowed, and then ran her teeth over her lower lip—"I meant "acquaintances.""

"I'm flattered." He smiled. "You care more about me than others?"

She gulped and didn't respond. Even under Cosmo's allurement, she still had her secrets. She wanted to tell him to stop, to break the tension somehow, but at that moment his outline pulsed again, deepening to a dark mauve. Her skin tingled in response and she gasped. She found herself leaning closer to him, her chin tilting to expose more of her neck. She could close the distance between them so easily. Rise onto her toes and…*If you wanted to, Charlotte. Which you don't.*

*Right?*

"Am I something more than a friend, then?" His voice rumbled into her ear, melting something inside her chest.

"I—" Her mind struggled against her heart. "You're simply enhancing the allurement with your words. And we should make a note that—that your color deepens when you're…Blast it, why do you have to be so…" She took a small step backward, and gestured to all of Cosmo.

His color deepened again, dark and sweet like blackberry jam. Was he blushing?

Charlotte huffed to cover a gasp, her heart pounding in her ears. She covered her eyes with her hand. "It is utterly distracting."

Cosmo took her hand, enclosing it with his own. He pulled her close again, placing her palm over his heart. "That is the point, my dear."

Her soul contracted and then expanded within her own skin. Was this what people felt when they fell in love?

*This isn't love.* The logical thoughts that were Charlotte's constant companions were somehow drowning in the flood of warmth coursing from her heart, but they were still there. *If this is love, then love must…be very…illogical.* Her breath hitched in her throat and her torso felt magnetized, pulling her closer to his body.

"You are the sun in my dark days," he murmured. "And you have captured my heart."

Blazing suns, swallowing was difficult. The tip of her tongue tingled with the sweetness of honey. She licked her lips.

He kissed her fingertips and her heart felt as if it had exploded, sending thrilling jolts through her veins. Delicious flames licked every nerve. The intimate touch blasted away something inside of her—a divider in her heart—and a thrill coursed down her spine, both exciting and terrifying. Was he feeling this way too, at least a little bit? Would this change things between them? Did she mind?

*Don't dwell, Charlotte. Cosmo may still be able to hear you.* He had never invaded her innermost thoughts and feelings—of that she was sure—but she was so off-balance from the tests that, for all she knew, she could have been projecting her feelings and thoughts in all directions.

*Pull yourself together. Breathe.*

A soft grunt sounded from several feet away on her left, and Charlotte blinked rapidly, at her suddenly clear her head. Mrs. Graviston was shifting in her chair. Charlotte squinted through the goggles and saw a glow around Mrs. Graviston's body, the color of mulberry wine. Had Cosmo been vamping her with a sleep charm this entire time?

Cosmo had leaned down toward her and was now waiting, his eyes searching hers as if asking for permission to close the remaining distance. Even though the fog was gone from her mind, everything inside Charlotte tingled like lightning. It would take so little to close the distance…

Her heart skittered. She shifted her weight to her toes, her heart pulling her closer—then she blinked, came to her senses again and leaned away. She released his hand and took a step backward. *Blazing suns, Charlotte. Almost lost your head there.*

"Th—thank you, Cosmo." Her words stuck to her tongue. Had it always been this warm in here? She pulled at her collar, which suddenly felt restrictive. "This should conclude our allurement test. Your declarations of love greatly enhanced the charm. Good thinking."

The allurement faded and his color lightened back to the steady periwinkle, although there were still traces of that rich blackberry-jam color clinging to his outline. He looked…disappointed. Then the expression evaporated and a mischievous grin broke across his face.

She wasn't sure what would have happened if she had closed the distance. The thought gave her the same thrill and terror that standing at the edge of the Cliffs of Dover had— curling her toes, knowing that if she took one step, she would fall.

But what if instead, she soared?

Blood hammered in her ears. *Blazing suns, heart. Shut up before he hears you.* Though, given his supernatural senses, the hummingbird pace of her heart, and his cheeky expression, he already knew.

She raised a hand to try to calm that infernal organ, and when her hand passed by her peripheral vision, it left a trail of purple.

"Cosmo!" she gasped. "I—I'm glowing."

"Radiant, as always."

"No, Cos." Charlotte took the goggles off and carefully fitted them on the vampire's face. He took in the sight and his jaw went slack. "Residual allurement affects," she said, rotating her hand in front of her face as if trying to discern traces of color without the goggles. "Fascinating. Do you think I was glowing the entire time? And why is the turquoise layer absent?"

"You're beautiful," he breathed. "Purple always was your color."

Her cheeks grew warm again, though he wasn't vamping her any longer.

"Brilliant!" He waggled his eyebrows. "Now we'll have to conduct the seduction tests again, but I'll wear the goggles."

She straightened her skirts, uneasy knots twisting in her stomach at the thought of losing control of her sensibilities again. She wanted to believe there was nothing to worry about; his allurement abilities were probably so enticing because he was one of the Coven's most powerful vampires. Probably.

Mrs. Graviston coughed and shifted in her chair again, causing Charlotte to jump and blush once more. She took a step backward, her restless hands flying to her hair, smoothing her dress, then repeating the actions. She closed her eyes for a moment and filled her lungs to capacity, pushing back the unanswerable questions concerning her feelings.

"I'm only joking, you know," Cosmo said, raising his hands. He was grinning broadly now.

She was surprised as slight sting of disappointment flashed in her chest. "Well, it isn't a horrendous idea," she said a little reluctantly. "These goggles and experiments deepen and broaden supernatural science." Yes. Science. These experiments were for science. "Another time, perhaps. We'll have to assume that these goggles work similarly on other supernaturals."

"We could call on someone from the Pack to try to seduce you, if you'd like, although they have no supernatural charming abilities."

"Splendid idea," Charlotte said, examining one of the forgotten cucumber sandwiches Tiller had sent in. "Send for several members so we can ascertain whether their signatures differ based on pack structure. Perhaps the duke's aura will be the most alluring." She popped the sandwich into her mouth.

Cosmo's features darkened for a moment at the mention of the duke, but he switched to a playful grimace so quickly Charlotte couldn't be sure she had seen it. He sauntered over to the sandwiches, inspecting them with mild distaste. "I could never understand the appeal of a hairy werewolf."

"Only because none have tried to seduce you." Charlotte stifled a yawn, then idly traced the goggle frames with her fingers. These remarkable lenses would drastically alter her line of work, especially if each supernatural did indeed leave a trail. No more tracking down clues or interrogating strangers—she simply needed to follow the bread crumbs.

Charlotte pressed her fingers to her lips as a thought occurred to her. "Do you think the soul-eater even falls into one of the supernatural categories? It will be blazing hard to track otherwise." She rolled her shoulders, which again felt heavy now that the excitement of the experiments had died down.

Tiller entered the parlour, bearing a small tea service, more cucumber sandwiches, and the promised raspberry scones. At the sound of the clinking dishware, Mrs. Graviston fully awoke, blinking ponderously.

Charlotte closed her eyes, focusing on replacing her mental block against supernatural attacks. She swallowed and only with Herculean effort reestablished most of her mental defenses. She bit down a sigh. It wasn't her strongest fortification, but after the night's events it was the best she could do. She bit back another yawn.

"This came for you, m'lady." Tiller handed Charlotte a thin piece of paper, which she immediately recognized as from the telescriber which she'd left on the hallway table. Any residual glamour from Cosmo melted away immediately. Was it Inspector Dawson? Had they found another corpse?

*Charlotte, I have secured tickets for the Zwilling airship's maiden voyage. If you are reading this you should be asleep. Go to bed.*

*—Aunt Hespa*

A third yawn crept up her throat, but she did her best to stifle it. Aunt Hespa would *not* be correct about Charlotte's current state of alertness if Charlotte had anything to say about it. But a small thrill of excitement hummed in her stomach. The maiden voyage of the airship would be very entertaining.

So many things to see and do. The yawn came back with a vengeance, and Charlotte lifted a hand to cover her mouth. Sleep. Sleep would make everything better. "Well, I'd best be off. Tiller, call an autocab, please."

Tiller bowed and helped the blinking Mrs. Graviston out of the parlour.

"Tommyrot," Cosmo said. "You're not going home by autocab at this hour." He shouted after the butler. "Tiller, don't call the cab. I'll take Lady Astley home myself."

Charlotte sighed. "You're still under house arrest." Her nose wrinkled at the phrase. "Besides, you know humans can't travel by mist."

Cosmo fixed her with his green eyes, his dark hair framing his stern features. "They can. *You* simply don't like the side effects."

"Who would want to be asleep for eight hours straight?" Charlotte yawned again.

"Right now, you would." Cosmo took Charlotte's top hat and gloves from Tiller, then put his arm around her waist.

"It drastically reduces my productivity," Charlotte said, allowing herself a small pout. As they stepped into the newly cleaned foyer, she winced—the wall now sported a gaping, cinder-lined hole.

"If I don't intervene," Cosmo said, completely ignoring the partially destroyed wall, "you'll run yourself ragged."

Charlotte turned away, blocking the charred crater from her vision and moved closer into Cosmo's torso. She told herself it was the state of the hallway and her general exhaustion that made her bury herself further in his embrace, not because she was curious what it would feel like.

"Don't forget my Tesla gun and the specter goggles." Charlotte's voice became more and more slurred. Hunting this soul-eater monster had really taken up most of her time. She simply didn't want to rest until everyone was safe from its dark power.

Cosmo cautiously took a step away from Charlotte, his hands up as if ready to catch her should she fall. Only after she'd shown him she was steady did he retrieve the goggles and ray gun. She stumbled a bit, but steadied herself distinctly aware of Cosmo and where his body had been touching hers.

Cosmo gave the goggles to Tiller, who stood sentinel at the door, Charlotte's hat and gloves in his hands at the ready. "No need to worry about the goggles," Cosmo said to her. "I'll bring them tomorrow, after twilight. Say, seven o'clock? Then we'll have a real monster hunting adventure."

Cosmo's voice reached her through the thickening fog of sleep. It took a moment for Charlotte to process his words, her brows knitting together. "You're coming?"

"Blazing suns! Of courth, I'm coming."

Charlotte smiled at the return of his lisp. They hadn't been on a proper adventure in years—not since Cosmo became the second-in-command to the Coven five years ago. He'd become so serious—especially in public. Charlotte suspected it was probably one of the reasons why Cosmo delighted in his hijinks so much— it was his way of letting off steam. She stifled another gaping yawn and let Cosmo lead her to the front door.

"But is it proper for Lord Wilmott to come on a monster hunt?"

"If it's proper enough for the Prince of Wales to grow a snout and howl at the moon, then I see nothing untoward in my joining you to hunt."

"It hasn't been confirmed that the prince is werefolk, you know."

"Not yet." Cosmo waved his hand, clearing the air. "Besides, I have to protect my investment. Those blasted goggles cost me half my fortune."

Charlotte doubted that, but before she could respond, another wave of exhaustion hit her full blast and she staggered. Cosmo easily caught her and scooped her into his arms, her limbs dangling like a puppet whose strings had been cut.

"Are you vamping me?" Charlotte could barely keep her eyes open. She rested her head on his chest, not even stopping to assess whether it was proper or not. "None of your mental…whatever it is you do." Her protestations sounded weak even to her own ears.

"Shh, my dear." He stepped out with her into the brisk London night. Howls suffused the air from Hyde Park, just beyond the Square. The Pack. Charlotte nestled closer to Cosmo's chest, and the same warm feeling from their allurement test wrapped itself around her once more. Was it residual charm from Cosmo's vamping, or was it because she was so close to him, and so incredibly tired? Her last discovery of the night was that she didn't care either way. Cosmo held her tight and the smell of spiced leather washed over her. A velvety blackness enveloped them both, and then Charlotte remembered nothing.

# Chapter 5

Charlotte shoved the last half of a raspberry scone into her mouth, crumbs spilling down her outer corset as she contemplated the circular questions that had been bouncing around her head from the moment she awoke in the late afternoon. What the soul-eater was; how to stop the creature; how to personally acquaint St. Bridgeman with the soul-eater to prove him wrong—the usual questions.

Charlotte wiped the crumbs off her hands. Her Aunt Hespa would have been mortified at the mess, but Charlotte was ravenous. Puzzling required brain food—preferably in the form of Cook's superb scones. Charlotte knew she'd indulged long enough, though. She had things to do.

Her staff usually carried on like a well-oiled Zwilling automaton, but lately there had been minor differences between her personnel she'd had to settle herself. Part of her appointment as Royal Monster Hunter included a large townhouse with attached land just south of

Holland Park in Kensington in the center of London. The previous Royal Monster Hunter had been old-fashioned and more than a little vengeful in his views toward supernaturals—views which some of the previous staff continued to reflect.

Charlotte pursed her lips. *First the staff, old girl. Then you can save the world.*

She sipped the last bit of her tea, the hot liquid infusing energy into her limbs. The china clinked as Beth, the newest maid in the Astley household, entered the room to clear away Charlotte's breakfast. Although, was it still considered breakfast if it was well past teatime and—blazes—nearing half past three?

"This came for you, ma'am," Beth said, handing Charlotte a calling card.

"Thank you, Beth," Charlotte said. The dishware clinked as the young lady replaced the tea service. "By the by, how are you and Howard coming with your full moon preparations? It's in a few days, isn't it?" Where had the last month gone?

"Tha' new hinging door with the pull release will work wonders when we shift. Ta." Her words were optimistic enough, but Charlotte spied Beth tugging at her sleeve attempting to cover the silver moon-shaped mark on the inside of her wrist.

Charlotte bent down and caught Beth's downcast gaze. It was unusual for any employer, let alone the Royal Monster Hunter, to employ supernaturals, especially ones so new to their afterlives—newborn vampires and werewolves could be unstable. Charlotte made a point to provide as many accommodations for her staff—human and supernatural alike—as they needed. The werewolves were given special consideration around the full moon, she usually made up the time difference in working hours by giving humans more time off. Hardly any employers did that for their staff.

"You needn't worry about hiding that here," Charlotte told Beth. "And soon you won't need to concern yourself with it at all. The mark fades within three transformations."

The young maid nodded her head and gave a tentative smile. "It's just tha', with the Council for Humanity raisin' all kinds of trouble, ya cannae be too careful."

Charlotte placed a gentle hand on her arm. "You're safe here."

A genuine smile grew on Beth's face, her usually cheery mood mostly restored.

"These came for ya this mornin'." She placed a stack of mail on the table top. Charlotte's fingers tapped the edges of the stack as she looked at them; the morning paper, a card from Mrs. Weatherton, and a letter from a distant relation. Nothing out of the ordinary, except…what was this?

A thick envelope crinkled, and she pulled it out of the stack and tore it open. Edges of cheap wood-pulp paper peeked through. The next penny dreadful in the Dick Turpin series! She clutched the book against her chest, trying to think of when she would next have some time to read it. The stories were ludicrously horrible fiction, but she simply couldn't help herself—it was so awful it was wonderful.

With a sigh, she set down the penny dreadful and turned back to the other envelopes. Nothing interesting. Then Beth produced a small package and additional envelope. The rectangular parcel was wrapped in packing paper and twine, with a small brass key looped through the knot and bow. She chewed on her lip as her fingers tugged at the string and paper.

The paper crinkled open and Charlotte gasped at what it revealed—a stunning glove box made of polished sandalwood with an intricate repeating flower and scroll border. On the top of the lid were three delicately carved ivory panels. Charlotte immediately recognized the symbolism in each panel, her fingers tracing each tiny masterpiece. The left panel depicted a waning crescent moon peppered with tiny craters and the profile of a wolf's head emerged from the side facing the center of the box. *Werewolves.* In the far right panel, the shrouded figure of a woman was shown next to an open grave. *Specters.* A blossoming rose flourished as the focal point of the lid, growing beyond its carved quatrefoil border. Tiny garnet drops, red as the blood they represented, adorned the edges of the petals and winked as they caught the light. *Vampires.* Simply put, the box was exquisite.

Charlotte placed the box on the table. "There was no other card with this item?"

Beth shook her head, her eyes wide.

The floor creaked as Charlotte moved to the edge of her chair. Whoever had sent it had very fine taste indeed—and knew her very well.

With the key pressing between her fingertips, Charlotte pushed it into the brass lock that was shaped like a heart inside a sunburst. A sharp sandalwood aroma wafted through the air as she opened the box and removed a second envelope secured with a small wax seal. Something oddly shaped lay in the box, covered with a silk cloth. Charlotte flipped the envelope over, then smiled as she saw the image on the seal.

Her fingers traced the Wilmott crest's lion, to which had recently been added tiny bat wings. Charlotte pulled away the cloth, revealing the goggles from the night before along with an additional letter.

*I meant to present the goggles to you inside this box but the box was still at the jeweler's and it seemed that you needed the goggles immediately.*

*Invitation almost secured. Can't wait to see St. Bridgeman's face.*

*—Cosmo.*

*P.S. I will call on you shortly after your supper. It's time to unravel your soul-eater mystery.*

A surprisingly pleasant sensation prickled the hairs on her arms, tingling as they traced the flourished calligraphy of Cosmo's signature. Had he vamped the paper? Was such a thing even possible? Holding the specs over her eyes, she scanned the letter. Not even a hint of purple. Hmm.

Emotions from the allurement charm last night trickled through her logic. He had been so deucedly handsome. His high cheek bones, athletic build, the way he always ran his fingers through his hair, mussing his rich brown locks—everything was suddenly endearing. They all coalesced into a perfect storm. She winced as her words from last night came back to her. Was he actually more storm than drizzle?

"He must like you very much to give you such a lovely thing," Beth said.

The spell broke. Charlotte looked up, almost surprised to see Beth still standing there. Charlotte rubbed her arms, trying to dispel the feeling. She closed the box gently and set it aside. Time to get back to the matter of her staff.

"Beth, please bring me the preparations list for the full moon, and have Mrs. Eden assemble the staff. I'd like to restock everyone's kits. And, may I say that I deeply appreciate your allowing me to observe your next transformation. The wolfsbane and valerian tisane will be ready by then and should slow the transformation, making it less painful."

Beth nodded her eyes again uneasy, then turned to finish clearing the trays.

Charlotte picked up the box with the goggles and retired to her study ready to work. She pulled out the list of full moon preparations, rechecked the condition of her Tesla ray, and assessed her salt and garlic stores—everything a modern London household should have. Her staff did much of this themselves, but it helped Charlotte organize her thoughts and gave her peace of mind knowing that even the smallest detail had been personally reviewed. Plus, with it being Beth's second transformation, Charlotte wanted to be certain that everything ran smoothly. Beth could prematurely snap and transform if put under enough pressure, and without the calming effects of the full moon, she could easily rampage. The household could quickly turn upon one of its own.

She tapped the paper against her lips in contemplation. They were prepared for all manner of known supernaturals, but how could she prepare her staff against a creature like the soul-eater? Was it shifter-based, or was it phantasmagoric in nature? She hoped the goggles could at least help identify what category of supernatural it was…and whether there were or could be more of them.

The biggest part of what had made the Origination so—well, horrific was an understatement—was that it had escalated. One vampire or werewolf could have possibly been dealt with quickly. No, it was the fact that each vampire or werewolf had also been changing other humans at alarming rates.

A chill raised the hairs on the back of Charlotte's neck. She'd been safely away at her family's country house when the Origination had reached its peak. Compared to London, the country had been relatively prepared by the time rogue vampires and werewolves appeared and turned on those who dwelt there.

Originologists theorized that the whole event began with a solitary vampire and werewolf who bit only a few humans themselves; then, much like the cholera outbreak fifty years ago, the human population was transformed at exponential rates each night, until the Origination reached its zenith in ten days' time. Confused newborn vampires, with a new all-consuming dietary need, slaughtered families and friends. Not long after, the newborn werewolves fought the blood-crazed vamps for territory—a time known as the Upheavals. With other "lesser" supernaturals like boggarts, goblins, and banshees appearing alongside the transformed humans, London was chaos incarnate for three weeks straight. Once the full moon had passed and the newborn vamps had been satiated on the blood of unfortunate innocents, their human natures reasserted themselves, and the supernaturals devastated at the destruction they had caused, submitted to the hatred and abuse of the surviving humans.

There were rumblings among the ruling class of retaliation against the supernaturals, even war. How could there not be with almost a third of the population either killed or transformed? War seemed imminent. However rumors began to spread that the Prince of Wales had been bitten by a werewolf and turned. The crown intervened. They issued a proclamation outlining basic supernatural rules and regulations, for life among the supernatural population, though little had been done for supernatural rights. But the Victoria and Albert Blood Clinic for the vamps and hunting territories for the werefolk had been established within London proper, along with a monthly delivery of large game from the countryside. These helped provide for a somewhat smoother transition to a new normal life for both the supernaturals and the humans.

And in the years since, no one had been able to solve the mystery of the Origination and of the supernaturals' beginnings.

"The staff is assembled, m'lady."

Charlotte rose, followed Mrs. Eden to the staff kitchen, and smiled at the people lined up before her. After the Origination, the Astley house had been one of the first to employ the newly turned supernatural population, in good part because Charlotte was one of the best-equipped to handle a rogue supernatural. The staff was a rag tag bunch comprising of two vampires, three werefolk, and an odd assortment of humans and other supernaturals.

The staff's supernatural abilities opened up new efficiencies and dynamics within the household, such as performing some tasks quicker and identifying the freshest groceries with their enhanced smell. Overall, Charlotte was quite pleased with the results.

She inspected the kit each staff was holding, though her mind kept drifting back to the soul-eater. Her ruminations snapped when she came to Mr. Bauen's kit.

"Where's your salt, Mr. Bauen?"

"Pouch got damp, m'lady, and dissolved half the salt," he grumbled while casting a glare toward a young vampire maid. "The other half is hard as stone."

The muscles on Charlotte's neck tightened and her heart sank. He was usually above any petty machinations toward staff members.

Mr. Bauen was one of the still-human members of her staff. His salt and pepper hair was now more salt than pepper. When had that happened? She could clearly remember him and her father discussing early autocabs and how they might be improved. He spent most of his spare time in the carriage house, tinkering and helping improve post-Origination life. It was he who had come up with the cleverly concealed spring-loaded doors, some of which had wooden stakes drilled into them while others housed small firearms—all of which were loaded with silver bullets. Thankfully, she'd never had to use them, but a young lady living on her own in supernatural London could never be too careful.

The young woman vampire—who obviously thought herself outside of Charlotte's peripheral vision—stuck out a crimson tongue in response to Bauen's glare.

Tension crackled through the assembled staff's movements and Charlotte spied angry sidelong glances between the half-dryad and the new boot boy. Mrs. Eden, the housekeeper, shifted her weight, her pinched features displaying her own disappointment with the staff's behavior.

Charlotte netted her fingers in front of her and released a measured breath. She'd never been a maid, but she certainly often felt like one, rushing from one mess to the next. Couldn't civilized society stay civil for five minutes?

Her heels clicked on the black and white tiles, and she lifted her chin as she strode in front of the gathered staff, commanding their attention. "The Astley household is a rare gem amid the residual strife and contention that continues to stain London. Your duty is to this house"— Charlotte paused making sure to catch each staff member's gaze— "and to each other."

Mr. Bauen dropped his gaze to the floor and a smug look crept across the vampire's face. Charlotte gave a mental sigh. Was her house a microcosm for larger politics in Parliament? Apparently this maid needed a stronger incentive.

Charlotte cleared her throat. "And finally, I must remind you that prejudiced and petty behavior"—she looked straight at the maid—"will not be tolerated unless one wishes a swift and most judicious termination of their post."

Now the young vampire dropped her gaze to the floor, having the decency to at least look sheepish. Charlotte dipped her chin, satisfied the matter would rest for now.

"Mrs. Eden, would you please—"

A rap at the door interrupted Charlotte's words.

Beth dipped a curtsey and left to answer the door. Charlotte pressed her lips into a thin line, anxious to continue preparing the staff.

Beth opened the door greeting the visitor. Though the entryway was around several corners from the staff meeting, noise from the street invaded the kitchen and the scent of animals and dust assaulted the nose. A man's grating voice ricocheted down the hallway. "Interested in…beware…Council for Humanity…"

Charlotte's breath caught and she held up a finger to silence the staff's murmurs. Her fingertips pressed against her wrist sheaths as she moved toward the door. What was going on? Only personal deliveries or callers should be using the front door.

"You're one of them!" the male voice snarled, followed by a rip and a sharp slap. Charlotte quickened her pace.

Beth was cowering against the base of the stairs, looking up at the intruder who was well beyond the house's threshold. He loomed over the young woman and Council pamphlets fluttered around his feet. "Please, sir," she whimpered. The sleeve of her shirt had been ripped open, exposing her forearm, and the silver mark flashed like a brand.

"Your kind cost me my job!" The man looked as feral as any newborn supernatural. His right hand gripped Beth's forearm. His left arm and face were a mangled mess of scars. Werewolf claw and bite marks. "You werewolf bi—" He slapped her again.

A red welt rose on the side of Beth's tear-stained face.

"That's enough!" In two strides Charlotte stood between the man and Beth.

The man blinked and stepped backward, releasing Beth. "This vermin," he spat, "is werefolk."

"Indeed," Charlotte said, her voice even-toned, despite the fury burning inside. Her eyes consumed the man's tattered suit, his mangled form. His life had likely been devastated by the Origination, and he'd never recovered. Someone he'd become a canvasser for the Council. A zealot.

She knew she shouldn't antagonize the man, but the words came unbidden. "She's also the best maid I've ever had. The only pest I see here is you."

The man's face turned purple and his scars white. "You know about this—this filth in your home?" Before Charlotte could react, he pushed past Charlotte and his fist cracked the side of Beth's head. Beth fell back against the stairs and lay gasping on the ground. Her breathing turned to rasping. Her fingers curled.

Charlotte shoved the intruder out of the way and knelt next to Beth. The maid's dark eyes were turning amber.

Blast. It was too early. There was no moon and this was only Beth's second turn. *No, no, not now.*

Charlotte whirled at the man. His barrel chest heaved, the smell of beer on his breath washing over Charlotte. Violent types like this only reacted to violence. So be it.

"Sir, I suggest you leave before I make you."

"Not without this." A growl hurtled from his throat, and he grabbed Beth's ankle and pulled. Her head bumped on the stairs and she groaned, her eyes rolling back in her head.

Charlotte wrenched his hands off of the girl and grabbed his collar to force him to look into her face. "Unless you want the rest of your body to match your face and arm, you will leave *now*."

Rustling from the hallway told her the entire staff was close by in the corridor.

The man's eyes widened as he saw the staff. "This whole house is infested." He shoved away from Charlotte and started trying to count the supernaturals in her household.

Beth's back arched, her thin frame contorting in pain. Her moans intensified.

Charlotte swallowed. Not enough time. "Mrs. Eden," Charlotte called behind her. "Get the wolfsbane and rosemary poultice. Louisa, start a lavender tea. Mr. Bauen, start an ice bath. Add lots of salt."

The hallway burst in a flurry of hurried but controlled activity. They knew what to do. This is what they'd daily prepared for.

The intruder scowled and advanced. "You're saving that filthy mongrel?"

Charlotte closed the distance between them.

"Leave." She threw her full fury into her next words. "Or I'll kill you myself." She slipped a knife from her sleeve and pressed it against his stomach. "I don't like to repeat myself."

The man hesitated. Was his stupidity inherent or an effect of the alcohol? She pressed the knife deeper, and the man gasped. He fled to the front door, placing a hand on the door frame. "The Council will know about this."

Beth groaned and doubled over, her teeth elongating. Panic clouded her yellowing eyes.

With a flick of her wrist, Charlotte's knife thudded into the door frame, grazing the tip of his fingers.

The man scuttled out the door and into the glaring sunlight, whimpering. Charlotte slammed the door shut, her chest heaving.

"Mr. Bauen," she shouted. "Secure the premises and ring the constabulary. I want that man in chains."

A guttural cry came from behind Charlotte. She whirled.

The skin around Beth's eyes began to darken with tiny hairs. She fought for each breath as her bones attempted to prematurely arrange themselves.

"I'm here, Beth," Charlotte said, dropping next to her writhing form. "Control your breathing…that's it. Deep breath in. And out. Help is coming."

Hours later and completely exhausted, Charlotte pulled out a chair in the kitchen and practically collapsed into it. Mrs. Eden sat across from her, a sheen of sweat across her brow. Mr. Bauen and the young vampire joined them looking just as worn, as did a few other members of the staff.

"Well, I'm knackered," Mr. Bauen said, mopping at his neck with a kerchief.

With the tea, poultice, and salted ice bath, Beth's transformation had slowed and then reversed. Even with Charlotte and her staff working tirelessly and the mix of remedies, it had taken nearly two hours before Beth was out of the danger zone.

Charlotte nodded and looked at each staff member. She fixed her gaze on the young vampire maid from earlier, who had worked tirelessly, carrying buckets of ice from the ice house to the bathing tub.

They had done it. They had saved Beth.

Exhaustion blanketed all of Charlotte's feelings except one.

"Well done," Charlotte said, allowing the pride she felt to reso-
nate in her voice. "Well done all."

# Chapter 6

"Cast off!"

The order from the aerial officer echoed along the promenade deck and down the line of sailors. The airship *Asteria* gave a groan and rose, stopping to hover fifty feet in the air. At this height, Charlotte could peer over the top of the Crystal Palace's iron frame and its many glass panels reflecting the noonday sun.

Airshipmen scrambled over the ratlines and rigging, their shouts lost among the clamorous throng. A pleasant swaying sensation wobbled through Charlotte as the *Asteria* caught some of the cross breezes, sending the deck rocking gently. Her heart rate jumped. She'd often envied Cosmo and other vampires their ability to mist and fly; this was the closest she'd ever get to replicating that phenomenon, and she intended to enjoy every moment. And hopefully a lunch with raspberry scones.

This respite would be perfect. A short but much-needed jaunt around London.

Two days had passed since Beth's near-transformation and taking a meal on London's first and only luxury airship liner was a splendid way to literally rise above one's problems. Waves of delight rippled through Charlotte and she leaned further over the railing, the buttons of her coat pressing against her stomach. Ground crew scrambled over the grass untethering more lines and stowing the gangplank.

"Charlotte, s-stay away from the rail." Beside her, Aunt Hespa and her lady's companion Minnie Zhou stood watching the beehive of activity.

Aunt Hespa and Minnie could not have been more different. Minnie's thick raven hair, loosely piled atop her head, put Aunt Hespa's graying plain chignon to shame. The older woman's severe attitude was reflected in her dark-blue traveling dress, its vertical lines accentuating its wearer's angles; Minnie's loose, pink ruffled dress emphasized her plump curves and brightened her smile and golden complexion. When they stood next to one another, Aunt Hespa towered over the shorter Asian woman; however, Aunt Hespa was holding tight to Minnie's strong arms, like a drowning woman clinging to a branch along a riverbank.

"Do you hear me, niece?" Aunt Hespa spluttered at Charlotte. "It would be very ungrateful of you to p-plunge overboard after *I* secured tickets for such an indecorous activity."

Charlotte sighed, then complied with her aunt's wishes. While the playful summer breezes tugged at her skirts, feelings of guilt, anger, and disappointment coiled in Charlotte's chest. The purchase of these tickets *was* incredibly thoughtful of Aunt Hespa, as she eschewed anything adventurous, and Charlotte felt pangs of sympathy that her otherwise commanding aunt was terrified the the point of stuttering. But warmth also bloomed inside Charlotte. Was Aunt Hespa finally seeing her niece as something more than a thorn in her prim and proper side?

Charlotte peered up at the large, rugby-shaped, lighter-than-air balloon hovering above them. If this steel-framed contraption could float above London, perhaps Charlotte and her aunt's relationship could rise to new heights as well.

"Thank you for the tickets, Aunt Hespa." The hope swirling in her chest rose above the other more selfish emotions. *Remember, small steps before big leaps. Make this easy for Aunt Hespa and it will pay dividends later.*

"Oh, you don't know what I suffer. If you comprehended the great lengths I took to ensure your enjoyment—" Aunt Hespa pulled out a white handkerchief and waved it in front of her until it looked like a bird in distress. "Minnie, my tonic."

Feat shot through Charlotte's heart. *Blazing suns.* Nothing, not even a horde of shambling lich, could spoil this trip...except Aunt Hespa's nerves. Charlotte screwed on her attentive-niece smile, praying that Minnie had indeed packed the tonic.

"Yes, of course," Minnie said, fishing out a small amber bottle from her reticule. She uncorked it and gave it to Aunt Hespa, who took a sip of the liquid and grimaced. Minnie returned the vial to its place and took Aunt Hespa's hand in her own.

As Aunt Hespa's companion, Minnie was obliged to comfort; but as Charlotte's friend, she was also obliged to glance at her behind Aunt Hespa's back and give an eye roll.

Charlotte smiled, then stepped closer to Aunt Hespa wrapping her arm around the thin-framed woman and pulling her into a gentle embrace. Her aunt was shivering despite the warm summer sun. *The poor dear.*

"How many trips has the *Asteria* taken?" Aunt Hespa's panicked gray eyes gazed past the prow. "They're saying it's an infallible airship; the statement lacks tact and humility. People should know that such superlative claims invite disaster."

"Perhaps I shall find a steward," Minnie said.

Charlotte nodded, recognizing the telltale signs of an "authority-only" solution. Nothing but reassurances from an aeronautical expert—or at least one of the staff—would calm Aunt Hespa's nerves.

Minnie departed, the breeze ruffling the skirts peeking beneath her beige traveling coat.

Aunt Hespa glanced between Charlotte and Minnie and muttered something about "their pity" and "...think they have me all figured out."

Charlotte squeezed her aunt's upper arm in succor, but Hespa's features twisted in discomfort at the gesture and she pulled away, carefully tucking her partially amputated limb under her traveling shawl. Like many of London's residents, Aunt Hespa had not come out of the Origination unscathed, but she was one of the few who still bothered to try to hide the damage. And she was still always uncharacteristically reserved around werefolk.

"Charlotte, please," Aunt Hespa said. "Sentimentality cannot compensate for authority."

Scraping the bottom of her well of patience, Charlotte pulled a steadying breath.

Aunt Hespa's hysterics continued and despite Charlotte's gratitude and hope of a better relationship, she was half contemplating throwing her aunt overboard. It wouldn't have been a subtle solution, but it would have stopped Aunt Hespa from ruining the one spot of enjoyment in Charlotte's entire week.      Fortunately, Minnie returned with the steward who began to explain much of what they had already read in the travel brochure.

"The airship will rise in stages until we reach the desired altitude. Some minor turbulence is to be expected. We will sail due north over the Thames, enjoying a bird's eye view as we circle over Highgate and the Abney Park Cemetery, which boasts over two thousand different tree and shrub var–"

"Weigh anchor!"

*Finally.* Charlotte bit her lip in anticipation.

The ship rose with the steady elegance of quicksilver in a warming thermometer. The crew doubled their efforts with every meter. The smooth oak deck pressed against her feet, defying earth's gravitational pull, and she hazarded letting go of the railing with one hand to grip the brim of her hat as the wind whipped her hair and stung her face. It was hard to keep herself in one piece—half of her wanted to present a proper societal front, while the other half wanted to raise her arms wide in abandon and shriek with delight like the gulls.

She restrained herself. Barely.

Behind her, Aunt Hespa, after recovering from the launch with a wave of her fan, maneuvered the steward away from the two friends and into a "discussion" about the safety of the *Asteria* and how she was sure the Queen herself would have some issues with their protocol.

After the dispute, which, Aunt Hespa had apparently won, she returned, her complexion healthy and strong. She'd simply needed someone to boss around. The steward, now sufficiently cowed, gave many "yes, ma'am's" and "of courses." Charlotte was altogether glad it wasn't her this time. Was this a sign of a change in their relationship?

"You said you had something planned for this outing, Aunt Hespa," Charlotte reminded.

Aunt Hespa's now-steady voice carried easily through the chilling air. "I've invited several people for lunch and you *must* behave."

All of Charlotte's sympathy evaporated like smoke, and the slight urge to toss her aunt overboard returned with a vengeance. "Behave" was code for "be nice to the man I've deemed marriageable, end this supernatural detective business, and have an army of babies."

"I've asked the steward to show us in to the dining room early." Aunt Hespa then turned on the man like a newborn vampire looking for first blood. "I have some extremely special guests for the luncheon, and as such, I expect them to be given the utmost attention." Aunt Hespa and the haggard steward moved away from the railing, leaving Minnie and Charlotte alone.

While Minnie laughed, Charlotte groaned. "I don't think I can stand another round of her machinations. Last time it was so dreadful I wanted to gouge out my own eyes."

"What about Lord Wilmott?" Minnie teased, her almond eyes alight with mischief. It was a favorite taunt of Minnie's but it annoyed Charlotte to no end. Why did everyone insist that two people of marrying age who were close friends had to be in a romantic relationship? Did platonic connections no longer exist? What was the world coming to?

"We are *friends*. Plus, he's still a vampire." Charlotte eyed her friend shrewdly, the air began whipping about them more. "Aunt Hespa would never approve."

Deep inside Charlotte's heart—in dark, neglected corners that she avoided—a longing for romance smoldered. The Origination had thrown off several Seasons, including Charlotte and Minnie's, but now the *ton* assemblage was back in full gear and they were both careening towards spinsterhood.

"Perhaps, we'll find a beau for you," Charlotte said holding her hand to her forehead and peering down at the crisscrossing streets below.

"He'd have to be a scrupulous one." Minnie waggled her gloved fingers like an evil wizard about to cast a spell. Since the Origination, she had had a mysterious gift of claircognizance which allowed her to view past details of an inanimate object. She had once touched an emerald brooch and used her ability to locate the duchess to whom it belonged. Charlotte had begged Minnie to allow her to perform experiments to see exactly where her limits fell, but she had demurred. Charlotte had been forced to accept that some people had serious deficiencies in their dedication to science. Though, Minnie's gift made her blazing hard to beat at cards.

"Oh, please," Charlotte wheedled, "use your powers."

"I don't know." Minnie looked towards the stern spying some shuffleboard tables and a game of quoits, but Charlotte was already dragging her stout friend to a cluster of deck furniture.

Minnie bit her lip and scanned the chairs. "These might be safe." She removed her glove. Charlotte glanced around. Aunt Hespa and the steward were still discussing proper luncheon protocol.

No sooner had Minnie touched the back of the chair when a shudder racked her body, her shoulders wriggling in disgust. "Ugh, a spider was here." She quickly replaced her glove.

Charlotte examined the deck. "I don't see anything."

Minnie shook her head. "Sometime yesterday. A spider crawled across the back." She pressed her gloved knuckles to her mouth.

"Your ability showed you...a spider."

Minnie squeaked an affirmative.

"From yesterday."

"It was this big." She raised her fingers. The offending arachnid had been the size of a penny. Charlotte pressed her lips between her teeth. "And that was only a day ago," Minnie continued, "which means it could still be somewhere close, making spider babies—no, making aerial spider babies. That can fly." Minnie's dark eyes grew round and she swallowed. "A legion of flying aeronautical spider babies."

The two giggled at the long-gone arachnid even if Minnie's was more nervous tittering than real mirth.

Aunt Hespa approached. "Charlotte, this man will show us to the dining room."

"Aunt, we are permitted on deck during the entire launch."

"We will retire." Steel edged her words, and she whirled around like the Duke of Wellington leading the troops into battle. Her bustled silk plaid skirts trailed in her wake.

Charlotte shrank inside. She took the wild, half-crazed-with-limitless-freedom part of herself and folded it away. When she spoke, her voice was hollow. "Yes, Aunt Hespa." She looked at the unburdened sky with all of London one last time before following her aunt into the dining room.

The Zwilling Company spared no expense as evidenced by the sheer elegance of the interior. The dining room's expansive walls were adorned with hand-carved white-painted wood paneling. The azure linoleum tiles, speckled with tiny silver stars, gave Charlotte the impression she was waltzing across the heavens. Small Tesla lamp sconces provided a warm summer-dawn light. The portholes were larger than an ocean liner's and offered an incredible view of the Thames winding like a green ribbon through London. The scents of the air changed from cool and soot-tinged to woody and sharp. The lemony scent of linseed oil and piney odor of the fresh turpentine paint filled the space, stinging her nostrils.

Waitstaff bustled around the room, seating guests and placing ornate tea services in the center of each table, while sumptuous buffet tables flanked the right wall. Within moments of being seated, Charlotte's stomach rumbled, warning her that if it was not attended to soon, it would cause problems. *Patience. Raspberry scones are coming.* She attempted to scoot her chair forward but instead bumped her knees into the table.

*What in the blazing suns?* She looked down at thick, sturdy bolts securing the furniture to the floor. The steward had insisted this would be a smooth ride, but doubts crept into Charlotte's mind. *Foolish girl. Never trust an advertisement.*

Two seats at their table remained vacant, but that didn't stop the staff from bringing the tea service. The Zwilling Company logo—a sun, moon, and two stars superimposed over each other—adorned the dinnerware.

Charlotte wasted no time in filling her plate with smoked salmon, chocolate éclairs and other assorted pastries from the tiered serving tower. Sadly, no raspberry scones were to be found.

Charlotte and Minnie fell into eating and swapping nuggets of gossip while Aunt Hespa continued to scan the remaining guests. After a moment, a tall, Romanesque woman bedecked in green brocade approached, her gray-blonde hair pinned loosely atop her head. Aunt Hespa stood and held out her hands. The newcomer's angled face accentuated her aquiline nose and commanding presence.

"Mathilda. This is my niece, Lady Charlotte Astley. Charlotte, this is Baroness St. Bridgeman."

Charlotte nearly choked on her éclair. Blazing suns, was St. Bridgeman here? He would ruin the entire trip for certain. She relaxed when a thin, unfamiliar young man nodded to her from behind the baroness, and she managed to hide her relieved smile.

Charlotte tried, but she couldn't help but feel immediate dislike towards the woman who had spawned her nemesis. The baroness wore a large opal necklace with strands of pearls rippling around her collarbones. An agate cameo ring shone from her left hand, and a glittering diamond bracelet coiled around her wrist. Charlotte wrinkled her nose silently judging the baroness and her absent (though still bothersome) offspring. They practically stunk of wealth.

Charlotte skin prickled. Aunt Hespa was glaring daggers at her. Was she supposed to respond? Charlotte swallowed the last bit of éclair, wincing as it crammed down into her throat. "Apologies, I didn't catch the name?"

Aunt Hespa sniffed, but the baroness smiled and gestured to the sticklike man behind her. "This is Mr. Ernst Hollands, youngest son of Lord Hollands."

Mr. Hollands, who had been sucking something out of his teeth, clicked his tongue and offered a bow.

Charlotte stifled a groan. *Mr. Hollands?* She thought she had preemptively dealt with him at Aunt Hespa's salon the month before. During a pause in one of Mrs. Brown's lectures, Aunt Hespa had made pointed remarks about Mr. Holland's many virtues: primarily, that he came from a landed family with several titles.

Charlotte had commented to her aunt about wanting more than additional titles in a marriage.

Her aunt had fallen silent and Charlotte had supposed that was that. But looking at the man before her, Charlotte had new reason to question her aunt's sanity. Did Aunt Hespa want Charlotte to court this man? His beaked nose and narrow face looked as if someone had squeezed him into an iron vise, pushing all of his features forward.

*I knew Aunt Hespa desperately wanted grand-nieces and nephews, but didn't she at least want them to be pleasant to look at?*

Charlotte dipped a curtsy. "What a pleasure." She shot Minnie a raised eyebrow.

Minnie stifled a giggle.

They all sat and talked of the weather (boring), the taste of the refreshments (mediocre), and small snatches of last week's gossip (yawn). Mr. Hollands answered with a flat monosyllabic replies, more focused on getting that stubborn bit of food from between his teeth than his surroundings. However, after his dental needs had been addressed, a torrent of banal conversation flooded from the man. Charlotte wished for an emergency, a rogue supernatural, for *anything* to appear and get her out of this highly awkward situation.

The one interesting thing during the luncheon, which no one else seemed to notice, was their tea resting unevenly in the cups. Everything slanted to the left by about five degrees for several minutes. The ship must have been turning for the return journey to the Crystal Palace.

Charlotte had her chin in her hand now, only pretending to listen. How cold was it on the observation deck now? What did London look like from the air? Could she see the coast?

"I have been fortunate enough as to have been distinguished by Lady Hespa Shelton," Mr. Hollands was saying in his pinched voice when Charlotte started listening again. "Her beneficence has allowed me a glimpse into this most illustrious group, where it shall be my earnest endeavor to demean myself with grateful respect towards her Ladyship."

Charlotte nearly rolled her eyes. No wonder her aunt liked this man.

Mr. Hollands turned the conversation to his football club (apparently his deepest passion) and was waxing eloquent about the proper dimensions of a football when the waitstaff returned. They began offering each table small plates of gingerbread, lavender, and tea biscuits.

As their server navigated the buzzing dining room, the ship gave a shudder, and his face screwed tight with fear. His sunrise-yellow eyes, a usual trait of werewolves shortly after a full moon, darkened with worry, but his movements were smooth as his predator's muscles helped him balance. He wore the same yellow armbands as few of the other airshipman.

Charlotte saw stark black letters stitched onto the fabric. Her blood chilled as if someone had dropped ice down her corset. The stitching read "SPN-W." "Supernatural-werewolf." Some companies refused to hire supernatural beings, and there was rampant mistreatment towards the employed ones, but to see such visible segregation in front of her reignited all the fury she'd felt at Beth's abuse a few short days ago.

"Here you are, miss," the yellow-eyed man said with a tremor in his voice as he set the tea on the table. If he'd been in wolf form, Charlotte was certain his tail would have been tucked between his legs.

As he bent to place Charlotte's plate of biscuits in front of her, the server next to him shoved into him, and the dish crashed to the floor, crumbs spreading everywhere.

"I say," Mr. Hollands complained, brushing scraps from his suit. "What a waste of a biscuit."

"Watch where yer going," the other server said, disdain layering his voice.

Charlotte flung her napkin to the table and stood. "That was no accident."

A superior in a white uniform rushed to the werewolf and hustled him off to a corner of the room. The head of staff appeared and wasted no time reprimanding the cowering werewolf, his words easily heard throughout the quieting dining room.

"Johnathan, you stupid dog. Did you think you'd get to eat the scraps of anything that fell on the floor? This is what I get for allowing you above decks. As soon as we land, you're off."

"My apologies, Baroness, Aunt." Charlotte brushed crumbs from her skirt. "Please excuse me."

Her feet were unsteady on the linoleum. Something was off about the dining room. Was it tilting more? She had no time to wonder, though. Justice needed to be served.

In the corner, the werewolf glanced from the head of staff to the man who had bumped him, then to the floor, never maintaining eye contact with anyone. The second server folded his arms, a smug smile pinned to his face.

The head of staff was so busy berating the werewolf, Johnathan, he didn't notice Charlotte standing until she tapped him on the shoulder. "Pardon me."

He turned, his voice suddenly smooth and appeasing. "Apologies, miss. I'll be finished in a moment."

"You are finished now." Charlotte held the man's gaze. He spluttered, and she moved between him and the werewolf Johnathan. "This man meant no harm. In fact, he has been a very attentive server to us. I insist you allow him to resume his duties."

"This will be handled. You may return to your table, miss." The head of staff sneered and stepped closer to Charlotte, blocking her view of the dining room. "This one must learn his place."

The dining room was now eerily quiet. Charlotte's fingers itched to grab a weapon. "Now, wait just a moment—"

"What is the meaning of this?" The strong voice of someone used to getting their own way sliced through Charlotte's retort.

The head of staff turned to the newcomer and both he and the werewolf each gave a small bow. "Baroness St. Bridgeman."

The baroness's eyes went to Johnathan's armband, and something stirred behind her cool mask.

Blazing suns, could this get any worse?

"Apologies for the trouble this one may have caused you." The head of staff's sycophantic voice grated in Charlotte's ears.

The ship gave a shiver, and the baroness's face tightened. Charlotte sighed inwardly, preparing to wage battle on two fronts.

*Blazing suns. The apple never falls far from the tree.*

"He has caused no trouble." The baroness's steady tone stated these words as irrefutable fact. "We are all quite well." Something flashed in her green eyes.

"Y-yes, baroness." The head of staff and the second server inched away, never taking their eyes off her before they escaped back to the kitchen.

Charlotte felt a shiver of fear snake through her veins—which was unusual, but blazing suns! Members of high society rarely ruffled Charlotte's feathers, but this woman did it with ease, and on behalf of a werewolf. Perhaps St. Bridgeman's apple fell farther from the tree than she'd initially thought.

The baroness unclasped her green reticule and pulled out two small calling cards that bore a shield with a crescent moon.

When she handed one to Johnathan, he stared at it as if unsure of what it was.

"This is my charity, The Preservation and Enhancement of Super-natural Society." The baroness's reticule closed with a snap. "Perhaps you could join us next Tuesday evening at my townhouse near Regents Park. You as well, Lady Astley," she said, handing Charlotte a second card.

It took Charlotte a moment to close her astonished mouth. "Of course, Baroness."

Johnathan stashed the card in the pocket of his suit, gave a curt bow, then, without a word, returned to the kitchens. His posture was slightly more upright.

Charlotte had a thousand questions tickling her brain. "Your charity is…unexpected," was the politest she could muster as she and the baroness returned to their table.

Aunt Hespa and Minnie stared at the pair, worry etched deep in Aunt Hespa's drawn features, curiosity sparking the latter's. Mr. Hollands, however, had somehow managed to cram a large slice of pound cake into his very narrow mouth and was helping himself to another, oblivious to the entire exchange.

"I know who you are," the baroness said as she sank into her chair, her voice low but still audible above the noise resuming in the dining room. "My son has…spoken of you."

Charlotte squirmed like a child caught with their hand in the sweet jar. What had St. Bridgeman said about her?

Aunt Hespa gripped the tablecloth, her eyes wide. Charlotte couldn't be certain of her aunt's exact thoughts but assumed it as something along the lines of, "Dear heavens, my niece will be publicly humiliated and kept from polite society and be rendered unmarriageable condemning herself to a life of lonely spinsterhood."

Charlotte forced her face to remain neutral.

"Trevor and I do not always share our beliefs," the baroness said, "But perhaps you and I do. Your aunt invited me to an evening of croquet in two night's time. Perhaps we could discuss more there?"

Aunt Hespa leaned back in her seat and closed her eyes, letting out an almost imperceptible breath.

Charlotte's eyes widened. A smile twitched at the corner of her mouth. Maybe this luncheon was worth all of Mr. Hollands' tedium after all. "That sounds lovely. Thank you."

They settled into their seats, each with a fresh plate of biscuits, Mr. Hollands munching steadily on the offerings. "Glad that was resolved," he said, crumbs spilling from his mouth with every word.

The ship jolted with a deep groan from below decks and Aunt Hespa gripped the edge of the table. The baroness placed a hand over her heart and the other pressed against her forehead. Charlotte's brow furrowed. This behavior didn't match the strong woman from moments before.

Another tremor rocked the ship and guests screamed. Charlotte glanced down at her saucer and teacup, noticing that the water was at a significantly higher slant, perhaps fifteen degrees.

The ship heaved again, sending silverware clattering against the floor, then steadied and leveled itself out. Guests froze, some half-standing, waiting to see what the *Asteria* would do next.

The baroness moaned and swayed in her seat, her skin greying. Her mouth formed a small "o" and her eyelids fluttered, then she collapsed into her chair.

"Mathilda!" Aunt Hespa shot to her feet. "Minnie, my tonic and salts!"

Charlotte leaned over, raised her hand to the baroness's forehead, then frowned. Feverish.

The guests murmured. Mr. Hollands clutched at his napkin. "Egads, she's succumbed."

The whole dining room lurched to the left. People screamed and grabbed at the tables. Minnie held onto Aunt Hespa, both women frozen in fear. "It's a vampire attack," Aunt Hespa shrieked. "It is!"

The tea services and dishware slid from the bolted furniture, crashing onto the floor and splattering cream and tea everywhere.

The ship continued to list slowly to the left.

Charlotte, holding on to the bolted-down table, glanced around. "Is everyone okay?" Minnie swallowed and nodded. Mr. Hollands held onto the baroness, keeping her securely in her chair. At least he was useful as a human doorstop.

Aunt Hespa whimpered, her terror-filled eyes finding Charlotte's.

"It's not a vampire attack," Charlotte said gently. "That makes no sense, and it's the middle of the day, remember? They would be reduced to ash."

Aunt Hespa nodded, apparently reassured by this.

Charlotte had no idea what she was going to do, but no one else was doing anything. "Stay here. I'll be back." If there was something supernatural happening, she could help. She then let go of the table.

Aunt Hespa screamed her name.

Charlotte slid down the slanting floor and landed with a thud on the white wood paneling. She lifted her skirts and secured them with a skirt-hike, causing her petticoats to bunch around her waist. She then raced along the wall, clambering through the dining room door and down the hallway, one foot on the floor and the other on the wall.

The bright summer sun blasted through the door leading to the observation deck. Charlotte scrambled onto the deck, her heart racing as she saw all of London below them tilting into view over the hand rails. Several airshipmen scurried fearlessly up the rigging. Men shouted orders, some hanging over open air hundreds of feet from solid ground, but a few simply stood in place, pressed up against the railing of the promenade deck, each looking in the same direction with an unfocused glaze in their eyes. The immobile airshipmen all wore yellow armbands.

Charlotte pulled herself along the railing to one yellow-eyed sailor and shook his shoulder. "Sir, can you hear me?"

No response. Just the empty stare past her.

"Sir." Charlotte shook the airman harder and was about to slap him, hoping that would have a stronger effect, when an electric humming behind her made her turn. Her throat went dry.

A massive green oval hung suspended in the sky a hundred meters off the port side. Green coils of energy wrapped themselves around a translucent chartreuse center, writhing in a constant tangle with the surrounding clouds. Blue bolts of lightning pulled the circumference of the storm wider with each passing moment.

It was like the blue lightening was pulling the sky apart, leaving a glowing green wound in its wake.

The hair on the back of Charlotte's neck stood on end. "What in the blazing suns?"

Gravity pressed against her and she clenched the railing tighter.

"Come about, starboard," someone shouted from the helm.

"Aye, Captain!"

The iron framework of the *Asteria* screamed in defiance as the ship continued to be drawn to port and directly into the storm. The crackling green energy pulled at the ship like a sea monster pulling them to their abyssal doom.

Wind whipped against Charlotte's hair as the ship kept turning and speeding toward the still-growing storm. The airshipman next to Charlotte still stared, his unblinking yellow eyes reflecting the thrashing tentacles of electricity.

Should she lash him to the railing? If the ship continued to tilt, would he even move to protect himself? She searched for something to tie him down, but to no avail.

A few guests who had managed to leave the dining room screamed.

"Five hundred meters," a sailor shouted.

Visions of the *Asteria* colliding with or being swallowed into the aerial vortex burned into Charlotte's mind.

"Four hundred meters!"

Blue lightning crackled, raising the flesh on Charlotte's arm.

Tendrils of energy snapped out toward the *Asteria* like a giant, ravenous squid.

"Three hundred."

"Brace for impact!"

"I've got you," she said, grabbing the airshipman, her muscles tight as she pressed them both against the sturdy railing. There was a roar of energy, and the center of the storm flared white, blinding Charlotte. She screamed. Air rushed past her ears whipping toward the storm.

Then with a deafening silence, everything stopped.

The storm shrank, collapsing in on itself, vanishing in a twisting mass of dark green energy. When it disappeared, it left most of the sky a cheery, almost harsh blue.

The tilting stopped. The ship lurched, groaned and began to right itself smoothly.

"Brace yourselves," someone shouted.

The deck swayed and bobbed back into its leveled position. Passengers cried in relief, some cheered, and murmurs of amazement rippled through the ship.

The airshipman Charlotte was holding moaned and sank to the floor. He shook his head as if clearing away cobwebs.

"Are you all right?"

"What. . .happened?"

Charlotte leaned in, checking the man for any signs of injury.

He pushed her away, the pressed his hand to his forehead as he staggered to his feet. He gave Charlotte an uncomfortable and mildly disgusted stare, the recognizable "how dare a woman save me" look before he scrambled away to rejoin the crew.

"You're welcome," Charlotte called after him. *Ungrateful cad.*

"Charlotte," someone shrieked.

Aunt Hespa and Minnie pushed through the passengers and embraced her.

While they fussed over her and she kept assuring them she was all right, worry quivered in her bones. In the ten years she'd spent living in a supernatural London, she had never seen anything like that storm. Had the Origination affected the weather and London was now to be plagued by supernatural storms? It had to be supernatural. What else could it be?

What in the blazing suns was going on?

# Chapter 7

After the *Asteria* landed, Aunt Hespa ordered the party to leave immediately as the newspapers had gotten word of the airship's trouble and she wanted to be away before anyone so vulgar as a journalist accosted her.

Charlotte found an autocab and pressed her aunt's address on the map of London engraved on a large copper plate. The automaton driver whirred to life and the gears inside the driving mechanism clanked with gusto. Aunt Hespa winced, distrustful of "soulless" automatons, but after what she'd just been through, she was more interested in the safety and comforts of home, and so she squeezed into the cab.

The ride was less a denouement of the events on the *Asteria* and more a diatribe on everything that displeased Aunt Hespa—which was a lot. Charlotte's shoulders pressed tight against Minnie's plump frame and allowed her buzzing thoughts to drown out Aunt Hespa's opinions on proper autocab programming and Minnie's routine responses.

What was that storm and why had it appeared? Had the supernatural airshipmen's entrancement happened because of it? No matter how much she deliberated over it, she couldn't come to a clear thought about its origin.

Charlotte turned the baroness's calling card over in her fingers, tapping the corners against her lap. *This*, too, had been a fascinating turn of events. How could she use this blossoming association to her advantage? She half-smiled at the fantasy of running into Baron St. Bridgeman at a crime scene and seeing the look of horror on his face when she revealed his mother was her new bosom sister. Charlotte added the image of the baroness disinheriting her son for good measure.

"Niece, are you listening?" Her aunt's strident tone cut through a scene of the baroness sending St. Bridgeman home like a scolded puppy.

"Yes, Aunt," Charlotte said, her posture reflexively straightening as she pinned a smile on her face. "Always."

Aunt Hespa's shrewd eyes narrowed. "This is your reminder of the croquet party I am hosting at my house in two nights' time. Mr. Hollands will be there. Please do not bring any of your"—she waved a hand over Charlotte while she searched for an adequate phrase—"detective trinkets."  "Mr. Hollands? Aunt Hespa, no, not again." Charlotte flopped so hard against the back of the cab's seat, the carriage rocked. Why did the woman insist on even more matchmaking when the last attempt—ending less than an hour ago—had been a disaster on multiple fronts? And with the same feckless man? Meeting with Mr. Hollands twice was two times too many.

She stared at the tiny copper plate engraving of Hyde Park, Chelsea, and the surrounding neighborhood. A miniature light flashed along the pre-programmed route. Blast it, they were still four streets away from Aunt Hespa's residence. Would flinging herself from the moving cab be too dramatic?

"Have you not seen Mr. Hollands?" Charlotte wove as much plaintive whining into her voice as she could manage. If her aunt insisted upon treating her like a child, then she would act like one. "The only remarkable bit of his personality is that he is *lacking* one—unless, to you, tedium counts as a winning trait."

Minnie squeaked a laugh from the middle of the trio but quickly covered her mouth.

"You *will* come." Even the Queen's Guard would have a hard time resisting Aunt Hespa's commands. "The baroness will also attend."

Charlotte bit her lip. True, another outing with Mr. Hollands would be horrible, but this might be an ideal opportunity to start befriending St. Bridgeman's mother and perhaps discuss Charlotte's own ideas for the preservation of supernatural society. *Could the mother of my enemy be my friend?*

The cab finally lurched to a stop in front of Belgrave Square, and her aunt stepped out of the carriage, the immense pressure from the tight squeeze as well as her domineering presence lessened. Aunt Hespa turned to stare at her niece, looking like one of those gothic villainesses in one of Charlotte's Dick Turpin novels.

"And you can leave your prickly nature at home, as well as your monster-hunting gear. You never consider what others will think of you—"

"I'm not prickly." Then she closed her eyes in frustration at her brusque tone. *Blazing suns, don't prove her right.*

Minnie placed Charlotte's hand between her own, giving her a reassuring squeeze.

Despite Minnie's efforts, Charlotte opened her mouth to offer an even pricklier reply to her aunt, when the welcome sound of her telescriber ticked away in its satchel. *Praises be! A murder.*

She moved to read the telescriber's paper, but Aunt Hespa reached into the cab and over Minnie with a speed Charlotte was not aware she still possessed. Aunt Hespa's hand blocked the text.

"Lord Wilmott is also invited." The woman's tone was flat, as if the statement were a horrible concession.

Charlotte's heart skipped at the mention of Cosmo's name. When Minnie sent her a teasing smile, she returned a little sniff of dismissal, but still heat streaked up her neck.

"Of course I'll come, as promised," Charlotte said in surrender, as if she'd ever really had a choice. Aunt Hespa would have wheedled and cajoled until she finally agreed. Again. It was a constant, odd sort of war of attrition between the two of them.

"My house at seven in two nights' time, please." Aunt Hespa removed her hand.

Charlotte immediately pulled out the roll of paper, her eyes devouring the message.

*Inquest at four STOP Draper STOP stray cat STOP Singh STOP*

Charlotte squeezed her fist, crumpling the paper as a familiar excitement percolated in her chest. An inquest was as good as a murder right now. Not only would provide an avenue of retreat—fortune willing—it might give her more clues about either the soul-eater or that strange storm.

Minnie moved to get out of the cab, but with a bolt of inspiration Charlotte grabbed her friend and yanked her back into her seat.

"Oof! What was that for?" Minnie smoothed her skirts around her ankles and glared.

"Aunt Hespa, would you object if Minnie comes with me to the draper's?" It tickled Charlotte that she wasn't completely lying about going to see a draper—the one Charlotte would see was less a retailer for fabric and more than a little dead. She leaned over her friend to close the door, not wanting to give Aunt Hespa any room to maneuver. She spoke through the window. "I'd like to see if they have any new ribbons. You don't mind do you, Minnie?" She batted her eyes at Aunt Hespa for top effect while Minnie narrowed hers at Charlotte.

"I suppose," Aunt Hespa said, sounding more surprised than anything.

Charlotte felt a slight twist of guilt at her lie, but if Aunt Hespa chose to be difficult, it was only equitable to return the favor.

She leaned forward, blocking the views of either woman, and scanned the small map, then pushed a button. A square lit up just outside Soho. As Aunt Hespa backed away, the cab lurched in motion. The latch closed with a loud snap and the large square window offered Charlotte a moment of petty satisfaction as her aunt's disapproving form retreated in the distance.

A short cab-ride later, the pair found themselves on an unassuming corner not far from Piccadilly. The pungent, tangy odor of automaton grease and horse manure hung in the air. On the ride over, Charlotte had refused to answer Minnie's questions, instead peppering her with talk of the *Asteria* to pass the time. The small but growing lump of guilt was now settled in her stomach like river sediment. She hoped that Minnie would remain calm during this informal inquest so that they could depart before any unsavory characters (like St. Bridgeman) arrived.

After stepping out of the cab, Charlotte turned in a slow circle to take in their surroundings, from the dust-colored sun lighting the few odd shops to the bustling crowd and the alehouse on the corner. The street was respectable enough. At least nothing screamed "dead body to be examined," or Minnie would never have exited the carriage.

Her friend's cherubic features dropped in confusion. "This isn't the milliner's."

Charlotte's insides squirmed. "Would you be very angry if I told you this was an inquest?"

"An inquest?" Minnie paled, leaning forward to whisper, "As in dead bodies?"

Charlotte guided her friend out of the street lest she be hit by a passing autocab.

"That is the definition of an inquest. And you don't need to whisper. Aunt Hespa can't hear you."

"Charlotte Astley," Minnie hissed.

Charlotte checked her pocket watch. Half past three. They would need to be quick if they were to leave before Singh and the rest of the peelers came. She made a mental note to thank Singh for tipping her off and delaying his comrades.

Singh's message "stray cat" was code for "district coroner's office" which was not the locale for most inquests; the majority were held in friendlier, and more familial locations, such as the home of the victim. Singh's note had a double meaning that stoked Charlotte's fires of injustice as well as flooded her with sympathy: the soul-eater's most recent victim, Mr. Oliver Draper, had a family who refused contact with any and all supernaturals—including their departed vampire son.

Charlotte grabbed Minnie's hand, dragging her towards a nearby building. "The coroner, Mr. Tollum, is expecting us and we have to be quick."

Minnie dug in her heels and stopped at the threshold of the door, just outside the dim hallway that led into the coroner's office. "Why do I have to come?"

Charlotte tugged. "Because I need you."

"Me?"

"And your powers."

Minnie turned ashen, her black hair framing her ghostly face. "Charlotte Astley, I am not touching a dead body."

Charlotte released Minnie's hand and stood in the doorway, waving away her friend's words. "But Oliver needs our help."

"Who is Oliver?"

"The victim."

Minnie shuddered, and even Charlotte noticed a chill coming from deep inside the hallway at her back, but she took her friend's hand again, and this time Minnie allowed her to pull her into the corridor.

"Whatever you discover about Oliver's last moments could help us find the truth about the monster that killed him." Charlotte said, giving her a reassuring smile.

Minnie's features softened, but a lingering air of disgust and wariness shaded her dark eyes. Charlotte guessed the immense unsettling portraits of people on the walls didn't help—those eyes seemed to stare into one's soul.

Charlotte reached behind Minnie and closed the door just as a large wagon laden with a dozen oak barrels stopped outside the alehouse. The street noise dampened.

Charlotte led her friend to the top of a flight of stairs descending into an unlit basement. She leaned closer to whisper in Minnie's ear, allowing a pitiful quaver in her voice. "Oliver had a wife and two children and took care of his sickly mother when he passed."

Minnie pulled away, her brow tight with suspicion. "You're making that up."

"Completely." Charlotte clutched at her friend's hand when Minnie made another weak attempt to escape back to the street. Charlotte gently drew her to the edge of the landing. "But somebody loved him and was devastated when he didn't come home."

Probably another lie; two in less than thirty minutes. *Where is your honor, Charlotte?*

Minnie grabbed her pink skirts and lifted them over the threshold, fixing Charlotte with a narrow glare as she passed. "You have no shame." And with that, Charlotte followed Minnie's short frame and clacking shoes down the stairs leading to the coroner's rooms below.

The pair made it to just outside the examination chambers before Minnie stopped. She stood as still as a statue, her eyes fixed on the chilly chamber. A large marble-topped table loomed in the middle of the lightless room. A rectangular window near the ceiling cast long shadows over something that rested on the table underneath a coarse white sheet. The floor was discolored with something dark and rust-colored. Charlotte shivered.

Minnie squeaked and clutched Charlotte's hand, her high voice filling the space. "This is much worse than spiders."

Charlotte peered into the dismal and (almost) empty room. Where was the coroner?

"Pardon me," a flat, colorless voice said behind them.

Both women shrieked and whirled around. Charlotte instinctively reached for her hairpins and jumped in front of Minnie.

A balding, gaunt-faced man stared at the two of them, his large eyes practically luminous in the dim light. He rubbed his long fingers over each other, their movements resembling a beetle's legs.

Charlotte lowered her hand and forced a laugh, one that sounded more like rocks falling than laughter. "Mr. Tollum. You startled us."

"Lady Astley." The coroner's voice was as thin as a knife.

Charlotte felt Minnie cringe.

"This is Miss Zhou," Charlotte said.

Mr. Tollum blinked once at her and once more at the trembling Minnie behind her before gliding into the examination room, his feet making no sound.

Charlotte glanced behind at her friend, who was pressed up against the doorframe, eyeing the toad-like man with wariness. "It's all right, Minnie. He always puts on dramatic and macabre airs."

Her words fell flat on her own ears.

Sighing, she followed the eerie man into the room. Not for the first time, Charlotte wondered how many people had been altered by the Origination and granted supernatural abilities but kept quiet about it, as Minnie did. Did Mr. Tollum have powers besides being the creepiest ghoulish coroner anyone had ever seen?

*Was* he a ghoul? Charlotte pressed her lips into a thin line as she eyed the man in the dim light. Ghouls *ate* dead bodies. She locked all the muscles in her body to stop from shuddering. She'd explore that thought if and when it was ever required.

The coroner crept up to the body with an almost reverent expression and pulled back the sheet, revealing Mr. Draper's face. The vampire's collar and necktie had been either cleaned or changed as neither of them bore the grimy water stains of the Whitechapel alley, and his dark suit, though rumpled, was passably clean.

It had been nearly a week since the soul-eater had taken Mr. Draper's life and his body had finally expired and was no longer whispering—a fact Charlotte was grateful for as Minnie was skittish enough already. As it was, the corpse had started to mummify, its brown skin ashen. For reasons yet unknown, vampire corpses, unless exposed to direct sunlight, became desiccated, accentuating every angle and feature. Mr. Draper was no exception—his hollow cheekbones and protruding fangs stood out in stark contrast to his parchment-like skin and rich dark curls, making him look otherworldly.

Charlotte cleared her throat. "His personal effects?"

The coroner pointed to a side table full of instruments and a small assortment of items laid out on a handkerchief. He then left, both women watching him exit the room as quietly as he had come.

"We've really got to put a bell on him one of these days," Charlotte said, echoing Cosmo's sentiments about Tiller.

Minnie let out a nervous laugh, her eyes darting to Mr. Draper on the table and then back up at Charlotte.

"I won't make you do anything you don't want to," Charlotte promised.

"Too late for that," Minnie muttered, moving to the personal effects and removing her gloves. "Just knowing that I'll be touching something that belonged to a dead man..." She edged around Mr. Draper, keeping her eyes on the assortment of his items, her voice strengthening as she moved away from the body. "I'm not promising anything either."

"Understood." Charlotte joined Minnie next to the table.

"Let's set some expectations based on reality, Charlotte. Mainly that I can see the *surroundings* of an inanimate object."

Charlotte nodded, poking at the pocket watch and odd bits of paper on the table. *At last, we're going to get a solid lead on this soul-eater.*

The dull noises of the street traffic outside punctuated Minnie's silence and hesitation. Charlotte folded her arms to keep from grabbing Minnie's hands, yanking off her gloves, and shoving a trinket into them.

"I can also only see within a ten foot radius of that object. Once anything or anyone leaves that area..." Minnie raised her hands and extended her fingers. "Poof."

"That's reasonable." Charlotte chewed on her lip. *Almost there.*

"And I can only see an object's surroundings from within the last few days."

Charlotte blinked. "Mr. Draper has been dead for five."

Minnie shrugged. "He's also obviously a supernatural and I can't see supernaturals. They don't..." She paused and pulled her fingers through the air as if trying to catch the correct word. "They don't reflect in the object's memory."

"Blazing suns." Charlotte stared at the objects, valiantly fighting back tears of disappointment. They had been so close.

A stillness crept into the room and Charlotte's heart, the only sound was Minnie's steady breathing.

*Another good lead blasted to ash. Stupid. You should have thought of using Minnie's ability sooner—*

"Pardon me," a cold voice said at Charlotte's elbow.

Both Minnie and Charlotte jumped.

Charlotte recovered first, her fists clenched, tempted to lay the short little man flat. "Mr. Tollum!"

"Terribly sorry, but Mr. Draper is due for his portrait in a quarter of an hour, and then the police will be here."

"Portrait?" Minnie raised a quizzical eyebrow at Charlotte, who pressed her lips together.

"Indeed." Mr. Tollum smoothed his suit front. "His daughter wants a postmortem portraiture."

Charlotte had never seen one taken, but she knew that some families wanted a memento to remember their loved one by after they had passed on. The family would often stage photos with the deceased, who would be propped up on a stand to appear more lifelike, while the living relatives would pose around them mimicking a formal portrait. The logistics of such a photograph made her skin crawl. Blazing suns, that was why the portraits in the hallway above had looked so unnatural. They were death portraits. A shudder threatened to sneak up Charlotte's spine.

*No, no uncomfortable feelings here. Logic, my dear.* Charlotte's anxiety receded as she said, "I am glad someone wants to remember Mr. Draper, though I assumed vampires couldn't have their pictures taken due to the use of mirrors during the process."

The coroner shrugged. "Is he a vampire anymore if he's dead?"

It touched on a deeper philosophical question Charlotte didn't want to think about and she caught Minnie's wide-eyed stare. Minnie wrinkled her nose, then studiously examined the door, clearly wanting no further involvement of any kind.

Charlotte didn't blame her. Death photography *was* an odd practice and she wasn't quite sure how she felt about it.

"I'll give you one or two more moments with Mr. Draper." Mr. Tollum retreated a few steps, but he apparently had no intention of leaving the two girls alone anymore.

The strain Charlotte felt earlier about this case returned, pressing against her chest. She turned back to the table with Minnie and dropped her voice until it was little more than a whisper. "I'm sorry. This was pointless."

"If you had told me where we were going beforehand," Minnie hissed, holding her arms wide to take in the cold chamber, "I could have been spared this… cellar of gloom."

She sounded so much like Aunt Hespa, Charlotte's hackles rose reflexively, ready to fend off Aunt Hespa's tide of criticism. Instead, she lifted the fox pin, twirling it through her fingers, and offered it to her friend. "Let's have a go, shall we?"

Minnie scowled but removed her gloves. Charlotte placed the pin in her hand. Minnie's eyes fluttered shut and her features slackened. "Nothing." She opened her eyes and held out her hand for the next item.

They quickly went through the green horseshoe and sun pins— why did this man have so many pins?—and Charlotte's hope dropped with each one.

Minnie shook her head, placing another item back on the table. "It's all dark with little flashes of light, which I assume are Mr. Tollum's lantern in this room."

The man nodded. Charlotte's shoulders slumped and she scuffed at the ground, aware of how childish she looked but not caring in the slightest. She had almost been one step closer to finding out the identity of the murderer.

Minnie gestured to the green horseshoe pin then replaced her gloves, clearly anxious to leave. "This one was the worst. Absolutely nothing. But it doesn't help that it's broken."

"Broken?" Charlotte's leaned forward.

"Well, this is only half of it."

"What does the pin actually look like?"

"I don't know, but it feels…incomplete. Besides, you can see here that the center was a pale green."

Minnie pointed at some small bits of leftover paste crusted against the ridge of the u-shaped rim. Charlotte grabbed the pin from the tray, holding the decorated end close to her eye. The other half of the pin had been broken off. Charlotte scowled at the item. *Give up your secrets.*

The jewelry offered nothing.

"I'm a bit chilled," Minnie said, already walking out into the hall.

"I'll catch up," Charlotte said, slowly replacing the pin on the tray. Minnie's retreating steps clicked up the stairs like a ratchet gear.

Charlotte wrapped her arms around her, trying to stave of the cold while pondering what to do next. Nothing worked for either problem.

"Lady Astley."

Charlotte jumped and vowed to purchase a substantial bell for Mr. Tollum. She pasted on a smile.

"I thought I'd mention it to you, but I didn't want to do so in front of the lady," he said.

Charlotte bristled but let her exclusion from womanhood slide.

"There were marks on the body."

Her gaze sharpened, fixing on the coroner and his large eyes. "Marks?" There hadn't been marks on any other victims.

"Around his torso, below the collar."

Charlotte strode to Mr. Draper and tugged at his collar, loosening his necktie. Mr. Tollum cleared his throat, likely at the lack of propriety.

*There.* Inches below the vampire's collar were circular abrasions approximating the size of a sovereign coin, the perimeter spotted and raised. Charlotte leaned over Mr. Draper, peeking down his shirt.

His chest sported more than a dozen similar circles, all beneath the clothing. The gooseflesh rose on Charlotte's arm. She had thought this soul-eater might be a mindless monster, killing for food. Was this evidence that the creature was intelligent? Charlotte whipped out her telescriber to send a message to the corresponding machine at her home. All these clues needed more consideration.

"Thank you, Mr. Tollum," she said, her voice echoing off the walls.

The man nodded, his jowls wavering, then he trotted back into the dark without a sound.

Charlotte climbed the stairs, and heaved a sigh as she stepped into the welcome sunshine. She was wholly unsurprised to discover that Minnie had already procured a cab. As she approached, the aged driver tipped his hat at her and she was about to join her friend in the carriage when a voice spoke from behind.

"Lady Astley. What are you doing at an inquest?"

Charlotte took her foot off the step and turned to see St. Bridgeman and Policeman Singh standing on the walkway. St. Bridgman's sandy-colored hair peeked out from beneath a too-tall top hat, emphasizing his narrow frame and drooping mustache. Blazing suns. She'd been so close to a clean getaway. She glanced up at Minnie, whose attention was captured by the speaker, an odd look of interest in her dark eyes.

"Once again, Baron, you have failed to grasp the obvious." Charlotte gestured to herself. "Monster hunter."

Charlotte heard Minnie shift in the cab, and the horse pawed at the cobblestones, probably as eager as Charlotte to be on their way.

"I can save you time if you'd like." Charlotte waved her hand at the coroner's behind St. Bridgeman.

"Tha'd be splendid. This is really just a formality—" Policeman Singh started.

St. Bridgeman scowled at the man, his mustache drooping. "I'll judge that myself. I prefer not to trust biased assessments."

Ooh, that rankled.

A sudden tiredness and desire to be home settled over Charlotte winning out any desires to exchange barbs with St. Bridgeman.

"Suit yourself," Charlotte said, hopping into the cab.

St. Bridgeman looked almost befuddled, as if he'd anticipated a skirmish. He narrowed his eyes, then turned to enter the coroner's. Singh gave Charlotte a small nod before following him inside.

"Who was that?" Minnie asked, craning her neck.

"No one of any importance," Charlotte muttered, settling in her chair.

People, passing traffic, and buildings lumbered past her view as the cab turned onto Piccadilly Circus. Charlotte and Minnie were both silent, watching the outside world, lost in thought.

The corpses' whispers. The pin. The marks. Nothing about this soul-eater was even close to making sense.

Charlotte's thoughts drifted back to the coroner's with Mr. Draper's body laying in the cold room.

"I'm not giving up yet," Charlotte whispered to herself as the streets of London flashed past. "Not by a long shot."

# Chapter 8

Charlotte smoothed her cream-colored jacket. The heat from the summer day had long since cooled to a temperature perfect for a garden party. The sweet smell of Aunt Hespa's roses lining either side of her doorway wafted around Charlotte as she stood on the doorstep. Satisfied with her appearance, Charlotte knocked on the door.

Moments later, the door opened so quickly a small gust of wind tickled the nape of her neck.

"Hello, Charlotte!" Minnie beamed as if they hadn't seen each other in months. A slight flush on her cheeks set off her light-blue peplum jacket and elaborately ruched double bustle.

"You look lovely," Charlotte said, stepping onto the foyer's painted checkerboard floor.

"As do you." Minnie ran her fingers over the fabric of Charlotte's skirt. "Surely your aunt can find no fault in your ensemble."

Charlotte allowed herself a rueful smile. "She means well," Minnie nodded consolingly. "Perhaps someday, she will trust you to dress yourself."

The two shared a conspiratorial giggle.

Aunt Hespa often demanded that Charlotte come over to accompany her and Minnie to events. Her aunt claimed it settled her nerves and also served as assurance that Charlotte didn't end up dead in a ditch or from an overturned carriage. Charlotte suspected that the real reason was to ensure Charlotte was appropriately dressed—as if she made regular habits of prancing around Piccadilly naked.

"Speaking of my loving aunt, what does the weather look like this evening?"

"Charlotte!" Aunt Hespa's strident tone ricocheted off the mint-green wallpapered walls.

Minnie pulled Charlotte closer to whisper, "Stormy."

Charlotte had no time to batten down the proverbial hatches before her aunt appeared, looming at the top of the stairs.

"Good heavens, child, what are you wearing?"

Charlotte glanced down. What could be wrong? Beth had worked tirelessly on her hair, now coiled and piled atop Charlotte's head in order to conceal the weapon-like nature of her wooden hairpins. In fact, Charlotte had just come back from the jeweler's, which had been another dead end for any clues as to Mr. Draper's broken pin, but she *had* managed to mount two lovely golden finials on the end of each hairpin.

Meanwhile, her emerald-green tiered skirt hid the daggers she had strapped to her calves, and the long V-shaped silk overcoat gave her access to the short rapiers hidden inside her corset. Even the floral-print fabric tucked under a ruffled bustle mostly covered

Charlotte's ray gun and telescriber holster. She'd taken extra care to allow for easily accessible weapons, while also keeping them out of eyesight.

Aunt Hespa blanched, placing a hand to her chest before pointedly averting her gaze. "You are exposing an inordinate amount of ankle."

"Aunt Hespa, it's croquet."

"No excuse. Minnie, please check for weapons."

Charlotte managed a brittle laugh. "Aunt, do you really think I'd bring weapons to a croquet game?"

The older woman narrowed her eyes. "You brought a skirt hike on an airship."

"Which I used to climb out of the dining room and save an airshipman."

"Also not an excuse. Minnie, please."

Minnie gave Charlotte an apologetic look and began searching her, starting at her forearms. Metal clattered onto the wooden entryway table as Minnie removed Charlotte's second favorite set of throwing knives. Cosmo still hadn't replaced the first pair from the faux banshee, high noon take him.

Minnie methodically moved to Charlotte's mid-section. Away went the rapier knives and the ray gun. It took Minnie a full five minutes to search Charlotte's bustle. All the while, Charlotte glared at her aunt.

Aunt Hespa gasped as Minnie lifted the dagger from Charlotte's boot. The older woman pressed a hand to her forehead. "You look as if you're trying to retake the Americas."

Charlotte sighed. "Pity. I was aiming for a look closer to Charge of the Light Brigade."

Minnie laughed but managed to cover it with a small cough.

Aunt Hespa's eyes tightened. "Men don't like sarcastic women. You will remember that won't you, Minnie?"

"Of course," came Minnie's automatic reply, her voice echoing off the painted floor as she searched Charlotte's other boot.

Charlotte eyed the small armory on the table and sighed, then turned back to her friend, pleading with her eyes to not take everything. Minnie stood and winked.

"Those are lovely hairpins, Charlotte," Minnie said. Charlotte's fingers itched to strangle her.

Her aunt leaned forward, scrutinizing the coils of Charlotte's dark hair around the accessories. Minnie's eyes twinkled, and she gave Charlotte a tiny gesture that clearly meant *be patient*.

"Yes," Aunt Hespa said at last. "Those finials are quite fetching."

After a minute of further scrutiny, Aunt Hespa declared they were ready. The maid, waiting in an unobtrusive corner for this moment, snapped to the woman's side with her jacket, and then the trio exited the house and made their way via Aunt Hespa's carriage to Hyde Park.

"What if something were to happen tonight?" Charlotte asked the occupants of the carriage at large, slouching. "You would be very grateful I had made preparations."

Aunt Hespa sniffed. "Mr. Hollands, Lord Wilmott, and the baroness will all be in attendance and I have procured one or two croquet lawns for our use and provided a small array of refreshments. I also believe the baroness is bringing her son."

"Baron St. Bridgeman?" Charlotte's stomach clenched as if she'd eaten spoiled oysters.

"That is the only son she has, yes," Aunt Hespa said warily. "I know your history with him and his views, but he is Mathilda's child, so be civil."

Charlotte's gaze pled with Minnie, who simply shrugged.

"I behaved on the airship," Charlotte whined. "What's the point of punishing me for good behavior?"

"You will act with perfect decorum or I shall never speak to you again."

*Do you promise*, was on the tip of her tongue, but even that was a step too far and Charlotte knew it.

The short drive to the Park lasted an eternity.

Once they arrived, it was immediately obvious that this was not the small party she had expected. Instead of the one or two lawns, as Aunt Hespa had initially claimed, four croquet lawns were set up, outlined with pale blue ribbons. Paper lanterns hung from the trees, casting delightful pink and yellow glows over the food and furniture and ornate area rugs. Plates of iced oranges, stewed pears, and crystallized fruits glistened amidst the serving stands of colorful molded desserts, meringues, and Victorian sandwiches. Several staff members, including Beth and others from Charlotte's household, stood next to the tables, ready to be of service.

It looked as if Aunt Hespa were preparing to entertain royalty, not a few acquaintances for croquet. Charlotte's wariness rose. Why would her aunt throw such an elaborate affair when it could have been a simple small garden party between friends?

Aunt Hespa turned to inspect the tables of food, and Charlotte caught sight of the empty sleeve, rolled and pinned near her shoulder. *You be nice to your poor aunt,* she scolded herself, shoving her suspicions back down. Aunt Hespa had had a much rougher go of it than Charlotte. With one arm, she wasn't able to participate in many social activities, let alone croquet, and if it weren't for Minnie, she would be forced to entertain herself with the unmarried nieces and old maids in want of a husband.

*Put on a brave face, Charlotte, even if you're screaming inside.* She had to make sure she didn't spoil any of this for her aunt.

Aunt Hespa immediately fell into lecturing the staff as they prepared to receive guests. Minnie standing dutifully behind the aging woman, gave Charlotte a small smile before turning her attention back to Aunt Hespa.

Not wanting to get in her aunt's way and having nothing else to do but wait, Charlotte took this as a perfect opportunity to read. A large pink-and-green wingback chair was begging to be used.

Charlotte swished over to the food table, made sure her aunt wasn't looking, and popped a sugared grape into her mouth. While she chewed, she turned her body, to block the book she'd squirreled away in a corner of the carriage from any glances her aunt may be throwing her way.

The book read *Mrs. Beeton's Etiquette for Young Ladies*, something Aunt Hespa could find no fault with if she did happen to catch Charlotte reading. However, it was a partially hollowed-out copy, containing the two latest Dick Turpin penny dreadfuls and enough decoy pages to allay suspicion if anyone decided to meddle.

Licking the last bits of grainy sweetness from her lips, she settled into the chair and cracked open her book. The first pages featured images of a dreadful house fire with several silhouettes trapped inside (delightful), a woman in a dead faint (typical), and a masked vigilante on a rearing horse whose identity Charlotte hoped was going to be revealed in this installment.

Charlotte was so engrossed, she didn't notice Aunt Hespa's approach until she was nearly upon her. Charlotte shoved the book under her bustle just before Aunt Hespa pulled her up by the elbow, then squeezed her arm as if it were a sausage, distaste wrinkling her nose.

"You need to eat something. You have no softness," Aunt Hespa said. "No man wants a woman who is sinew and gristle."

"It's muscle," Charlotte grumbled.

"They'll want that even less." Aunt Hespa looked down and frowned. She snatched the book that was peeking out from behind the apparently insufficient bustle. "A book? At a party?"

Blast it all.

"You're already upsetting your delicate feminine balances by playing detective." Aunt Hespa gestured wildly, her lace trimmings ruffling with the motion. "Do you want to further endanger and ruin your reproductive constitution with all the reading you do?"

Charlotte reached for the book, but Aunt Hespa had already maneuvered it into Beth's hands, and the maid immediately took the offending object to Minnie.

Charlotte's ire nearly bubbled to the surface, but she adopted what she hoped was a soothing tone. "So far, reading has done nothing to stop my monthly courses—"

Aunt Hespa chittered like a trapped pixie, a blush rising through her pinched cheeks. "Your feminine humors are in danger," she hissed.

A sharp hotness rose in Charlotte's chest, but she swallowed it. She took a steadying breath, her corset tightening against her ribs, and looked her aunt in the face and spoke as gently as her suppressed temper would allow. "If reading actually did disrupt one's feminine courses, there would be libraries on every corner and you would never see a woman without a book in her hand."

"Hear, hear," Minnie said from behind the older woman, raising the confiscated book in one hand like a banner.

Aunt Hespa opened her mouth, a tirade on Charlotte's childbearing duty surely ready to burst forth.

"Excuse me, ma'am." Beth's petite voice cut across any response her aunt had been about to make. "Guests are arrivin'."

The woman snapped her mouth shut and gave a disapproving hum. Her countenance changed as she caught sight of a middle-aged couple disembarking their carriage. She shot one more warning glance at Charlotte before sweeping off to receive them.

Minnie sidled next to Charlotte. "Actually, it would be a capital method to indicate interest in someone. If a woman had a book in her hand, it would be a very clear signal that she was not willing to engage in further conversation; but if she were *without* a book, it would indicate her desire to interact."

"It would certainly revolutionize flirting and society as we know it."

The pair watched Aunt Hespa greet a few more guests to the party.

"Can I have the *Dick Turpins* back?" Charlotte asked.

Minnie shook her head, mischief in her dark eyes. "Not before I read them first."

Charlotte pouted. "But they were just going to unmask who really kidnapped Miss Murray's daughter."

Minnie smirked. "I'll be careful not to bend the pages when I read them." The shorter woman passed the book to Beth once more, then moved to join the gathering party.

Charlotte sighed. This evening was already off to a bad start. No book. No prospects for entertainment (save Cosmo, and who knew when he would arrive), and now no food—not completely, because the food looked incredible, but Charlotte wanted to avoid eating for a while just to spite her aunt.

"Of course you remember my niece," Aunt Hespa's voice carried over the lawn.

Charlotte pasted a smile on her face and moved towards the guests her aunt was speaking with. Blazing suns, it was going to be a long night. "Lord and Lady Dharma, so good to see you again."

An hour into the party and Charlotte's genial smile was wearing thin. Mr. Hollands had arrived, and she had been sure to exchange the necessary niceties, and avoid further talk of football, but so far the event had been a tedious affair. Where was Cosmo? If anyone could save her from death by boredom, it would be him. She also had no opportunity to speak with the baroness, since her disagreeable son was always near his mother. This hinderance had done nothing to improve her mood.

When Cosmo finally made his appearance, Charlotte moved towards him as fast as was socially appropriate, her green dress trailing in the grass behind her. What had taken him so long? Tendrils of his vamp mist dissipated, and his smile widened as Charlotte approached. His dark hair curled by his ears, and his cravat was impeccable. Although he looked as he always had, something about him was different tonight. Charlotte couldn't quite put her finger on it.

Before she could reach him, an unctuous voice said, "What took you so long, Lord Wilmott?" The speaker was a woman with delicate features and glowing creamy skin the color of hazelnuts. She held her hands out to Cosmo. The elongated torso of her dress combined with the vertical floral pinstripe pattern accentuated her narrow waist, giving her frame a lithe grace.

"Miss Patel," said Cosmo, taking her hands in his.

Charlotte stopped in her tracks. So *this* was Miss Patel. Cosmo had recently mentioned a young vampire who had taken a keen interest in him. Charlotte had encouraged Cosmo to befriend her, thinking Miss Patel to be a young debutante whose substance was frills and naïve enthusiasm, but this was…Charlotte didn't quite know *what* Miss Patel was, but she did know she didn't like the way the young woman was smiling at her friend, her dainty fangs just visible over rose-colored lips.

Charlotte readjusted her course to a table of food, and she slowly assembled a small plate of fruit because she was hungry and most definitely not because she was eavesdropping.

"So good to see you," Cosmo was saying. "I wasn't aware you'd been invited."

"It's my last party before I'm homebound, and I'm determined to enjoy it."

Charlotte turned to watch Cosmo and this newcomer out of the corner of her eye. Miss Patel moved closer to him and dropped her voice. Charlotte had to strain to hear.

"I have a few ideas on how to make the most of this evening. I know it's tempting to read my thoughts, but try and refrain." Miss Patel ran her fingers across her temples, tucking a stray piece of dark hair behind her ears. The move emphasized her elegant neck.

Charlotte tightened her grip on her plate.

"Oh?" Cosmo said. "I do hope they involve croquet."

Miss Patel giggled into her hand. Cosmo offered her his arm, and they moved towards a lawn which had just become free.

Charlotte looked away, trying to organize her thoughts. She noticed Mr. Hollands standing near Minnie and Aunt Hespa. Aunt Hespa caught Charlotte's eye and gave her a pointed look that clearly said, "Attend to your duties. Your duties being Mr. Hollands."

Charlotte glanced back at Miss Patel and Cosmo. He was still smiling at her as she spoke animatedly. Charlotte didn't know why, and Miss Patel had certainly never given Charlotte any personal offense, but there was something about the poised and cheerful vampire she didn't like.

Time to take action. Charlotte strode toward her aunt. Mr. Hollands may have had the personality of a sack of potatoes, but he could most likely play croquet. When she reached her aunt, Minnie, and Mr. Hollands, she wasted no time in addressing the man directly.

"Mr. Hollands, I noticed you have not yet played a game of croquet. I'd be most pleased to play a set with you."

Aunt Hespa's eyebrows raised in interest.

Mr. Hollands swallowed the biscuit he had been eating and sucked his teeth loudly. Charlotte, trying not to wince, smiled wider.

"I would prefer a game of football; however, I know that it is not an established sport among your sex—"

Minnie choked back a giggle.

Charlotte's gaze drifted back to the croquet lawn. Cosmo was laughing at something Miss Patel had said. Charlotte narrowed her eyes, turning her attention back to Mr. Hollands, who was, amazingly, still talking. Good grief, how long did it take to agree to a game of croquet?

"—and while your sex is still new to certain physical activities, it is happy for you that I possess the talent of teaching with delicacy."

Charlotte blinked. "I beg your pardon?" With his last statement, she moved "playing croquet" lower on her list of to do's, though she still kept an eye on Cosmo and Miss Patel.

Mr. Hollands pressed his hand to his chest. "I have often observed how little young ladies are interested in learning new sports and also have a penchant for bending the truth particularly when they play"—he stepped closer to Charlotte; she resisted the urge to back up—"and there can be nothing so advantageous to women as to have a patient instructor who keeps them from the pitfalls of"—he leaned in to whisper—"cheating."

Mr. Hollands smiled, as did Aunt Hespa.

"I await your instruction," Charlotte said through clenched teeth and a forced smile. She placed her plate of food on a table while Mr. Hollands bid a lengthy adieu to her aunt, who was beaming at the both of them.

Minnie came to stand by Charlotte and hissed, "What are you up to?" Worry creased her almond skin.

Cosmo and Miss Patel were standing close together now. Somehow their croquet mallets had become entangled.

"Nothing."

Minnie followed Charlotte's gaze. "Liar."

Charlotte sighed and started towards Mr. Hollands, who was waiting at the edge of the food tables to escort her to the croquet lawns. "Nothing too drastic," she whispered.

Minnie trotted alongside her friend. "Charlotte, I have to tell you something—"

"Not now, Minnie. I'm on a mission."

"But it's about tonight and Mr. Hollands."

"Later. Right now, I'm pleasing my aunt and…." She glanced at Cosmo and Miss Patel, who were now playing with another couple. *Blast*. Asking Mr. Hollands had taken longer than expected. "…and I am about to be instructed in the marvelous game of croquet."

"But—"

Whatever Minnie had been about to say was swallowed up by Mr. Hollands's greeting. "Believe me, my dear Lady Astley, that your humility, so far from doing you any disservice, rather adds to your other perfections."

Out of the corner of her eye, Charlotte caught Cosmo's green eyes flashing at her and Mr. Hollands.

Charlotte slowed her pace and smiled. "Did you say 'perfections,' Mr. Hollands? I noticed you used the plural of that noun. Humility is one of my greatest virtues, so much so that I never take notice of the others."

She batted her eyelashes in what she hoped was a coquettish manner. Mr. Hollands stood a little straighter, his prominent nose lifting at Charlotte's attention. Cosmo frowned.

"I try to give compliments in the impulse of the moment," Mr. Hollands said, "but indeed, you do have many other perfections."

Perhaps her aunt was onto something with having an unabashed flatterer near her at all times. She couldn't play with Cosmo and Miss Patel, but perchance a croquet game with someone who thought she was perfect wasn't so bad.

It was worse.

Endless flattery, while an agreeable concept, did not work well in practice. Especially coming from the resonance of Mr. Hollands's pinched voice.

After the glow of Charlotte's "perfections" had worn off, she was left with little to do other than try and play this game of croquet as fast as possible. Except her ball refused to go through the designated wicket, which were entirely too small for any ball, and once that was accomplished she was forced to aim for an impossibly thin stick in order to end the game. In short, Charlotte was terrible. What she really wanted to do was swing the mallet hard using her socially unfashionable muscles and send the ball as far into the shrubbery as physics would allow. As it was, no matter how softly she tapped the infuriating ball, it still went anywhere it pleased.

Mr. Hollands offered croquet advice, coming annoyingly close every time. Aunt Hespa, who was watching their game closely, was immensely pleased each time he did. Her placation was Charlotte's one consolation. Minnie's expression, though, grew more concerned with every passing minute.

Miss Patel and Cosmo had finished their game ages ago while Charlotte's dragged on into eternity.

"Well played, Mr. Hollands," Charlotte said when he was finally able to escort her back to her Aunt.

"Perhaps another game," Mr. Hollands said, "after you've had some rest. It is most strenuous for a lady."

Charlotte merely grimaced.

Aunt Hespa's smile lifted her usually serious features, and she warmly welcomed Mr. Hollands back into her circle of guests. The man turned his attention back to her aunt, and the pair joined others in enthusiastic conversation.

Charlotte wanted to collapse.

Minnie sidled up to her, offering her a glass of lemonade, which she took gratefully. The refreshing, sweet drink left the perfect pucker sitting at the back of her throat.

"Who invented that game and why is it popular?" Charlotte glared at the other players, some of whom seemed to be actually enjoying it.

Miss Patel, with her gazelle-like figure, and a small group of guests were chatting among themselves in a settee while also watching the other players. Cosmo was standing beneath the chestnut tree, his eyes scanning the crowd. He caught her gaze and smiled, moving towards her and Minnie. Charlotte still couldn't quite tell what was different about him tonight.

She took another sip of her punch. The now-large crowd appeared to be enjoying themselves. Aunt Hespa certainly had been more than satisfied Charlotte's attention to Mr. Hollands. Despite some minor annoyances, Charlotte considered the evening an overall success.

"You're not helping yourself, you know," Minnie said to Charlotte, taking a sip from her own drink.

"I fail to see how." Charlotte gestured to the party. "It's been well-attended, I paid Mr. Hollands special attention and I've been a dutiful niece and pleased my aunt. That is the very definition of helping myself."

"*Bonne soirée*, mademoiselles." Cosmo bowed and offered Charlotte and Minnie a plate of variety of shortbread biscuits he had gathered from a nearby table. "Miss Zhou, you look lovely tonight. Even lovelier than me," he said, pressing a hand to his elaborately embroidered waistcoat.

"Thank you, Lord Wilmott," Minnie said, smiling.

Charlotte took one of the biscuits and immediately began nibbling. Its buttery crumb coated her mouth and she hummed her satisfaction. "Very good. Thank you, Cos."

He inclined his head in acknowledgment.

"Charlotte, listen." Minnie maneuvered her frame in front of Charlotte, blocking Cosmo, her round face as serious as a vampire at dawn. "I was trying to tell you before, but you went and dug your own grave and then danced on it."

Charlotte frowned.

"This isn't just a croquet party. It's your pre-engagement party."

# Chapter 9

The noise around Charlotte suddenly muffled as if she were underwater. Everything shot out of focus, and instead of being surrounded by gilded members of the laughing and gossiping ton, their forms turned into amorphous, impressionistic blobs. Even the lanterns' glow fuzzed against the night sky.

Someone dressed in light blue with jet-black hair was saying her name. Minnie?

Charlotte blinked and shook her head. "I'm sorry. I think I just hallucinated. Could you repeat that, please?"

"This is a pre-engagement party," Minnie said, enunciating each word.

"Pre-engagement?" Cosmo gave a laugh that was more bark than anything else. His green eyes were moving from Charlotte to Minnie, burning with an intensity Charlotte had never seen before.

Minnie quailed under Charlotte and Cosmo's combined stare. "It's more like a pre-pre-engagement party," she squeaked. "I saw the sample invitations for the actual pre-engagement party, and Hespa is getting really desperate, which goes without saying, but the invitations are on the most luxurious paper with a large scalloped edge and a Greek key pattern along the outside. I was trying to tell you earlier that Hespa wants the *ton* to see you and Mr. Hollands as a couple."

Minnie twisted her fingers together, and Charlotte placed her hand on her friend's arm. "Pre-engagement party." She could barely get the words out.

"Yes," Minnie said. "And you just played a very lengthy game of croquet with Mr. Hollands."

"But that's because she's terrible at it," Cosmo said.

"I wasn't that bad," Charlotte said, slapping him hard in the arm.

"Well, I overheard Hespa saying to the baroness that you were being deliberately bad as a tactic to spend more time with Mr. Hollands."

Charlotte's heart dropped into her boots as Minnie continued. Cosmo huffed and ran his fingers through his hair.

"Invitations are being printed for a party next month which would be the official pre-engagement affair."

Charlotte paled. "Next month?"

Her friend nodded and bit her lip, then she backed up to allow Charlotte some space.

Charlotte wanted to sit down. Aunt Hespa had pulled stunts before and had tried to foist her in eligible men's paths, but Charlotte had been able to spot them a mile away and avoid them.

She turned to Cosmo and gripped his arm, her other hand pressed to her forehead. At her touch, he lost control of his form for a moment, small tendrils of mist rising like steam from his collar.

"Engagement party?" he murmured, taking in their surroundings as if with new eyes.

Charlotte spotted Baron St. Bridgeman standing near the croquet lawn, eyeing the crowd, his too-long sideburns drooping in disapproval. He wore cream-colored trousers with a matching silk jacquard vest and jacket. And all of her frustrations at the evening, at Aunt Hespa, and at St. Bridgeman closed in on Charlotte. The expansive lawn was suddenly too small, her corset too tight. Her breath came in quick gasps. Why was it so hot all of a sudden? She tugged at the frill of her neckline, trying to get more air.

She glanced back at Minnie, who was now gazing at the party with an odd expression on her face. She was obviously as distraught about this news as Charlotte. Perhaps if they put their heads together—she, Minnie, and Cosmo—they could solve this problem.

"Minnie, how do we fix this?"

Cosmo turned to their small friend as well. "Minnie?"

The shorter woman continued to stare somewhere.

"Minnie, are you listening?" Her friend's evident apathy at her situation was like a slap in Charlotte's face. Didn't she care? Hang on, what was she looking at? Charlotte couldn't tell—there were too many people.

"My engagement?" she prodded, nudging her friend's shoulder.

Minnie's mouth twitched in the corner and a dainty flush colored her apple cheeks. She blinked and then gave a quick glance at Charlotte, her gaze quickly returning to whatever had held her attention. "Yes, it's bad, but it's not happening tonight."

Charlotte folded her arms. "And?"

"We have time, we'll figure it out," Minnie answered, the dreamy haze blanketing her features and voice once more.

Charlotte looked at Cosmo, who frowned and shrugged.

"Who is that?" Minnie finally asked, distinct notes of interest weaving through her voice. The crowd parted and Charlotte realized that she was looking at Baron St. Bridgeman. "He was at the inquest, was he not?" She produced a fan out of nowhere and placed it in her left hand.

Charlotte's stomach coiled. The left hand? Minnie was using fan code? She wanted an acquaintance with *him*?

"You mean St. Bridgeman?" Cosmo said, squinting in that man's direction. "That *is* a fine vest, I must say. Could use some additional embellishments, but not bad."

Charlotte glanced at Cosmo's own flamboyantly embroidered vest, a dark silk jacquard with a cornucopia design and flowers exploding from the horn. The swirling florals made Charlotte's eyes spin, so she turned back to St. Bridgeman, her horror at Minnie's piqued interest washing away everything else. She *did* have time to resolve Mr. Hollands and her forced engagement, but her friend being attracted to her nemesis? Something had to be done.

As if he sensed their combined stare, St. Bridgeman turned and raised his glass at the trio. Cosmo returned the gesture. Charlotte smiled, but it felt more like baring her teeth than anything resembling friendliness.

St. Bridgeman's gaze lingered on Minnie, who was still obviously holding her hand in the "I wish to know you better" left hand. Something like interest sparked in his eyes. To Charlotte's horror, Minnie's blush spread across her nose and face.

Now it was Charlotte who stepped into her friend's line of sight. "No. Absolutely not."

She looked over her shoulder. St. Bridgeman was now weaving his way through the crowd in their direction. He barely seemed to notice Charlotte, only smiling at her friend. How very dare he!

Minnie waved her fan in front her of face. "He must always look distinguished. He did at the inquest. And his mustache is quite attractive."

Had her friend gone mad?

"Minnie, he's the thorn in my side. And no his facial hair styling is all wrong."

Minnie ignored her, moving past her towards the insufferable man.

Cosmo bent to whisper in Charlotte's ear, words probably meant to reassure her. "Charlotte, what is the harm? He is not always pleasant, but he's no monster."

"He's"—Charlotte searched for an appropriate comparison to a monster—"he's a politician!"

Neither Cosmo nor Minnie paid any heed to Charlotte.

Instead, Cosmo caught up to Minnie. "Would you like me to introduce you?"

She nodded, her face aglow with anticipation.

Disgust snarled in Charlotte's stomach as she trudged behind her friends. Was there no loyalty anymore? She stepped in front of the pair, before they could embark on introductions..

"I forbid it," she said. "Minnie, his views on supernaturals,"—Charlotte dropped her voice to a hiss—"a community which you are a part of, should immediately set you on your guard."

The blush washed away from Minnie's face. "Right. But you said his mother is favorable towards supernaturals. Perhaps she could change his mind?"

There was real longing in her words, and Charlotte's stomach clenched again, this time for a different reason. She recognized that same yearning in her own heart: to be married and have a family. But not with just anyone and certainly not with the likes of Mr. Hollands or St. Bridgeman.

Minnie squared her round shoulders and straightened her short frame. "I'm still going to enjoy myself."

"No, no, no."

"Yes, and I'm even going to flirt. And I'll like it."

Charlotte threw her arms wide as if to block Minnie's path. "I…I forbid it." Charlotte attempted her best Aunt Hespa impression and was both satisfied and horrified at how accurate it sounded. And then she knew she had overstepped. Even Cosmo lowered his brows, a scowl forming across his features.

Minnie turned with fire in her eyes. "You cannot."

Charlotte backed away, feeling deflated and hollow. This garden party was awful. She was awful.

"If you try anything, remember the two daggers and lock picking set I overlooked," Minnie said. "Perhaps I'll recall my oversight to your aunt."

"You wouldn't," Charlotte said her eyes narrowed.

"Or I could tell you the ending of *both* Dick Turpin books."

Charlotte folded her arms and watched Minnie and Cosmo walk steadily toward St. Bridgeman. And she found herself following reluctantly in their wake. Perhaps she could still find a way to be the voice of reason.

As the two friends approached St. Bridgeman, the baroness joined her son.

Charlotte wanted to stamp her feet and howl. Blast. Now she'd have to join the group, be nice to St. Bridgeman, try and talk about supernaturals without insulting the baroness's detestable spawn, and try to stop Minnie from falling for the man and his horrible mustache.

The conversation was disastrous. Charlotte twice attempted thoughtful dialogue with the baroness but was so distracted by Minnie and St. Bridgeman it was near impossible. Cosmo saw Charlotte's predicament, and perhaps feeling sorry for her, tried to solve the problem by inviting her, Minnie, and St. Bridgeman for a game of croquet. As if St. Bridgeman's politics weren't bad enough.

Perhaps Cosmo was actually punishing her.

Charlotte's playing was, if anything, worse than it had been with Mr. Hollands. She was so annoyed, she accidentally sent the ball into a thicket of lilac bushes. *Please just make this end.* She stormed over to the immense shrubs, their rich perfume giving her an instant headache. She pushed branches thick with purple flowers out of the way.

"How can I help?" Cosmo asked, joining her, and she knew he wasn't referring to finding the lost ball.

Charlotte used the mallet to separate some branches. "I need something to do other than watch Minnie flirt with *him*."

Cosmo stepped closer to Charlotte and dropped his voice. "You could flirt with me."

Charlotte turned to him and raised an eyebrow. Was he serious? His expression was difficult to read, and she didn't know how to take his comment until a joking smile broke across his face.

She let out an exasperated huff, then pressed deeper into the bushes.

Aha. There it was. She leaned down, reaching for the ball with her mallet. Small branches poked into her side as the lilac fought to keep its prize. She tapped the ball toward her. Just a little closer. *Got you!* Her hand closed around it and she stood, but a twig snagged on the fabric along her waist, opening a hole in the fibers that would most certainly need fastidious mending. "Blast. Beth will not be happy with me."

"The evening is almost over," Cosmo said, placing a hand against her back, leading her back to the game.

Charlotte cried. St. Bridgeman and Minnie had taken full advantage of her absence and were engaged in an impromptu lesson on how to properly aim the ball.

"Like this?" Minnie asked, staring up at St. Bridgeman, flashing a bit of ankle as she bent to aim.

Heat rose up Charlotte's neck. "That brazen hussy," she hissed to Cosmo.

Then the Baron brushed the back of Minnie's hand supposedly helping her adjust for the target wicket. Charlotte gripped her mallet so tight the flesh of her palms pinched.

"I need a drink," she said to Cosmo.

Minnie's laughter at something St. Bridgeman said followed Charlotte as she left the lawn. Cosmo produced a glass of liquid and pressed it into Charlotte's hands. As she drank, she took in the press of people, Minnie enjoying herself with that horrible man, and then the approaching Aunt Hespa and Mr. Hollands. Panic clawed inside Charlotte's chest and she pressed her free hand to her heart, hoping to calm its racing rhythm. *Please, not now.*

"Do you need anything else?" Cosmo asked.

Charlotte gulped her lemonade, choking as the acidic drink hit the back of her throat. "I need this evening to end," she said reaching for a napkin. "You don't happen to have a herd of stampeding elephants on hand, do you?"

Cosmo rubbed his chin. "Not elephants but would hobgoblins do?"

Charlotte tilted her head at him and gestured for him to continue.

"Tiller was helping the neighbors with a hobgoblin infestation. I can see if I can gather some up."

Charlotte raised her eyebrows. Hobs were mischievous, but no more than a naughty household cat would be—simply an annoying nuisance. She nodded slowly. "Hobgoblins would be perfect. Anything to stop"—she swept her arms wide—"this."

Cosmo winked, transformed to mist, and then flew away, leaving Charlotte to fend for herself.

Half a torturous hour later, Charlotte was finally able to excuse herself from the lackluster conversation with her aunt and Mr. Hollands and found herself sitting on the bench underneath a tree, where the party was visible to her but the foliage obscured her from the crowd. Black mist gathered beside her and Cosmo materialized, a smug look warming his features.

"Where have you been?" Charlotte hissed, poking him in the ribs. "I just escaped from Mr. Hollands. Did you know his football team is sponsored by his father's mining company?"

Cosmo's smile faded.

"Did you also know that I don't particularly care for discussing mining companies?" Charlotte's jaw hurt from her clenched teeth.

"I apologize," Cosmo said. "It took a while to convince Tiller to load the hobgoblins into a cart. These ones have quite a nasty streak."

Charlotte shifted in her seat and furrowed her brow. "Unusual, but no matter."

"I even ran into an exterminator as he was leaving next door and took a few off his hands. See that bloke over there?" Cosmo pointed to a cart with a nervous-looking driver standing near it. "He's going to open the cages."

Even from the distance, Charlotte heard snarling and growling coming from the wagon. The driver shifted his weight, his eyes fixed on Cosmo. Her friend gave a small nod, and the man opened several cages, then hopped onto the driver's seat and drove off like the devil himself was after him.

Hundreds of short, thickset creatures with knobby ashen skin poured from the carriage and onto the lawn. Gristly grey hair streamed from their heads, trailing past them as they scurried towards the croquet party, drawn by the large crowd of people and the smell of food.

Cosmo held his hands out as if to embrace the snarling horde. "The perfect distraction!"

A woman screamed. Hundreds of fiery, beady red eyes turned towards her. Now Charlotte could see that the creatures each had a small red fabric hat on the top of their head.

Charlotte's blood chilled. "Oh, no."

In seconds, the creatures charged the party, swarming over the first food table. Several took up forks and knives. Some tossed plates like circus jugglers. Guests shouted and pushed each other to escape the flying dishware.

"Those are redcaps!" Charlotte scrambled to her feet, hiked her skirts up, and ran towards the party. "Redcaps," she shouted to the guests.

"Redcaps?" Cosmo said, running behind her, as hundreds of the tiny creatures scrambled towards him and Charlotte and the crowd in front of them.

The cry of "redcaps" echoed through the party. The large gathering then scattered into a strangely organized chaos, pushing outward from the raiding redcaps like oil on water, each member of the group keeping a careful distance from one another. Charlotte felt a swell of surprised satisfaction and pride. After ten years post-Origination, even these nobles seemed to know basic defenses and protection against the more minor creatures. Redcaps were attracted to heat sources, and a crowd of the aristocracy bunched together at a pre-pre-engagement party fit that category. Spreading out was the best strategy.

That didn't mean it was done very gracefully. Several guests ran to a nearby fountain, the women hiking their skirts scandalously high as men helped them into the chilled water. Some small groups of guests stayed together, but never in clusters larger than three.

The redcaps didn't seem to mind—they were currently too occupied with the food. Within moments, the delicate refreshments and entremets had disappeared into the bellies of the horde or acted as throwing ammunition. Custard and chocolate flew overhead and guests dodged to avoid getting creamed.

As her guests scattered, Aunt Hespa remained frozen, her composed demeanor as demolished as her desserts.

"My table," she wailed. "No, stop! Unhand me!"

Two of the creatures tugged at the woman's skirts, threatening to unbalance her entirely. Charlotte raced to her aunt, grabbing a pillow from a settee on the way, and thwacked at the redcaps until they released the clothing.

"Charlotte!" Aunt Hespa pointed.

Charlotte whirled around and raised the pillow at a redcap who had launched itself at Aunt Hespa. The tiny monster's sharp teeth shredded the decor, sending strings of beads and clumps of cotton raining down on the lawn. Charlotte swung the cushion, launching the creature into the air.

Aunt Hespa, her breath coming in short gasps, rested a hand on her niece's arm. Charlotte gave her a reassuring smile.

"Charlotte! That was American cotton." The older woman moaned, a deep frown setting in her face. "The cost of the pillow alone—"

"The pillow?" Charlotte said, dropping the tattered remains. Why did she even bother?

A redcap, wearing a ceramic fruit bowl on its head like a knight's helmet, screamed shrilly and charged at the two women. Charlotte grabbed a plate from a table and scooped the running creature up, sending it flying over the wrecked dessert buffet.

"Get to the fountain, please!" Charlotte pushed her aunt in the direction of the fountain and watched to make sure she made it there. Several other guests moved into the trees and bushes. Charlotte spied St. Bridgeman herding Minnie away from the park, an arm protectively around her shoulder.

Blazing suns.

Some of the guests were less fortunate. A man yelped and kicked at one of the creatures, but two more scampered over to him and began gnawing on his shoe. Two young ladies were shrieking and pulling at the skirt of a third woman, which had snagged on one of the wickets. An older couple were being harassed by small troupes of roving redcaps, who snapped at their heels and brandished silverware and serving platters like shields and swords.

Charlotte took in the scene. The little beasts were too spread out for her to do anything about them.

"Cos, get the monsters corralled," she shouted.

He began darting from redcap to redcap, herding them away from the edges of the lawn and closing their ranks.

Something hot dropped on the back of Charlotte's hand, burning her, and she cried out.

Rubbing the spot, she looked up. Several redcaps were swinging from the tree's branches, and a few were stoking the small flames inside the paper decorations. Many lanterns were already engulfed in flame, and searing wax was sprinkling from the trees.

"Bollocks." She needed a weapon. If she'd had her corset rapiers she could have easily dispatched this lot. "Find something, Charlotte," she murmured, dodging more hot wax.

There! She bent and grabbed a discarded croquet mallet, then used it to pull down the flaming lanterns. Cosmo joined her in stamping out the fires. They needn't have tried. Drawn to the heat, redcaps swarmed the fallen decor, ripping it to shreds, and extinguishing the flames.

A man cried out in pain and fell, a couple of redcaps scrambling over his back, tearing at his jacket. Charlotte lunged, swinging the mallet. With a solid crack, the creatures sailed across the lawn.

Charlotte smiled. Perhaps croquet did have its merits. She twirled the mallet in her hands, noticing the balance. *Whack.* Yes. This aspect of croquet was most satisfying.

"Don't hurt them," one of the male guests in the fountain cried.

"They're only redcaps," a woman shouted. "They're not actual people."

Charlotte continued swinging at the little brutes, who were now ripping into the furniture and gnawing on table legs. The woman was correct—redcaps, like pixies, banshees, and other minor Origination creatures, were not altered humans and their bites, though dangerous, were not transformative in nature. So she had no qualms about hitting the evil little creatures as hard as she could.

*Whack.* That was for St. Bridgeman and Minnie.

*Whack.* That was for Mr. Hollands and this whole confounded party.

Cosmo appeared in a dark mist beside Charlotte and began pitching the creatures over his head left and right. For one brief instant, underneath shrieking, flying redcaps, their eyes met, and Charlotte smiled. Actually, this was perfect. She was fighting monsters with her best friend, and they made such a good team. For one flawless moment, redcaps sailed over the lawn like rice at a wedding.

Then the beasts ran out of furniture, lanterns, and dessert tables to destroy. En masse, the horde turned to the closest heat sources: Charlotte and Cosmo. Well, only Charlotte really because Cosmo was an undead vampire and therefore less of a heat source.

The pair stood back to back. Hundreds of beady red eyes and matching red caps moved toward them. Charlotte swallowed at the sea of snarling grey and crimson. They would try to kill her first, then spread out, hunting down the rest of the guests, fountain camouflage or not.

"We'll have to banish them," Charlotte said.

Cosmo hurled two more of the creatures away. "Banish them? As in from the realm?"

"No! From this mortal plane." Charlotte knocked a redcap on the side of the head. A few spindly hands reached for her stick, but she pulled it from their grasps. "Oh no, you don't. I don't know, Cos! I'm no spiritualist. I just know it works."

"Excellent," Cosmo said, swiping at group of redcaps who were forming a crude tower attempting to gain height and attack Charlotte. "How do we do that?"

"Ouch!" Charlotte raised her heel to stomp on the monster that had just bitten her ankle, its sharp teeth piercing the leather on her boot. "You don't know how to deal with redcaps?"

"No, I always call you."

Had they not been in the heat of battle, Charlotte would have made a scathing reply. Instead, she gave a column of redcaps a hard swing, grunting with the effort but sending the creatures tumbling onto the heads of those behind them. "You have to quote scripture."

"Scripture?"

"Yes." *Whack*. "Quote a holy text and bash them on the head with something. Observe."

Cosmo turned as Charlotte raised her mallet over her head.

"'As I walk through the valley.'" She brought it down on the top of a particularly ugly redcap. The tiny red hat exploded, and the creature was enveloped in a cloud of heat and light. A small charred spot of grass was soon all that remained. "Like so."

The other creatures chittered excitedly, drawn to the heat from their banished brother. Dozens of redcaps with more behind them scrambled over each other and Cosmo to get to the heat source.

"Get off, get off! No, not my vest!" The beasts' nails pulled thread loose and tore scratches in the embellished, expensive fabric. "Um, lead me…lead me into…Charlotte, I don't know any scripture!" His dark hair fell across his worried eyes as he ripped the monsters off his shoulders before they could get closer to her.

"'Lead me not into temptation,'" Charlotte grumbled and swung again, aiming for a creature on Cosmo's head. *Flash*. Of course he wouldn't know any scripture. Many supernaturals had been banned from any religious edifice or grounds. Cosmo hadn't been to services in years.

The redcaps swarmed around her, nearly knocking her off her feet and she brought the mallet down her in a sweeping arc to clear some space, sending several flying. She heard Cosmo behind her, swinging a silver platter he'd found in the grass.

"'But soft, what light through yonder window breaks?'" *Flash*.

Charlotte whirled. A small blackened circle of earth was smoldering by Cosmo's feet.

"It worked!" The vampire wore an astonished but definitely pleased look on his face. A redcap came sailing over Cosmo's shoulder, aiming for Charlotte.

"'Shall I compare thee to a summer's day?'" He swung his platter at the creature, catching it on the head. *Flash.*

Charlotte turned back the group of swarming monsters. "I said holy text, not literature. 'Deliver me from evil.'" *Whack. Flash.*

"'Out, damned spot,'" Cosmo cried. Another burst of heat and light bloomed and then disappeared. "You know, I think they like Shakespeare less than scripture. That one took out two. This is all tho exthilerating!" Cosmo's fangs had extended.

"You're ridiculous," Charlotte said, but she was smiling. "Let's see how they feel about Austen. 'It is a truth universally acknowledged.'"

The redcap she'd hit on the head vanished, as well as two others near it. Hmm. Perhaps it was time to experiment.

"'I am no bird, and no net ensnares me.'" Ten bright flashes came up in succession. Charlotte laughed. "They really don't like Bronte."

"'It wath the betht of timeth, it wath the wortht of timeth.'" *Flash. Flash.* "Blatht, only two."

"Try Poe."

"'Quoth the raven, "nevermore."'" Cosmo's silver platter clanged followed by an enormous burst of light and whoosh of heat. "Ha! I think we have a winner."

A handful of the more brave partygoers joined in, swinging mallets and other objects while reciting passages. A few moments more of solid whacking, and with some literary help from Poe and Bronte, soon Charlotte and Cosmo were standing in the middle of a blackened, smoldering lawn. Several of the guests who had assisted returned to their companions to help them from the fountain. Charlotte wiped her brow and dropped her mallet.

She turned to see Cosmo. Dark smears of soot swathed his porcelain skin, but his eyes were alight. He cracked a grin and a relieved chuckle bubbled up in Charlotte's throat. Soon both of them were consumed with gales of laughter. A handful of guests cheered and began to mingle together, murmuring and babbling about the fiasco. Some were obviously shaken, but they seemed to be collecting themselves well enough. No one appeared to have been seriously hurt.

Charlotte wiped her eyes and leaned against her friend. "Cos, I'm so lucky to have you."

A strange look crossed his face for a moment, and he gave her a gentle smile she hadn't seen before. Such an unfamiliar look from her longtime friend made Charlotte uneasy.

"Ah, well, you're lucky I am well read. As is Aunt Hespa." Cosmo chuckled, his fangs retreating slowly. "Where did the old girl end up?"

Charlotte pointed to the fountain.

"What have you done?" Aunt Hespa's shriek pierced the air, stopping all chatter.

The woman approached the edge of the scorched circle and stepped over the demarcation between lush green grass and blackened earth. Her entire face twisted in disgust.

Charlotte lifted her soot stained mallet in her hands and twirled it once more. "All in a day's work for a monster hunter."

Cosmo coughed behind her.

"And her esteemed associate," she said.

"How could you?" Aunt Hespa dropped the still-wet hem of her dress and dabbed a handkerchief to her eyes.

Charlotte allowed her arm to fall, the mallet suddenly twenty pounds heavier. "It's my job."

Minnie moved to stand beside Aunt Hespa, the bottom of her blue skirt gathering soot. Baron St. Bridgeman followed Minnie, and Charlotte couldn't help but think he looked smug. The guests were now all staring at Charlotte.

She looked down, suddenly seeing herself through their eyes. The bottom inches of her dress had been torn or gnawed off, and both of her ankles were exposed, including a few inches of stockinged flesh above the boot. Her dress was no longer the beautiful cream and emerald-green ensemble; it was stained with ash, wax, and custard. She pressed a hand to her hair, tucking several dark, tangled strands behind her ear, and wished the still-smoking ground would swallow her up.

"Your job," Aunt Hespa said, her voice quavering, "is part of the problem."

# Chapter 10

Despite the warm afternoon, a fire burned vengefully in the grate in her father's old study. An anonymous package had arrived earlier that day containing an advertisement for the removal of redcaps, a clipping from the society pages describing what had happened at last night's party, and a stack of leaflets from the Council for Humanity. Charlotte fed the last bits of offending paper into the flames, then stood and dabbed her handkerchief against her perspiring forehead.

Beth was resting in her bedroom. She had recovered enough to work the evening croquet party, but with the redcap debacle, she was spent.

Charlotte had sent someone to her aunt's to retrieve her weapons. She had no desire to face her aunt's wrath or criticism at the moment. Or hear Minnie talking about how attentive St. Bridgeman had been to her during the redcap attack last night. Her friend had done plenty of that in the carriage ride back to Aunt Hespa's. Once she had her weapons back, everything would be in order.

"These arrived for you." Mrs. Eden entered the study bearing a large bouquet of exquisite blooms. Blue hyacinths mixed with white and yellow daffodils, their sweet fragrance filling the room.

*You must allow me to tell you how ardently I apologize. I will arrive for evening tea.*

*—Cos*

Charlotte smiled. "Thank you Mrs. Eden. Please place these in the parlour. I'll receive Lord Wilmott there when he calls."

Mrs. Eden nodded, then disappeared out the door with the flowers and down the stairs.

Charlotte walked to the wide window in her late father's study and took a deep breath. Leather and book dust filled her nostrils, melting away the last of her tension as she settled into the large chair behind the cluttered desk.

She placed the goggles on the table, determined to tinker to her heart's content. Spreading gears across her worktable and getting her fingers slick with grease would make Charlotte as happy as a selfie frolicking in the sea foam.

Several hours later, she leaned back in her chair, pleased at the result of her labors. With the addition of a handful of polished brass cogs, the goggles were now not only more functional but a great deal more fashionable.

She sipped on long-cold tea as she took in the hazy London evening outside the study window; the sun was nearly down and the other half of London's population stirred, making preparations for their day—or rather, their night.

Charlotte stretched, picked up the goggles, and moved downstairs into the parlour anticipating Cosmo's arrival. She'd just settled into her seat when suddenly the doors burst open, causing Charlotte to practically jump out of her skin.

He clapped his hands together. "Are we feeling rested and ready to hunt a monster?"

Charlotte's heart raced at the initial shock, and then willfully refused to return to its normal pace. She was instantly aware of the rumpled state of her dress and hair. She placed the goggles over her eyes, clicking the lenses to purple. No, Cosmo wasn't vamping her; then why was her pulse all of a sudden refusing to cooperate?

"I noticed you received my flowers," he said smiling, glancing at the large bouquet.

She nodded, suddenly feeling uncharacteristically shy. "They are lovely."

Silence threatened to spread between them until Cosmo cleared his throat and spying the glasses, picked them up examining them, his usual exuberance returning. "Marvelous!" he said. "I simply adore what you've done to the specs. Tell me—when you wear them, would you say I look magnificent or heart-stopping?"

She coughed, ignoring the question. "I was hoping we could work on the soul-eater case."

Cosmo nodded again, this time so enthusiastically that his dark curls bounced against his brow. He fell into pacing around the tea table, his boundless energy making her dizzy.

"Can I offer you a drink?" Charlotte's fingers curled around the neck of the decanter. Perhaps some *vin de sang* would curb some of his restlessness. She had shivered when she'd first ordered her staff to purchase the drink, but it was worth every penny when she saw the grateful looks she received from the calling vamps.

And it was insurance. If for some reason the vampires' thirst overcame them, hopefully they would have enough capacity to consume the *vin de sang* before anything—or anyone—else.

Cosmo accepted a glass without slowing. His presence altered the atmosphere until it was nearly tempestuous. As Cosmo's mental powers washed over her, Charlotte swallowed and, reflexively, her training took over. For each crash of emotion he sent out, the barrier in her mind pushed back. Thank the heavens, Sir Isaac Newton's laws applied to both the mental and physical world, or she'd have been at quite a loss. As it was, she took a leisurely sip of tea and smiled, amused that Cosmo wasn't even aware he was vamping.

"We need to...we need..." He stopped pacing and looked at Charlotte. "What do we need?"

"A plan?" she supplied. She took another drink. Cosmo was excited enough to give himself a heart attack.

He took to pacing again. "I've been up all night—I mean, of course I was up all night. All day, too, if we're really being honest. Lovely flowers in your hair, by the way. Did Beth do that?"

Charlotte's hand reflexively went to the braided twist she'd had to arrange herself with Beth so worn out.

"In any case, what sort of plan? While I was re-arranging the furniture in the sitting room, I thought of the last soul-eater's victim, you mentioned him when we tested the goggles..."

He continued, gesturing wide with his hands. His most recent house arrest must have been harder on him than she'd thought.

Louisa, one of the human maids, entered the room with another bottle of *vin de sang* to supplement the first. She looked flushed. The bottle trembled in the woman's hands as she set it on the table. "W-will that b-be all, m'lady?"

"Wait a moment, Louisa. I'd like to demonstrate a point."

Louisa had her hands behind her back meekly, though she bounced on her toes, unable to remain completely still. Charlotte's staff were going to suffer from cardiac arrest if Cosmo didn't calm down. She walked to Cosmo and lightly touched him on the arm, pulling him from his thoughts.

"Cosmo, please stop sharing."

He stopped mid-sentence, his eyes briefly searching her face. In an instant, the cogs clicked into place and he bowed his head, looking sheepish. A small curl of hair fell into his remorseful eyes and Charlotte resisted the urge to brush it away. He inhaled deeply, then straightened. Charlotte knew the moment he'd gained control of his emotions when Louisa *whooshed* in relief. Her hands hung by her side, like a puppet whose strings had been loosed.

"My apologies." He bowed to both Charlotte and Louisa, every inch of him Lord Wilmott. Charlotte nodded her thanks to him, her heart pushing heat through her chest. *Ever the gentleman.*

Louisa accepted Cosmo's words with a wobbly curtsey of her own.

"That will be all, Louisa. Thank you."

After another curtsy, Louisa left.

Cosmo, now fully in control, stood rooted to the floor and cleared his throat. "Again, my apologies. I should have noticed your discomfort. Where would you like to start with the soul-eater?"

Charlotte stifled a smile. "Perhaps you could assist me in deciphering these clues." She opened the notebook from the study and spread out her papers.

"The great Lady Astley is stumped, is she?

Charlotte waved him away. "Do you want to help or not?"

He clapped his hands together, then cracked his knuckles. "What have we here?"

"What do you make of 'holy' and 'ink?'"

"Blazing suns, Charlotte."

Cosmo ran his fingers through his dark hair then pulled it forward in a wavy bunch. "Ink, holy…do you think it refers to holy ink? Perhaps scripture?      "There is nothing particularly religious about the other aspects of this case, though," Charlotte said, thens sipped the last of her tea.

Cosmo paced and Charlotte briefly wondered if her carpet might wear out before the night was over. "Thinking about the case is getting us nowhere," he said, slapping the back of his hand against the other. "We need to catch the soul-eater in the act. But how can we know where it's going to attack? Perhaps the locations are correlated. We need a map."

"My current working theory is that each word relates to the location in which the victims were attacked. The locations I have now, show no pattern. But I think St. Bridgeman's map does," Charlotte said, pouring herself more tea.

"What do you mean, 'St. Bridgeman's map'?" Cosmo stopped pacing and folded his arms. "What if he still believes the world is flat? What use are his maps to us?"

Charlotte stood and gestured as she spoke, all of her frustration at the case woven through her words. "I'm actually not entirely sure it *is* a map, but I believe he has not only been tracking the location of the soul-eater, but also has key evidence about the creature before I became involved. He carries a notebook with him and has it almost whenever I see him. "

"How do you know this?" Cosmo's tone belied the way he casually leaned against the wall.

"If you are referring to whether I know what information is contained inside the notebook, Policeman Singh caught a glimpse over St. Bridgeman's shoulder."

Cosmo shook his head, clicking his tongue against his teeth.

Charlotte shrugged. "I may or may not have asked him to do so. From what Mr. Singh said, it seems to contain relevant material. He only saw information I already know, but there was much more writing. I only wish I could get my hands on it."

A whoosh of air blew past Charlotte brushing stray tendrils of her brown hair across her face. She stood, looking around, but Cosmo had disappeared. She rammed the goggles onto her face. Where Cosmo had been, a long trail of lavender and turquoise glowed. *What is he about?*

Before she could fix her hair, with another gust, Cosmo was back, trailing purple and sea-green particles behind him. He leaned against the table, folding his arms in a deep pout.

"Cos, what in the blazes are you doing? Where did you go?"

Cosmo cursed, slouching further. "It's not in his study."

"What's not? Wait, whose study?"

"Bridgeman's map of London, you silly bird."

"Cosmo! Breaking and entering? You just got off house arrest!"

"Don't fuss. They weren't home. He did have several disturbing illustrations, though." Cosmo shuddered. "I don't see what is so appealing about octopi and squid."

Charlotte rapped her knuckles on the table. "Blasted man. He has more information than he's letting on." Her stomach soured at the thought. "We need to know everything he does."

Cosmo's palm smacked his fist. "I could vamp it out of him."

Charlotte patted Cosmo's hands. "Vamping the head of the anti-supernatural legislation is—how shall I put this?—sheer lunacy. You might as well stake yourself. Besides, I can be persuasive too." Her fingers drummed against the ray gun at her hip.

"You're going to shoot him? But you have terrible aim." Charlotte started to protest, but Cosmo shrugged in mock apology. "I was two feet in front of you and you couldn't even hit me. What makes you think you can persuade Baron St. Bridgeman?"

"That's not fair and you know it. I'm an excellent shot."

He raised his hands in defeat, smirking like a Cheshire cat—something she pointedly ignored.

"And as for convincing St. Bridgeman, perhaps I'll use my feminine wiles."

Cosmo bolted upright, paced away, then gripped the back of the chair. "You would actually flirt with him?" His voice was a few pitches higher than usual.

Flirting was one of her favorite hobbies, but pretending to be attracted to *St. Bridgeman*? She suppressed her growing nausea and swallowed hard. "For the greater good, yes."

Cosmo closed the distance between them, so close Charlotte had to look up to see him properly. "That man is not worthy of any attention from you, real or otherwise."

"Why, Cosmo, you sound positively jealous."

His playful eyes suddenly darkened and then softened with an emotional intensity she had never seen before. It sent a different set of chills racing along her skin. "Jealous of a man receiving your attention? Why, Charlotte. I don't limit myself to envying that man alone."

She quirked an eyebrow.

"For example," Cosmo gestured to her hair. "My jealously extends to your flowers."

She touched the delicate purple asters tucked into her weaving braid. The side of her mouth curved up. "My flowers?"

Cosmo stepped forward and lifted her other hand, his fingertips brushing along its sensitive skin.

"'If I had a flower for every time I thought of you…" He raised her hand to his mouth. Instead of kissing the back of it, he turned it over and brushed his lips against her palm. Charlotte's breath caught somewhere near her collarbones. "'…I could walk through my garden forever.'"

"Tennyson," she murmured, her heart expanding against her ribcage.

Her brain protested faintly. *Careful, old girl.*

"But no less true, *ma moitié.*" His thumb swept across the inside of her wrist. He stepped closer, mere inches away. Her mouth dried. He stood there, so close to her, and in an instant, he had changed from her best friend into…something deeper. Some may have only seen his vampiric beauty, but to her, Cosmo Wilmott was the most important person in her life. He leaned closer still, and her lips parted.

A small vibration at Charlotte's hip made her jump, breaking the spell. Cosmo exhaled slowly and strode away to the side table to refill his drink. Charlotte's thoughts clawed for order but they were thick as syrup, falling through her fingers. He hadn't been vamping—of that she was certain.

She had feelings for Cos. There was no doubt about it now. But what was their depth—simply a spring puddle? Or something more profound, more piercing?

Charlotte mentally brushed away her emotions, her heart erratic. It was folly to not know one's own feelings, but these could be analyzed and catalogued later. There was a telescription to attend to. Her fingers scrabbled for the device.

It was from Scotland Yard. *Barghest spotted,* it read.

A barghest? Her mind snapped into focus. There hadn't been a barghest sighting since the Origination. Charlotte's fingers flew across the telescriber's letters. *Where?*

*Piccadilly.*

Charlotte paled. The Circus was werewolf territory. Another murdered supernatural—and so soon?

*Coming,* she replied.

She shoved the telescriber back into her pocket, then ran into the study for her notebook.

Cosmo set his glass down on the table and straightened when she returned. "What is it? What's happened?"

Charlotte rang for Mr. Bauen and told him to bring her auto around and to program it for Piccadilly. She turned to face her worried friend.

"It's a barghest," she breathed.

The color drained from his face.

If there was a barghest nearby, it could only mean one thing: a werewolf had been killed. Werewolves were so new to this world, and so little was known about them, but it was evident that with their regenerative powers, none had yet died from natural causes. That left two possibilities: either a werewolf had been murdered by another supernatural or a human, or—Charlotte's fingers tingled— it could be the work of the soul-eater. This could be their chance to stop the monster.

Charlotte raced to the doorway, Cosmo following closely behind. She turned to face him as she donned her outerwear. "Meet me at the Circus."

Cosmo nodded, his expression deadly serious, then, exploding into mist, he darted out the front door. Not for the first time, Charlotte wished that she could travel by mist with him without the bothersome soporific effects.

She adjusted her goggles atop her hat and made sure her weapons were securely fastened—corset knives, wrist knives, ray gun, salt vials.

Moments later she perched in an autocab hurtling toward Piccadilly, her heart urging the cab faster.

159

# Chapter 11

Tesla lamps shone like muted stars deep in a nebula of fog. Occasional noises muffled by the damp vapor set Charlotte's senses crawling. Piccadilly Circus was usually a bustling thoroughfare smelling of dusty horses and sharp motor oil. The deserted landscape was alien, made even more so by a single lit sign, that braved the murky night and cast a yellow glow over the cobblestones.

*I might as well be on the moon*, Charlotte thought. She shivered despite the mild temperature. This was just like a scene out of a penny dreadful.

The fabric on her calf-length bustle hissed against the leather seat of the cab as she exited the vehicle. She told the driver to wait. He nodded, obliging by pulling out the programming card, and the autocab's buzzing engine died, giving way to the voiceless night. Charlotte turned, then gave a sharp intake of breath.

The alabaster form of a barghest glowed like the moon between the buildings.

Charlotte had only been ten during the Origination period, and while she hadn't seen the ghostly white dog, she'd heard stories of its nightly prowls over the bodies of dead werefolk. Its chilling howl pierced people's hearts like death's silver scythe. People had thought barghests were the ghosts of werewolves returning to haunt. However, John Watts, founder of the Gentleman's Ghost Club, discovered that the ghost dog simply howled at werewolf deaths and was not hostile.

Policeman Singh and Inspector Dawson approached Charlotte from where they had been waiting, near the center of the Circus. Singh tugged at his mustache, and Dawson chewed his lower lip.

"Good evening," Charlotte said to the two men, though her gaze barely left the barghest.

The ghostly being turned and padded down Shaftesbury, then rounded a corner just out of sight.

Charlotte frowned. Where was it going?

Cosmo emerged from the shadows nearby. He tapped at the top of his hat.

*Oh, the goggles!* She rammed them onto her face and flipped the tiny lever designed for tracking specters, throwing the world into a harsh blue light.

"It's in there," Dawson said to her and Cosmo, pointing at a respectable apartment building off the street. He turned to Charlotte. "It's behaving oddly. Keeps coming and going, in and out."

"Has it howled?" she asked.

He shook his head and Charlotte let out a breath of hesitant relief. The barghest only howled at the moment of death. No one had died—yet.

"Wait here and watch for anything unusual," Charlotte said to Dawson and Singh.

The two men nodded, a little too eagerly. Singh looked especially grateful for the order.

Charlotte stepped into the townhouse with Cosmo following behind her. The entryway seemed intact. She looked to her left and jumped when she saw movement, her hand dropped to her Tesla ray.

"Mirror," Cosmo said, tapping the glass. "Bit jumpy tonight, are we?"

"Nice reflection," Charlotte whispered, nodding to the empty space in the mirror where her friend's face should have been. He bared his teeth and she stuck out her tongue.

She left her hand resting on the comforting outline of her gun. She was ready for whatever lay ahead. Hopefully.

The barghest's immense form stood on the landing of the first stairway. Wisps of iridescent blue smoke rose from the beast's body like fog from the Thames. Its frame glowed robin-egg blue through the goggles. Under the aura, hugging the barghest's silhouette, was that turquoise layer—the same one she'd seen around Cosmo. Charlotte's heart skipped a beat. The barghest was closely tied to ghosts and death which was why the blue specter lenses on the goggles revealed its glow. But what about that turquoise outline? Perhaps it was a signature tying all supernaturals together. She made a mental note to record her findings later.

The barghest paced at the landing. Charlotte's fingers itched, wanting to reach out and touch the hauntingly beautiful creature. A pity it was the harbinger of something so terrible.

The spectral creature pawed at the ground, whining and pacing as if bothered by something. Charlotte's heart beat faster. As she watched, the ghostly dog turned and padded up the next set of stairs.

Charlotte took a tentative step from the entryway onto the stairs, then hesitated. Where and what was it leading them to? She shivered, her mind sparking with conjecture.

"Ladies first," Cosmo whispered beside her.

Charlotte nodded. She debated whether or not to use her pistol, already loaded with silver bullets, or her Tesla ray. After a moment's hesitation, she unholstered the Tesla and reached for the small pouch of salt attached to her thigh. Her hand brushed the sheath containing her second favorite set of throwing knives. She cursed herself for not bringing her cruse. If the barghest was leading them into a dangerous situation with a spectral-based supernatural, then Bath water would be able to slow it down more than a salt or knife attack.

Careful to tread lightly, Charlotte moved up the stairs, crouching and ready to react. Cosmo ascended beside her effortlessly. She glanced down. He hovered only an inch or two off the ground, his feet wreathed in black smoke. Charlotte grit her teeth. Blazing vampires. At least he wasn't using enough power to severely increase his thirst.

Once they reached the top of the stairs, they turned left and up. The spectral dog walked the length of the hallway, pausing at a door. A glow crept under the threshold from inside the room. The barghest looked back, fixed Charlotte with an icy stare, then continued forward, passing through the door and into the room beyond. Charlotte hurried to the door.

She looked at a grim-faced Cosmo next to her. His fangs had grown, pushing into his lower lip. He nodded, reaching down for the door handle.

*One*, Charlotte mouthed, gripping her ray gun and the salt pouch tighter. *Two. Three.*

They burst into the room, Cosmo turning left and Charlotte to the right.

Through the goggles, the room glowed a pale blue with whirling teal streaks. Charlotte squinted against the intensified light. It must be residual from the barghest, she thought. Although, it hadn't left a trail on the stairs. Perhaps it had already entered this room before she'd arrived?

The barghest sat next to a human-sized shape on the ground, its unblinking cobalt eyes boring into Charlotte. The form lay at its feet. Charlotte turned a lever on the goggles, and the fallen figure glowed a deep maroon. The same turquoise outline hugged its outline, though both the burgundy glow and turquoise were very faint. *Werewolf.*

Charlotte tasted a metallic tang in the back of her throat and a chill ran through her. Even without the barghest's direction, they would have easily found the corpse. The werewolf woman had been mid-transformation when she'd been killed, making her glowing, mangled body all the more grotesque. Both the body and the pooled blood glowed a currant red with the identical thin turquoise layer outlining everything.

Charlotte tore off her goggles, running to the body. When she reached the corpse, her knees thudded against the floor. She was dimly aware of a wet sensation soaking through her clothes.

Charlotte shuddered as she surveyed the damage. This couldn't be the soul-eater, could it? Not one of its victims had been mutilated like this woman.

"Are you okay, Cos?" her thin voice croaked from her lips, concerned for him in the presence of so much blood.

He nodded and waved her off, but his hollow expression echoed Charlotte's own emotions.

The smell of the fresh blood and torn flesh battered against Charlotte's mind. This poor woman had been literally ripped apart. Bile rose, burning her throat and her stomach churned. *Professional, remain professional.* Charlotte had seen bodies drained of life and victims brutalized and broken by supernaturals…but nothing like this.

She stared at the woman's face—virtually the only untouched part of the body—and bit back a gasp. The werewolf's pupils were tiny dots in seas of white. And were her lips moving?

*No, it couldn't be.* Charlotte bent closer to the woman.

"Holy, holy…"

Charlotte's heart dropped. So it *was* the soul-eater. But why mutilate this victim and not the others?

"Charlotte." Cosmo's voice was tight.

She looked up. The barghest was moving away from the body to another part of the room. Charlotte blinked hard, glancing again at the horror before her, then rose and walked to Cosmo, placing a hand on his arm. He swayed, looking as if he would be sick.

"Cosmo?" She shook his arm, and Cosmo paled, his body becoming rigid. She followed his gaze across the room, fearing what she'd find. The barghest was still pacing, but this time it was at the foot of a crib.

Crib? Her eyes flitted around, taking in the room completely for the first time, noticing the stacking blocks and wooden toys in the corner behind the door. Her blood froze. This was a nursery.

Cosmo approached the bed, then knelt on the floor beside the it with a strangled sound. Charlotte crept toward the crib as if in a trance, a lump in her throat making it hard to breathe. The fingers of one hand curled around the frame, and the other covered her mouth as she choked out a gasp.

It wasn't one child, but two. Two small bodies. Identical looking twins with cherubic faces, appearing as though they had fallen asleep in each other's arms. Twin brothers.

It all clicked like automaton gears. A werewolf mother and twin boys—the first natural-born werewolves since the Origination. It had been all over the papers at the beginning of this year—perhaps nine or ten months ago.

"No. No, no, no!" Charlotte whispered.

Dark hair wreathed their peaceful faces. At a glance, they could have been sleeping. One faced up and the other curled around his brother. What chilled Charlotte the most were the eyes. The boy facing up had the same white eyes as his mother—milky white orbs staring into nothing.

Cosmo rose from the floor and stood beside Charlotte. She shivered and couldn't hold back a sob. He rested one hand on her shoulder, then his other found hers when she gripped his shirt. She hadn't been fast enough; she was too late to help any of them.

The white-eyed boy's mouth moved. Charlotte gritted her teeth, forcing herself to lean closer to the small body, the fabric of her bustle swishing as she did.

"Brohwee," the boy whispered, forming a word his infant mouth should not have been able to speak. Charlotte leaned closer, puzzled. Had she misheard?

"Brohwee," the toddler repeated, his tiny lips moved his twin's curls with each puff of air. She tried valiantly to retreat behind safe logic of the child's confusing word, to connect the clues.

Brohwee? Brolly? Did the child perhaps mean 'umbrella?'

Her fingers brushed against the soft blanket placed in the crib and she took a shuddering breath. This was usually the part where Charlotte brought her detached scientific enthusiasm to the forefront to record details about the deaths. She covered her face with her hands. She wouldn't be needing to make any notes about tonight. These images would be forever inscribed into her memory.

She turned to take in the room once more, hoping observation and logic would fortify her against the devastating scene laid before her. But hearing the whispering child and the murmurs from the mother's corpse shattered all her barriers and hot tears spilled from her eyes. "You poor little dears." Her strength fled and slumped to the floor. Cosmo knelt beside her and put his arm around her.

As she looked at the floor, the dark stains on her hands from the mother's blood caught her eye. Her fingernails dug into her palms and tears burned down her cheeks.

Charlotte stood and reached down into crib to touch the children, her hand trembling as she moved. Her fingers smoothed away the hair from one's face and then gently closed his unseeing eyes. Something deep inside ached to hold the boys and press them close as if an embrace were all it would take to make things right again. Instead, she the pressed her hand against the back of the second boy, whose arms were wrapped around his brother.

The body shifted under her touch and she started, not daring to breathe. The baby gave a shuddering gasp.

"Cos, this one is alive!" Her heart soared. She checked his breathing. It was not deep, but neither was it the same shallow panting of his brother.

Cosmo put a hand to his chest. "Thank heaven!"

Charlotte pulled the babe into her arms, relief and joy infusing her with warmth. He whimpered, his eyes fluttering open, at first completely black, but within moments fading to blue. His eyes, his beautiful blue eyes, focused on Charlotte. Then he screwed his face tight, and then he howled, his cries high and piercing. They were the most glorious wails she had ever heard.

The barghest's gaze followed the babe in her arms, tilting its head at the cries.

Charlotte pulled him closer, bouncing and instinctively shushing him, unrestrained tears now spilling down her face. What this poor child must have gone through. Why had his eyes been black? Did it have something to do with them being twins?

But why would the soul-eater consume this boy's brother and not him? Surely a toddler cub would be much easier to overpower than a fully-grown werewolf—so why spare one and not the other?

Realization hit Charlotte like the blast of a Tesla ray. The soul-eater didn't *choose* to not consume this boy. It had been interrupted.

Which meant, it was probably still here.

"Take him." Charlotte pushed the still-wailing baby into Cosmo's arms. Cosmo took the child and began humming a lullaby. Within seconds the boy's crying had subsided.

Charlotte wiped her eyes, then donned the goggles. The dead baby's body and the body of his mother still glowed a faint maroon and turquoise. The barghest, sitting at the foot of the crib and watching the goings-on, emitted a spectral blue color. However, there was no trail from the dead mother to the crib. Which meant the hazy turquoise aura hanging like a fog around the room wasn't from the barghest.

It was from the soul-eater.

*Stupid, foolish girl.*

"Charlotte?" Cosmo's whisper cut through the silence.

The barghest disappeared.

She turned toward Cosmo and gasped. "Cosmo, there's a trail. A deeper teal one from the boy." She squinted, trying to pick out the brightest and most recent soul-eater trail. "Perhaps it will lead us to the soul—"

"Charlotte." Cosmo's voice cut her short, his tone sending chills down her spine. She froze. He was pointing behind her. She turned as though on a precipice. Her eyes followed the glowing trail and her words died on her lips.

Crouching in a corner of the ceiling was a writhing black mass. It appeared to be a ball of condensed smoke, continuously billowing and collapsing in on itself. Each tendril—no, tentacle—would extend, sliding from the center, then solidify, and then disintegrate into smoke, as if searching for something.

Like all the other supernaturals, this creature had two distinct colors surrounding it, which flowed over and around its dark silhouette. Silvery blue light haloed the monstrosity, however there was also a thick turquoise aural glow. A spectrally based life-form.

Charlotte couldn't help herself. "Fascinating," she breathed.

A pair of narrow ochre-yellow eyes glowed from the center of the mass, peering at Charlotte. Air hissed through Charlotte's teeth. It could see her.

Her hand flew to her blaster and she pulled it from its holster, her finger gripping the trigger.

"Why hasn't it attacked yet?" The floorboards creaked as Cosmo shifted behind her.

"Perhaps because we haven't attacked?" *Or because we're armed.* Her fingers ached to shoot, but she kept her gun at her side, ready.

The creature's eyes darted from Cosmo to Charlotte following their exchange.

Fear and excitement trembled through Charlotte. At any other time she would be loath to destroy such a unique creature. But the thought of the babe in Cosmo's arms and the dead twin and mother hardened her resolve. As singular as this creature was, if it was going around eating souls—well, that just wouldn't do. Her chest tightened, as did her finger on the trigger.

*Neutralize it first, old girl, if you can. Second rule of monster hunting.*

At that moment, icy fear lanced through her stomach and she doubled over, paralyzed. She tried to raise her ray gun but her arm wouldn't respond. What was happening?

The creature descended from the ceiling, approaching Charlotte. An aroma of stale dust filled her nostrils. Her stomach heaved and her chest turned to lead. Fear and panic swirled as she tried to fill her lungs, and fight off her growing lightheadedness.

Cosmo groaned. From the corner of her eye she saw him drop to his knees, an arm wrapped protectively around the child.

The creature paused, its eyes shifting between Charlotte and Cosmo. It changed course gliding toward her friend and the child. Its top half condensed into an elongated humanoid shape, smoke wreathing the lower portion of its body. Spindly fingers caressed the air as it skimmed the floor toward Cosmo and the crying child. As it distanced itself from Charlotte, the paralysis left her in small degrees. Her body gulping mouthfuls of air.

Cosmo was on his knees, one arm holding himself up from the floor while the other still cradled the child. His eyes and the tendons on his neck pulled tight. Someone whimpered, and Charlotte wasn't sure if it was the child or her friend.

A smoky tentacle slithered toward them.

It wanted the child. It was still hungry.

"You c-can't…have him," Cosmo whispered. He fell onto his side, curling around the baby, his jaw beginning to slacken. The soul-eater bent over him and the boy.

The unnatural fear abandoned Charlotte completely. A primal rage roared through her soul. The sudden adrenaline calmed her mind.

She stood, raised her ray gun and fired.

The beam hit a solid tentacle, blasting it off. The creature shrieked, and the smell of burning flesh flooded the room. Through the goggles Charlotte could see the severed tentacle, still solid and now dull and dark, writhing on the floor. She aimed again at the monstrous mass above her, waiting for the blaster to charge. The gun's hum rose several pitches. *Charge, you worthless thing!*

She aimed for the soul-eater's torso. Suddenly, its form wavered, transforming into a glowing sea-green cloud. For a fraction of a heartbeat, Charlotte was fascinated again. Its liquid movements lent the creature a predatory grace. The soul-eater's outline blurred and flashed white, then returned to the original pale blue and turquoise glow. The creature circled behind Cosmo.

"Charlotte," Cosmo growled though his teeth, struggling to stand. The child started wailing. "It disappeared."

Camouflage. Clever thing.

"Not for me," she murmured. She fired off three low-level blasts in quick succession, not waiting for the full charge. The soul-eater barely dodged the first blast. The second and third hit, but the low-charged blasts did little damage. The creature screamed and it backed into the corner where the barghest had been.

A few more quick blasts and Charlotte's ray was out of power—useless until she returned home to charge it. She hurled it at the soul-eater. A tentacle swiped it aside.

The soul-eater hissed and lunged for her, jumping over Cosmo. Charlotte ducked and the monster flew overhead. It landed behind her.

*If this creature is spectral, let's see how it handles basic ghost protocol.* She tore open a salt pouch and threw the whole thing at the soul-eater.

The monster's form scattered as the salt hit its mark. The resultant bone-shattering cry pierced Charlotte's brain. Her hands flew to her ears and she doubled over. Cosmo curled himself around the boy.

As soon as the scream had subsided, Charlotte straightened and pulled on the lowest part of the steel supports in her outer corset. Two long, thin daggers emerged.

Fragments of the creature coalesced in the corner, and the soul-eater swooped again. Charlotte slashed, the air whistling as the knives cut towards the monster, penetrating the cloud. *Please find the body.*

The daggers stabbed something solid in the center of the mass.

The creature shrieked again and lunged for Charlotte's face. One of the tentacles wrapped around her goggles, covering her vision and knocking her off balance. Her heartbeat thrashed in her ears. *Bad, bad, very bad!* She hacked blindly but failed to connect with anything.

With a wrench, the soul-eater ripped the goggles from her face. They hit the floor, and Charlotte cursed at the sound of breaking glass. She blinked her eyes, then widened them in the dim room. Blazes, the monster could be anywhere.

"Cosmo, keep to that corner."

The vampire, who was next to the crib, pressed his back against the wall, sliding toward the corner behind the door.

Charlotte whirled on her heels, the daggers held high and ready.

A dim glow caught her attention. The blades were covered in some faintly glowing teal liquid. The creature's blood—proof that the monster was a mix of corporeal and spectral elements.

Charlotte walked forward, regrouping the handles of her weapons, keeping her eyes trained on the floor. Tiny drops of luminescent turquoise led toward the crib.

"Oh, no you don't." She raced forward, stabbing at the air above the crib. Her dagger again connected with something solid. The soul-eater screeched becoming completely visible. Its cloud form was greatly diminished, almost transparent, revealing the bits of its corporeal body. Was that…black fabric? Charlotte blinked, then pulled her arm back for another lunge.

Suddenly, the nursery door burst open and a short, pug-faced man wearing a dark suit ran into the room. Something about him looked familiar, but Charlotte hadn't the time to do more than register that fact. The man's terrified eyes darted from the fallen woman, to the crib, then to Charlotte and Cosmo and he froze when he saw the cloud. Was this the father?

No time to think about him now. Charlotte thrust the dagger towards the cloud.

A sudden blast of unnatural fear rocked through Charlotte, paralyzing her again. The man crumpled to the floor and a thud sounded as Cosmo fell to the ground. The soul-eater hissed again and withdrew to the nursery window and flew into the night.

The terror gripping her heart suddenly dissipated, but it was still several seconds before she could right herself.

The man rose to his feet and stumbled to the woman's body in the center of the room.

Charlotte ran past the man, snatched the broken goggles, and rushed to the window. It was dangerous to turn one's back on an emotional werewolf, but she needed to see where the soul-eater went. The left lens was shattered, but the right still worked faintly—the soul-eater had left a trail of turquoise weaving through the streets headed west towards Kensington.

"Blazes!" Charlotte pulled herself back into the nursery and turned to face the newcomer. He was hunched over his wife's body. In the aftermath of the soul-eater, the corpse still whispered "holy" over and over.

"Liza," the man fell to his knees. "My sweet Liza." He cradled Liza's head in his lap. The man brushed his wife's matted hair from her face.

Charlotte's heart broke. She took a few hesitant steps forward, unsure of how best to comfort him, and one of the floorboards creaked.

The man stopped his wails and snapped his wild-eyed gaze to Charlotte. He lunged and grabbed at Charlotte's skirts, stained with werewolf blood, and gave a feral snarl. "Where are my boys?"

"Your son is alive," Charlotte said, dropping her weapons and raising her hands. She looked at Cosmo, who pressed the child protectively against his chest and eyed the man warily.

The man's gaze fell on the boy, then onto Cosmo's face. His nostrils flared. "Vampire!" His teeth and jaw began to sharpen and elongate.

*Not good.*

Cosmo, with his back to the wall, slid from the corner, moving toward Charlotte, keeping his eyes on the werewolf.

"Murderer!" The man leapt up, pointing a blood-stained finger at Cosmo. "Give me back my son!" He probably would have attacked Cosmo on the spot if the vampire hadn't been holding his baby.

Cosmo stopped in his tracks. He shifted into a defensive stance.

Charlotte lunged between them, her hands held out to the werewolf. "Please, sir, let me explain." She opened her mind to Cosmo, hoping he was listening. *Give him the child!*

Heavy footfalls sounded from the landing. A well-dressed, sophisticated black man entered the room. His barrel-chested frame seemed to take up the entire doorframe. A dark, short-trimmed beard covered a strong jaw. His brow deepened into a scowl, then he grimaced as he took in the gruesome scene. Charlotte had never seen him before, but his command of the room was apparent from the moment he stepped in.

"Your Grace, impeccable timing as usual," Cosmo said. His words were light, but the tone was forced—Cosmo kept his gaze locked on the werewolf father.

As the father lowered his eyes to the floor in obvious—and probably reluctant—deference to the newcomer, the cogs clicked into place. This was the Alpha of the London Pack, Duke Maximilian Westerton.

The duke's eyes lingered on Liza's form and the crib, then he turned to the father. "Johnathan, what has happened?"

Johnathan? Charlotte's mind snapped the pieces into place as she studied the his face. The *Asteria.* He was the server. The one the baroness had helped.

"This vampire has—has—" A lost look washed over Johnathan's face and his voice broke. He pointed to the form of his wife.

The duke turned back to Charlotte and Cosmo. A hard look settled on his dark features. "This is unfortunate, Wilmott."

Charlotte hadn't realized the two men knew each other. But of course they would being leaders in their respective spheres. And both belonging to the House of Lords.

*Unfortunate?* What was His Grace talking about? Did he think Cosmo had done this? Charlotte shifted her weight, her eyes darting between Cosmo and the duke. Her stomach tightened. *Protective instincts for the Pack will override any rational thought.* Her mind jumped back to the Upheavals, and she could see future events snapping into place as they unfolded around her.

"Your Grace, Johnathan—stop!"

Both werewolves ignored her and began to transform. Johnathan's face twisted in pain as his bones shifted, their structure rearranging. His hands curled and the fingers melted together. The blood from his fallen wife stained his paws.

"It wasn't Lord Wilmott!" Charlotte yelled, but they didn't pay her any mind.

As the duke transformed, Charlotte sucked in air, completely amazed. She had seen werewolves transform before, but never the alpha, and the scientific side of her mind was more than a little awestruck. In most werewolves, the transformation was unsettling at best, as body parts shifted from human to wolf, but the control and grace with which the duke transformed was both beautiful and terrifying. His broad nose and jawline gracefully elongated, his ears disappearing into his hairline. His dark hair thickened over his head and face and turned silver. Within moments, he stood with a human body but an almost completely lupine head, as regal as the Egyptian god Anubis.

The duke's piercing yellow eyes fixed a predatorial stare on Charlotte. "Where is the other child?" His voice growled around his still-sharpening canines.

*So* now *he wants the pertinent information.* Charlotte swallowed, her throat instantly dry. Her fingers itched for her silver-tipped corset knives, which were still on the ground. This could go wrong in so many ways unless she could calm these two down immediately, before they fully transformed. *They only want the boy. Why hasn't Cosmo given them the child? He must still be protecting it. Blast his paternal instincts.*

Cosmo was standing still, his arms wrapped around the boy, angling the wailing toddler away from the werewolves—which was precisely the wrong thing to do. To the Pack, it would look like he was taking the baby away, not protecting it.

The child thrashed in Cosmo's arms, its chubby arms and legs thrashing. Its face screwed tight as it wailed.

The duke advanced with his hackles raised and a growl building in his throat.

Filling its lungs, the babe let loose waves of wails.

Cosmo bared his teeth and elongated fangs.

Charlotte's training told her to neutralize Johnathan and the duke and explain later, but her feelings condensed into a hunch. She had to do something no one had done before—ignore the alpha.

"Pardon me," Charlotte said, clearing her throat and stepping between Cosmo and the werewolves with her back to the half-transformed Westerton.

The duke stopped growling. "What are you doing, woman?"

Charlotte did not answer. She took the baby from Cosmo's arms. He willingly relinquished the child, but his green eyes flashed with fear, and she could see his fangs still elongating.

"None of your nonsense, Cos," she whispered under her breath. Then she pivoted and took quick, confident strides to the alpha, who had frozen mid-transformation and now almost backed up in surprise. "Your Grace, this was not the act of a vampire. I can prove it." Charlotte offered the boy to the alpha, whose sharp eyes widened.

Then she turned her head to the side and dropped her gaze, exposing her neck.

The duke's head tilted as he assessed Charlotte's act of submission. After a moment, the silver fur retreated and his features returned to normal. His chest heaved, and only the slightest sheen of sweat indicated there was any discomfort from the transformation.

Johnathan followed suit, his bones snapping loudly back into their human arrangement. He did not look pleased, but kept glancing at the duke.

Charlotte sighed. The crisis appeared to have been averted. She scowled at Cosmo, whose fangs had retracted and he seemed back to his normal self. His shrug and sheepish grin only slightly mollified her irritation. *Men.*

The duke shook his head, blinking. His fists clenched and then relaxed, and his shoulders dropped any remaining tension. He stepped forward, shooting Cosmo one last withering look, then gently took the child from Charlotte's arms. He handed the baby to Johnathan.

Johnathan buried his face in the child's curls, releasing a shuddering breath. "Romulus."

"Explain why I must spare Lord Wilmott's sorry afterlife," the duke said to Charlotte, "before I change my mind."

Charlotte took in his glare and stern features. He was surly, but at least he wasn't about to kill anyone…for now. "This was the work of the soul-eater."

"That creature that's been killing supernaturals?"

She wasn't surprised he knew about the monster.

"We can track it with these." She held up the broken goggles. "Here is its blood. And here." She gestured towards the floor, where drips of the dark liquid had scattered around the room. "The goggles identify supernatural signatures, and the soul-eater's blood glows turquoise when you look through them."

The trail took them close to Liza's body, and Charlotte became very aware of Johnathan standing in the corner by the crib. He swayed back and forth, clutching his now-sleeping son. A deep ache tore within Charlotte as she followed Johnathan's gaze to the remains of his family, still and lifeless before him. She swallowed, offering him the only thing she could give to help. "Perhaps we could relocate?" she asked the duke, gesturing to the room, her voice mostly steady.

The duke glanced around and his expression softened.

Charlotte walked to Johnathan, who held Romulus in one arm. Careful not to disturb the sleeping babe, Johnathan reached down with his free hand to stroke the dead child's face.

"I'm sorry," Charlotte said. She glanced down at the small, still frame. The words sounded insignificant in the face of such carnage.

The duke came forward, gesturing for Charlotte to step aside, and she was once more struck by how large this man really was and how close they all had been to exchanging blows. Between herself, England's best monster hunter, and the alpha of the pack, Charlotte wasn't entirely sure she would win—at least, she wouldn't be left whole and fully functional. The duke turned to Johnathan and they spoke a few whispered words.

"Many thanks, Your Grace," Johnathan said. "I will come shortly. I'd like to stay with Liza"—his voice broke, dying to a whisper—"and Remus a bit longer."

"We will hunt this creature and destroy it. I promise." The duke nodded to Johnathan, then turned to Charlotte.

"Before we retire to the parlour," she said in hushed tones, "look through these." She handed the duke the broken goggles.

He obeyed and his body stiffened as his world infused with blue. He inhaled deeply, perhaps tasting the air. After a moment he returned the goggles to Charlotte. Then he and Charlotte and Cosmo left the nursery, closing the door softly behind them.

The trio entered the parlour and Cosmo turned on the Tesla lamp—entirely for Charlotte's benefit, as both vampires and werewolves could get along fine in the dark.

Charlotte released a breath. There was no point in hiding anything. In her experience, good working relationships were built on mutual trust. She explained to the duke everything, from the victims and their whisperings to the attack this evening. As she laid evidence and facts before the duke, gratitude for her calm logic washed over her—his stance and general demeanor were less aggressive and more resigned.

"Why would the soul-eater harm such a prominent figure? The queen herself recognized the twins' birth. And why assault a werewolf so near transformation?" The duke rubbed at his beard. "The full moon is tomorrow and the werewolf could snap, as Eliza did, and attack the creature."

Charlotte's mind spun around the question and she spoke slowly. "There was no forced entry. Nurseries are notoriously stuffy as the highest point of the house. It was possible the window was open and the soul-eater seized its chance. Most predators are opportunists and would consume what they could."

She looked to the duke and he nodded his confirmation. Charlotte continued. "Perhaps it was simply random circumstance that led the soul-eater to this home in particular. It is a prominent werewolf neighborhood. As for the timing of the attack and the full moon, I don't mean to sound garish, but maybe the soul of the werewolf has a higher nutritional value?"

Charlotte grimaced. The duke cleared his throat and greyed slightly. Cosmo shifted uncomfortably.

"From this encounter, we have learned several things," Charlotte said. "It has the ability to shift into a diaphanous form. It can manipulate and increase one's fear—it even blasted through my mental fortifications. But"—she raised a finger—"it has physical limits to its influence and can only affect someone within a certain radius." Charlotte ticked the next items off on her fingers. "It bleeds. It can camouflage, but it can be tracked with these." Charlotte pointed at the goggles in the duke's hand.

"Which are partially broken." The duke frowned and gestured to the left side of the goggles.

"Temporarily," Cosmo corrected. "I have prototype parts at home."

The duke dropped the goggles in Cosmo's outstretched hand. He then folded his own arms and lifted an eyebrow. "I suppose you have a plan to catch the foul creature."

"I do," Charlotte said, raising her chin. "But I have an errand for you."

"Charlotte," Cosmo said, clearing his throat. "The Duke of Keighley does not perform errands."

"Perhaps not, but Maximilian Westerton, Alpha of the London Pack, does. Especially if it means protecting his own. Is that not so, Your Grace?"

Charlotte glanced at the duke, whose mouth turned up ever so slightly at the corner. "Call me West," he said to Charlotte. Then he turned to Cosmo. "Unless I'm mistaken, this *is* the Lady Astley you've spoken of?"

"The one and only," Cosmo said.

The duke's smile broadened. "I like her. Is she always so bold?"

"This is tame," Cosmo murmured, rolling his eyes.

Charlotte smacked him on the arm.

The duke chuckled and turned back to Charlotte. "I'm at your disposal. What do you need?"

Charlotte spared a smirk for Cosmo before continuing. "When the soul-eater fled, it flew towards Kensington, but it may have gone further afield than that. We need confirmation of its direction and that it didn't double back. We wounded it, so it shouldn't be too difficult to follow. I'm assuming you know its scent."

The duke nodded and stood. "Of course. I'll send word either to Lord Wilmott or to you, Lady Astley."

"Thank you, West," Charlotte said, standing as well. The three of them moved from the parlour and exited the house. Charlotte turned to close the door, but a noise made her pause. Weeping. From upstairs in the nursery. She closed her eyes, then pulled the door shut.

A few wolves had gathered in the street, pacing, their nails clicking on the cobblestones. The barghest had reappeared as well and sat facing the house, as if waiting—but for what Charlotte didn't know.

The duke tipped his hat to Charlotte. Then, with a masculine grace, he transformed. Within moments, where West had stood, there was now a large silver-haired wolf. The alpha lowered his head, and tiny bits of dust swirled as he sniffed the ground. The other wolves padded over to West. He raised his head and, as one, they all loped silently into the night.

The barghest took no notice of their departure, its eyes wide and impassive as a marble statue. Shivers crawled down Charlotte's spine as it stood sentinel. How long was it going to stay here?

From across the street, both Inspector Dawson and Policeman Singh approached Charlotte and Cosmo.

"Seems you had a right hard time of it," Dawson said, glancing first in the direction of the remaining werewolves then at Charlotte's clothes.

Charlotte glanced down and saw her skirt and bustle askew, and several lace accoutrements ripped beyond repair. She could only imagine the state of her hair. Dark rust-colored stains hemmed the fabric, and she shuddered, her heart wrenching again.

"You don't know the half of it," she said flatly. "This fellow and the alpha almost single-handedly started another Upheaval."

Singh's eyes widened. "Cor, wha' did you do tha' for?"

Cosmo opened his mouth, but Charlotte beat him to it. "Just two hotheads blowing off steam." It wasn't entirely true, but the thought of explaining everything right now was too much.

Cosmo sniffed, then smoothed his vest, overlooking the torn pockets and fraying silk.

Dawson's mustache twitched then he looked over Charlotte's shoulder at the barghest. "What do you s'pose it's waiting for?"

"The right time, most likely," Charlotte said, turning.

"Beg your pardon?"

"Bodies expire some time after their souls are stolen. That may be why it's behaving so oddly. The bodies up there are neither alive nor dead."

Policeman Singh's gaze moved from the barghest to the upper windows of the townhouse. "When d'you suppose they'll expire?"

Charlotte smoothed her skirts and hastily re-pinned her hair. "Difficult to say. The soul-eater has never drawn blood before, that we know of, nor has it ever consumed such a young soul."

"Why did the soul-eater draw blood now?" Inspector Dawson rubbed the back of his neck. "Why not before?"

An epiphany struck Charlotte's mind with the force of a Tesla bolt. "Bread crumbs," she whispered.

Dawson leaned forward, his face knit in confusion. "Did you say bread crumbs?"

"Hansel and Gretel," Cosmo said. "Breadcrumbs."

The inspector scowled. "What do two German kids and their bread have to do with this case?"

Cosmo folded his arms. "You don't have any children, do you?"

"Do you?" Dawson blustered.

"I happen to be extremely well read." Cosmo straightened his vest and brushed his hair from his face.

"Yes, Lord Wilmott has only recently finished his Alphabet primer and is anxious to begin his grammar books." Charlotte patted Cosmo's arm. "His letters are adequate, but his spelling is atrocious."

Policeman Singh's hand covered a cough very similar to the one last night in front of St. Bridgeman. Charlotte's mouth twitched at the corners, while Cosmo's turned decidedly down.

"Gentlemen, I believe the victims have been leaving us clues. Condemning clues leading to the soul-eater. That's why the soul-eater wanted to destroy the bodies. However, it failed in its goal."

Dawson, still eyeing Cosmo, spoke to Charlotte. "What clues were they?"

Charlotte pulled out her telescriber and flipped it open, scanning the pages for her list. "'Holy,' 'ink,' and now 'brohwee.'"

Dawson scowled. "What in the blazes is this last one?"

"Nonsense?" Cos suggested.

She shook her head. "Think like a child, Cos. Some words are difficult for the very young to say. 'Brohwee' could be a child's version of 'brolly.'"

She rolled her shoulders, attempting to dislodge the chilling image of the dead white-eyed babe whispering. She came to herself. Blast. There had been that fabric under the soul-eater's smoke form. She'd forgotten to tell West about that.

The chief nodded and rubbed his chin, staring at the buildings across the street, lost in thought.

Cosmo leaned over Charlotte shoulder. "How could a soul-sucking monster be connected to an umbrella in any way?" As Cosmo spoke, he sent a puff of air that tickled against her skin. A shiver slipped down her spine. *There's just an extra bite in the evening chill—that's all.* At least, that was the lie she chose to tell herself.

Policeman Singh chimed in, jolting Charlotte's fuzzy brain into gear. "These clues 'holy' and 'ink,' must've been important enough tha' the soul-eater wanted to destroy the bodies. We should look into those first."

A small noise from a window on the opposite side of the street made the group pause. A face peeked from behind the window's curtains.

Cosmo turned to Charlotte. "Lady Astley, perhaps we should retire to Wilmott House to further discuss these matters more privately."

"Lord Wilmott is correct, Lady Astley," Dawson said. "We will need to process and contain the area. Plus, I must interview Mr. Johnathan. Tonight, unfortunately."

"But, we've almost got it. I can feel it." Charlotte hated the whine in her voice. The clues had failed her. If the duke didn't catch the soul-eater or at least come back with something significant, she was utterly stumped. "Can't we puzzle it out here just as well as at Wilmott house?"

Cosmo leaned in close and lowered his voice. "Baron St. Bridgeman is sure to be here shortly."

Charlotte's eyes widened, then narrowed. "Of course, it is late. By all means, let us retire. I've seen enough atrocities for one night."

Cosmo winked. "See you soon." With a burst of darkness, he rose into the night.

For the second time that night, Charlotte fought back a pleasant shiver. *This is not the time nor the place.*

"Lady Astley," Dawson said, "we'll be by tomorrow to take your statement."

"Very good, Inspector. Tomorrow."

She walked briskly to her autocab and told the driver the Wilmott house which he punched into the programming tin. As he replaced the apparatus, a howl tore into the night, melting Charlotte's bones.

She leaned out of the cab, facing Johnathan's house. The barghest stood on all fours, mist swirling around its paws. It threw its head back and howled again, each new cry building on the last. Liza and Remus. Their bodies must have died. A second howl mingled with the death cry, more human but more haunting. Johnathan.

Charlotte entered the autocab's carriage, and it lurched into gear and raced from the square. She leaned back in the cab, silently promising the family that no matter what it took, she would avenge them all.

# Chapter 12

No, no, no. If the words point to a location, then St. Mary's Church is the most logical for 'holy.'" Charlotte rearranged the scraps of paper over the map of London.

The Tesla lamps at the Wilmott house hummed into the early hours. Cosmo raked his hands through his hair, glowering at Charlotte. Even disheveled, he was still dashingly handsome.

"Why not the All Souls Church?"

Charlotte added sugar to her tea and stirred, satisfaction warming her more than the drink had. "Because the spires of St. Mary's could be seen from the Spitalfields alley."

Cosmo sighed and rubbed his chin. "Yes, a closer proximity to the scene of the crime would make sense. About 'holy' and 'clouds'— could it mean 'holy clouds' like an avenging angel? Or even St. Paul's Cathedral. It's the highest holy point in London and could appear to touch the clouds." He fell into pacing. "But what about the octopus?"

"Octopus?"

"Remember?" he asked. "There were several drawings of octopi and squid-like creatures in St. Bridgeman's study, along with sketches of clouds and smoke."

Charlotte frowned. A wriggle of memory invaded her mine, and she grasped for it. Clouds. Tentacles.

The strange storm she'd seen aboard the *Asteria*. Could it have something to do with…

*No*, she thought, *it couldn't have.* The storm had appeared long after the soul-eater began its attacks. Still, she couldn't shake the feeling that there might be a connection. She filed the thought away to examine later.

"Well, I suppose the soul-eater resembles an octopus with all those tentacles," she said, turning back to the issue at hand, "but how would that help us stop the thing?" Her hands smoothed her napkin, as if ridding it of wrinkles would present a solution to this madness.

"Blazing suns if I know."

"Cos, this might confirm that St. Bridgeman is a lying jack-a-nape—"

"Something you already believed."

"—and he knows far more than he has let on." She settled deeper into her chair and sipped her tea, feeling surprisingly calm and ready to tease the answer out of this puzzle over the next several hours. She was also enjoying the show.

Cosmo was barely holding himself together. Literally. He stopped pacing and reached for his own cup, but his hand passed right through it. He growled, attempting to grab the drink three more times.

Charlotte choked and coughed into her tea.

He took a deep breath, narrowed his eyes at the offending china, and finally grabbed the handle.

"Let's take the clues separately," he said, still glaring at the tea cup. "Clouds…clouds. You might need a brolly if there are clouds. But you need one all the time in London. There are clouds in the sky, smoke clouds from the factories. Blazing disgusting when you accidentally fly over one."

Charlotte counted on her fingers. "Smog and mist could be considered clouds. Cephalopods have ink *clouds* they release to escape predators."

Cosmo practically slammed his cup down on the saucer. "I've got it."

Her eyebrows rose.

"A giant octopus will attack St. Mary's Church."

She rolled her eyes. "Before or after it amasses an army of souls?"

"After, of course." He fell into his pacing once more.

Charlotte looked over the biscuits on the side table and set several onto her plate. "Let's move away from the clues. You look like you're about to have a fit of the vapors, and I don't think they have invented *sal de sang* for vampiric nerves." She nibbled the shortbread. "Besides, you're coming apart at the seams."

Cosmo stopped in his tracks, looking at his rumpled clothing. His outline solidified quickly, and a wicked grin stole across his face. "You're right. My valet would stake me if he saw the state of my neckwear alone." Then he gave Charlotte a sidelong glance that experience told her not to trust in the slightest.

*What are you about, Lord Wilmott?*

His skin slowly began to take on a golden sheen. Heat washed through Charlotte, too fast for her to stop. She gritted her teeth. *It's only a vampire glamour and nothing I haven't seen before. What's the fuss about?*

But then Cosmo started glowing like an over-charged Tesla bulb. His coiffure and cravat not only returned to pristine condition, but his hair color intensified and shimmered from a deep chestnut to a rich walnut. His skin smoothed to a porcelain finish. His jacket tightened visibly at the shoulders and, even worse, strained the buttons down the front. Within moments, Charlotte was staring—ogling, if she was honest—at the most overwhelmingly handsome man she had ever seen, supernatural or otherwise. Her heart nearly blew a fuse.

She stopped chewing, clutching the half-eaten biscuit, certain she looked like a simpleton —but she couldn't look away. And why would she ever want to?

Now *that* was a man.

A thought flashed like lightning across her foggy brain. *Where are those blasted goggles?* On second thought, they would tint everything lavender, and Charlotte wanted to savor every minute detail. Blazing suns, he was handsome.

And had he just increased his physical strength and stature? That was unusual for a glamour. Not that Charlotte minded. In fact, she gained a deep appreciation for the fine quality of Lord Wilmott's excellent tailor.

"Too much?" Cosmo asked.

Charlotte swallowed the piece of biscuit and nearly choked. Her chin dipped in a single nod, dislodging crumbs. Aunt Hespa would've had her hide. She cursed, wiping bits of food off her lap.

The impish twinkle in Cosmo's eye sparked her irritation. He knew exactly what he'd done. She had to squash her own mischievous impulse to raise the stakes and lean in to expose her neck. Perhaps she might even press her hand against her throat and increase the blood flow to that area. See how the vampire liked that move…

She shook her head. Perhaps they *had* been spending too much time poring over clues.

Cosmo's vampire glamour decreased, the golden glow around him fading completely and far too quickly.

Charlotte blinked, dazed. Had she fastened her outer corset too tight?

"I, um…need a…thirsty." *What is wrong with me?* She stood, pressing her fingers against the table to steady herself, then strode over to the side board and poured herself some Madeira, downing it in one swallow. The fruity wine stuck to her throat.

*The case, Charlotte.*

*Yes, of course. High noon take Cosmo.* She tucked a wisp of hair back into place, then turned to face the blessedly normal-looking vampire. "If you'd stop your antics then we could stop that monster."

He nodded, though the mischievous glint didn't leave his eye. "I believe we were discussing the possible tactics the giant soul-eating octopus might use to attack the church."

Charlotte bit back a retort. They had to solve these clues before the soul-eater took another victim. "Let's take a step back and look at the bigger picture."

He took an exaggerated step backward. "Go on."

She rolled her eyes but continued, grateful her brain had reasserted itself and they were back on track. "Don't you think it odd that only the slums have been targeted? Or at least, only the poorer areas. No one of note, with the exception of the twins, has been attacked. "

"The attack on those pups certainly has more political weight than anything else so far." He folded his arms, finally looking serious.

"How would this affect St. Bridgeman's bill?"

"His Council for Humanity will most likely argue that people are not safe if they don't know who their neighbors are. If something stronger than the known supernaturals is attacking the supernatural population, then who *is* safe? After all, it didn't just attack me—it attacked you, too, even though you are human."

She rubbed her forehead. "I was an armed human." Cosmo opened his mouth, but she beat him to it. "St. Bridgeman has to be involved somehow. These werewolf murders might tip the political scales in his favor. Curse the Council for Humanity." She paused. "What should our next move be?"

He threw his hands up. "I'm no politician."

"You sit in the House of Lords."

"Not as much as I should," he said, pointing a finger. "You can thank the mandatory house arrests for that."

Charlotte returned to her chair but did not sit, instead taking a turn around the table, her fingers tracing the edge.

"Here's a bigger-picture thought," Cosmo said, pivoting on his heel to face her. "Perhaps it's a known supernatural creature exhibiting powers we were unaware of."

"Such as?"

"Could it be a lindworm?"

"No scorch marks."

"Griffin?"

"Nothing was stolen from the victims."

"What about a ceffyl dŵr?"

Charlotte's fingers pressed against her temples. "Cos. A water horse demon?"

"It was in the news!"

"It was a hoax."

He grabbed his glass of *vin* and slumped in his chair, sipping sullenly.

"We do know that it is related to specters," Charlotte said. "But how that helps us, I don't know."

The pair had been arguing and rearranging the words on the tabletop until Charlotte's eyes crossed. They had to be indicating a church. What else could those words mean? She plopped down again at the writing desk and idly twirled the paper knife. Holy ink, holy clouds. The knife spun over her fingers. *A holy umbrella?* Twirl, twirl, twirl. She suppressed the desire to stab the tabletop. What was she missing? Twirl, twirl—her fingers fumbled and the knife dropped, slicing her thumb as it went.

Cosmo was at her side in a blur, deftly catching the knife before it hit the floor. Charlotte cursed, then sucked at the stupid injury. Cosmo gently pulled her thumb out of her mouth. Red welled up from the slit. "Holy saints of monsters and men, woman. You fight devils and demons but are undone by a letter opener."

Charlotte's breath caught, her muscles taut as a new idea appeared. "Say that again."

"'Undone by a letter opener.'"

"No, the first part."

"'Woman?'"

"No! 'Holy saints of'…whatever it was." The idea kindled a small ember of hope in her chest. Perhaps this was it.

Cosmo kissed her thumb. What was this man doing? She was trying to crack this case.

His lips moved from her thumb to her hand. "You taste like sunshine," he murmured.

"What if the clues refer to the next victim?" Charlotte asked, testing out her idea.

Cosmo came to himself, blinking hard. "The next victim?"

"We've got it all wrong." She stood with such force it nearly knocked him to the ground. "Mr. Draper gave us the word 'holy,' and what could be more innocent and holy than young children?" Each word could lead them to the next victim, and perhaps they could lie in wait and stop the soul-eater before it attacked.

"What do you make of 'ink' then?"

Charlotte's enthusiasm dimmed, then she remembered a detail from the alley. "Mr. Draper did have ink on his fingers." As soon as she'd uttered the words, she realized how thin her brilliant idea had been. *Everyone* had ink on their hands at one point or another.

"What about the duke's findings?" Cosmo asked. "Didn't the soul-eater flee in the direction of the St. Bridgeman estate?"

"We must wait for the duke to confirm, which I'm certain he will." Charlotte stood and crossed to the window, frustrated at how each clue had led them nowhere so far. "St. Bridgeman is involved some-how." She folded her arms and lifted her chin. If she was wrong about his involvement, they would find themselves back at the beginning with no answers and all the questions.

Cosmo scrunched his brow. "As slimy as that man is, none of these clues point to him."

"He could be in league with the creature," she said, some of her angry energy returning. "Perhaps he *is* the soul-eater. We both know he's as soulless bas—"

"Charlotte Glynis Astley. The mouth on that face."

She blushed both from the slip of her tongue and from the sud-den searing thought of her mouth pressed against Cosmo's. Her skin tingled. What would it be like to kiss him? She'd never been properly kissed before, only once by a tipsy prat at a soiree. Then she'd punched him. But Cos would be different. Another thought prickled her mind, and her mouth quirked: would his fangs hinder or enhance the experience? She chewed on her lip, eyeing his mouth. How would it affect their relationship?

She blushed deeper when he caught her staring. She did a quick check on her mental blocks, thanking her lucky stars she'd taken the time to learn such an essential skill, though she still had to press her fingernails into her palms to clear her head.

*Your emotional diversions will wear you out, Charlotte. Stay on the case.*

She cleared her throat. "St. Bridgeman may or may not be the monster, or even in league with it," she said, "but he knows more than he's letting on. We're clearly not getting anywhere."

"But there wasn't anything else in his book besides what I already told you."

She scowled. She had to warn Minnie about St. Bridgeman. But what if St. Bridgeman caught on that Charlotte knew about his secret? No, she had to capture and stop him before he could do anything to her friend.

She mentally calculated the risks. Her friend would not be spending time with St. Bridgeman this late at night, so she was safe for the next few hours at least. Aunt Hespa would require Minnie's complete focus during most of the day tomorrow, so St. Bridgeman could call upon Minnie only when other people would be present, and Charlotte doubted the soul-eater would strike during the daytime. Charlotte also knew that St. Bridgeman would be preparing for his mother's dinner party tomorrow night; that meant he would probably not have time to call on Minnie tomorrow anyway.

Perhaps . . . could he have invited Minnie to the dinner party?

Charlotte placed her hands on her hips. "Then we'll have to ask him in person. At the baroness's party tomorrow night." She checked the wall clock. "Tonight, I mean."

"Blazing suns!" Cosmo's face lit up. "About time for some good, old-fashioned vamping."

"No, Cos. This has to be done legally. You're in deep enough water these days as it is."

He slumped into a chair. "You take the fun out of having supernatural abilities."

"I, however, have no compunction in following something as mundane as rules." She gave him a sidelong glance. "Back to the dinner party—did the Great Cosmo Wilmott manage to secure an invitation for the best monster hunter in England?"

His pout deepened, and his voice had a surly edge. "I tried, but I regret to inform you that even though it is his mother's party, St. Beefwit specifically stated that I was not to extend an invitation to you. He said my invitation was based solely on my leadership rank in the Coven."

She folded her arms. "Blast it. How will I execute my master plan? That was the linchpin."

He rubbed his chin. "You must go the party, but how will you secure an invitation? It's not as if St. Bridgeman would extend one to you willingly."

Charlotte gave him a gentle shove, unable to stifle a grin. "Then I will have to do something that is infinitely more fun than actually being invited."

Cosmo rolled his eyes but chuckled. He stood closer, his scent filling her head. "*Carpe diem*, if you must. But Charlotte, don't kill anyone too important."

Just then, a chorus of anguished howls pierced the night. The Pack's lamentation washed through Charlotte, and she closed her eyes. "No promises."

# Chapter 13

"Will tha' be all, miss?"

Charlotte examined herself in the mirror. After last night's events with the soul-eater and puzzle-solving late into the night, she was relieved her eyes had only minimal dark circles. Beth had crafted a practical but exquisite hairstyle using the elongated wooden hairpins. Elaborate curls piled atop Charlotte's head concealed the pins' lethal nature.

"What do you think?" She rose to face Beth, the enormous peacock-blue and green bustle and train swishing softly with her movement. She smoothed her black silk trousers, which peeked through the shorter front of the skirt. "Am I prepared for dinner with the enemy?"

Beth's face showed momentary surprise. It was unconventional to ask servants their opinions, particularly if they were so new to the household, but Charlotte valued their perspectives. After all, no one made any discoveries by being conventional.

"Aye, m'lady. You smell especially nice tonight."

"I smell?" Charlotte's eyebrows quirked and Beth blushed, her hands flying over her mouth.

"No—I mean, yes—but not poorly." Beth knit her fingers together, obviously hesitant to continue.

"I confess, I'm not very aware of how keen a werewolf's sense of smell really is." Charlotte smiled reassuringly. She also strongly resisted the urge to sniff herself. "No need to be embarrassed. Please go on. "

Beth inhaled deeply, then spoke quickly. "You do smell, but everyone does. Smell. Wha' I mean is, everyone 'as a distinct smell. Sommat tha's personal to them. Take Mr. Bauen. 'E always smells of oil and metal. Cook smells of pepper and parsley."

Charlotte waved towards her vanity. "I don't wear any specific perfume."

Beth gave a shake of her head. "No, but ya still have a smell."

She was curious in spite of herself. "And what is it?"

The color on Beth's cheeks rose. "Soap."

"Soap?" That wasn't so bad.

"And Cook's raspberry scones."

Now it was Charlotte's turn to blush. So Beth could smell her one weakness. "Fascinating. I haven't had one since yesterday."

Beth's words seemed to be coming easier at Charlotte's encouragement. "Takes a day for most smells to fade. Though if the smell blends in with its surroundin' ones, it's harder to trace."

Charlotte made a mental note to rub herself in London soot if she were ever being tracked by a rogue supernatural.

"This may be a personal question, so please forgive me," Charlotte said. "But do you remember smells of people who have come calling?"

"It's not as if I'm sniffin' every visitor, but some are 'ard to ignore. Lord Wilmott positively reeks, 'specially right after his two weeks are up. Like someone gave coffee to a cat, then tied it in a bag."

Charlotte snorted. It was a fair assessment. Especially at the end of his house arrest. "Thank you, Beth. You may go."

Beth retreated from the room, the door clicking shut behind her.

Pushing aside thoughts of Cosmo, Charlotte went over the plan again, pacing around the table while tracing her fingers along its rim. It was ridiculously simple: infiltrate the baroness's party, then get answers from St. Bridgeman. Because it was a dinner party, she could arrive in her own carriage and enter the household. If she was brazen enough, she could "stumble" upon the dining room without seeming too brash. After dessert, when everyone returned to the drawing room, she needed to get St. Bridgeman alone, but how to do it without compromising propriety? Details, details. She only required a moment—it would be the perfect opportunity to field test her truth serum. Her fingertips tingled in anticipation.

It would all depend on her timing and the effectiveness. Could she pull it off without getting forcibly removed from the St. Bridgeman estate? Her hand dropped to her ray gun, one finger tapping the metal grip. *I'd like to see them try.*

A rap on the door broke through her thoughts. Beth entered, bobbing another curtsy. "Lord Wilmott to see you, miss."

"Does he smell like a coffee-drunk feline?"

Beth barked a laugh. "No, m'lady. 'E's right proper. Like wet lichen on the moors with a touch of mint."

"Now you have me exceedingly curious. It will take immense personal restraint, but I'll refrain from sniffing His Lordship."

She was rewarded with another smile from Beth.

Charlotte pressed a hand to her hair one last time. "Thank you. It seems your talents are as varied as they are extremely helpful. I'll see him in the study."

Beth blushed deeply, then curtsied and left.

After completing the finishing touches on her toilette, Charlotte entered the study. Cosmo stood and smoothed his embroidered wine-colored waistcoat. "Cos, what are you doing here? The party starts in a few minutes. How can I meet you there if you don't go?"

Cosmo folded his arms across his chest. His hair was slicked into chestnut waves. An image of his glamourized expanded physique snapped through Charlotte's mind. Heat crept up her neck. She shook it off, ordering her heart to behave. Tonight was about answers, not muddying the waters.

"How will you meet me there, when you haven't been invited?" He rocked on his heels, obviously pleased with himself.

"Pish— a minor detail." She moved to the large secretary desk and opened the upper cabinet, pulling out an oblong box and opening it to reveal a velvet-lined interior and two throwing knives. She placed the blades in their leather sheaths, then held them out towards Cosmo, who snorted and mumbled something that sounded suspiciously like "emancipated women."

"These are my *second* best pair, you know."

He laced the sheaths to her wrists. When he finished, she pulled down her specially altered sleeves concealing the weapons. Only the tip of each handle was visible and within easy reach.

"I'm not sure we're going to same dinner party," Cosmo said dryly. "Is Armageddon upon us?"

Charlotte waved her hand. "Hardly. It's only a ray gun, my *second* best throwing knives, and an unregistered substance of my own creation—all key to our operation tonight." She grabbed her reticule, satisfied at the reassuring weight of her arsenal. The serum sloshed inside its stoppered bottle. It had taken her a full three weeks to extract the requisite amount of henbane and corkwood and three more to find a proper medium in which to carry the oils.

The vampire's mouth curled into an *O*. "Marvelous! What illegal thing do you have planned?"

"Nothing actually illegal, per se. It's hard to have a law against something no one else knows exists."

"An intrigue! Do tell." Cosmo leaned forward. Mischief sparked his green, beautiful eyes.

She took a step back. "I'll not have you involved in any way. At least, not directly."

"Stop teasing." He offered his arm. "You'll give me a lisp."

"I'll let you know what to do when the time is right."

The clock struck seven.

Charlotte wrapped her arm around Cosmo's, noting how pleasant it was to have him so close. She allowed herself to be escorted to the doorstep.

He waggled his eyebrows. "Pity I have to attend by myself."

"I'm coming. Besides, you'll have West to keep you company."

Cosmo's brows lowered. "How do you know West is invi—"

"Just go." She pointed a finger in the general direction of the St. Bridgeman estate.

Cosmo heaved an overly dramatic sigh—he'd likely perfected it during his house arrest—then winked, misting, and vanished in a velvet cloud of smoke.

Charlotte watched the cloud rise swiftly above the rooftops, then she spun on her heels and closed the door.

"Howard, call an autocab, please. I have somewhere to be."

Lights glowed from the St. Bridgeman estate, surprisingly warm and inviting against the dark sky. Its large brick facade lay nestled between the silhouettes of formal and informal gardens. A glass building—either a conservatory or a butterfly house—jutted out at the back of the grounds.

Appreciation for the aesthetic nature of the estate grew as Charlotte's autocab rumbled up the drive. The smell of recently watered gravel mixed with the mechanical smell from her autocab's engine, and Charlotte inhaled deeply. Excitement and apprehension waltzed inside her. Tonight was the night. Tonight she would have answers.

She stepped from the autocab, inhaling the damp smell of earth—and wet dog. The werewolves had certainly arrived. The rain had started during the duke's hunt of the soul-eater and had continued on and off since. Though the werewolves hadn't found the monster, West had confirmed its direction toward the St. Bridgeman home. He had just informed her via the telescriber network, mentioning in his note that the soul-eater had the distinct smell of burning food. He'd also mentioned his invitation to the St. Bridgeman dinner party, indicating that he'd call on Charlotte tomorrow to further discuss the soul-eater.

The look on the duke's face when he saw Charlotte at the party—uninvited—would be priceless.

Armed with the repaired goggles, her ray gun, knives, and several other hidden weapons within the folds of her bustle and outer corset, Charlotte felt ready for anything. Her autocab pulled onto the St. Bridgeman estate, crushing the gravel beneath its treads. She stepped out. As she walked, she clutched her reticule and double-checked its illegal contents, making sure the serum vial hadn't cracked.

*Time to get answers.* She clenched her jaw and ascended the stairs, to the estate.

St. Bridgeman's butler raised his eyebrows at her unannounced arrival but did not hinder her, and she made a mental note to tell Tiller of his superior butler-ing the next time she saw him.

She could practically smell the ostentatious decorations before she saw them. As she walked into the estate, the marble entryway immediately chilled her. Even the warmth of the lights did little to quell the cold atmosphere. Pale-green and white stone swirled around each other in a circular pattern, with spirals reaching outward. Four immense red and brown pillars dominated the sides, supporting an arched ceiling. It was obvious that the atrium was meant to mimic the famous Kedleston Hall, but unfortunately, the St. Bridgemans of the past had been too ambitious—instead of open and grand, the entryway felt oppressively imperious, as if patronizing the viewer.

Charlotte sniffed, pushing against the emotion. She hated feeling patronized.

Muffled clinking what was most likely the dining room told Charlotte the staff was nearly done setting the table and bringing out the food. Perfect timing, she thought. It speaks of infinitely good breeding to never miss dessert.

She trailed the butler to the drawing room, nearly treading on his heels. Propriety dictated that Charlotte wait to be seen, but waiting had never been her strong suit—especially not when it hampered her search for the truth.

Her breathing quickened. *Square your shoulders, Charlotte.* Years of her governess's coaching revolved in her mind. She imagined a string pulling taut from her toes to the top of her head, straightening her and drawing her shoulders back and down. *There is power in one's posture.*

"Lady Charlotte Astley, madam," the butler announced to the guests in the drawing room. The chatting stopped and all heads turned.

St. Bridgeman nearly toppled over, barely catching his glass from falling. Charlotte raised her eyebrows in what was a general approximation of innocence. She stepped only a few feet into the expansive room. It wouldn't help to appear more bold than she already was.

A Tesla-lit chandelier drooped from the center of a ceiling radially painted with sea plants. White filigrees decorated the ocean-blue walls, and sage-green drapes stretched from floor to ceiling. Gilt-framed portraits of dour-faced St. Bridgemans glared at Charlotte's gauche behavior.

The baroness stood. The woman, elegant in jewel green, lifted her chin a fraction, her only visible sign of surprise. Charlotte was again struck by the similarities between mother and son—both with piercing blue eyes and aquiline noses.

"Oh dear. You have guests tonight." Charlotte's sharp eyes took in the intricately patterned carpet, the elaborate scarlet-velveted furniture, and the people sitting on them. No wives, only high leaders in the supernatural society. *This isn't a drawing room,* Charlotte realized. *It's a war room.* A quick scan revealed not only several influential members of the House but many leaders in the supernatural community. What in all the blazing suns would possess St. Bridgeman to invite such a large amount of supernaturals to his house at the same time? Of course, the baroness would likely have handled all the details for the evening, including the guest list. Perhaps the baroness meant to show outward support for her son, but was able to pursue her pro-supernatural stance via her charity. Or possibly this gathering was meant to inure St. Bridgeman to supernaturals. Either way, there was a political move here…somehow. Party leaders Sir Kimball and Lord Stanton mingled with West and his second-in-command, Beta Morainne.

Minnie was not there and Charlotte let out a small breath of relief.

West caught her eye and raised his glass to her. Cosmo grinned and winked. Charlotte's chin dipped infinitesimally in return greeting.

St. Bridgeman's jaw flapped before he found his voice. "Yes. Yes, we do."

Charlotte sighed, allowing her posture to slump somewhat. The upper lip of her outer corset pinched the flesh beneath her shoulders. She hoped she looked half as put out as Cosmo had last month when Tiller had refused to allow him to release a colony of rabbits in the house and train them to fetch his slippers and daily post. "I had hoped to discuss matters of the Citizens' Council for Humanity with you, Baron St. Bridgeman."

Cosmo stepped forward gliding over the rich carpet. "You must stay, Lady Astley. I'm sure it's no inconvenience to St. Bridgeman. He's always willing to save humanity."

Members of the group shifted, glassware clinking loudly. The baroness stared, as unreadable as a sphinx.

Charlotte waved a hand. "This is an unfortunate twist of fate."

St. Bridgeman glanced at his mother, then turned to Charlotte and narrowed his eyes. "You are overdressed for a happenstance social call."

A thin man in the corner, nearly concealed by an overgrown potted palm, squeaked at St. Bridgeman's rude comment and then began nibbling on his handkerchief. Charlotte took note of him. Must be a shifter of some sort—either that, or he had a terrible nervous habit of devouring linens.

Charlotte smiled at St. Bridgeman, though it felt like a grimace. "'One should either be a work of art, or wear one,'" she said to the room at large while gesturing to her peacock-blue dress, the outfit complementing her dark coloring and accentuating her hips. "At least that is what Mr. Oscar Wilde says, though I am partial to both."

A few quiet snickers broke the silence and the tension lessened.

Cosmo stepped forward, brushing his lips against the back of her hand. "Lady Astley, you are a masterpiece, as always." He retained her hand and with a flourish, strategically led her further into the room. "Wouldn't you agree, Baron?"

*The saucy rogue.* Delightful tingles danced across her skin even after Cosmo released her hand, and she blushed.

St. Bridgeman's scowl deepened, the corners of his large mustache making him look like an emaciated angry walrus. He opened his mouth to retort, but the duke stood from a settee in the corner and the room grew silent.

"Lady Astley, the St. Bridgeman family is known throughout the realm for their gracious and warm hospitality." A smile broke through West's dark beard, and his somber yellow eyes told the entire room he enjoyed placing St. Bridgeman in such an awkward social position. "They would not begrudge a dear friend of mine a place at their table."

All eyes darted the length of the room to the baroness and St. Bridgeman.

The baroness gave a tight smile, her features inscrutable. She inclined her head in West's direction. "Your Grace is too kind. Lady Astley is, of course, welcome at our table. How could I refuse Hespa's niece anything?"

St. Bridgeman nodded too quickly. "Of course. The St. Bridgeman family is not one to flout tradition." His words did not match the apoplectic coloring on his face. How was Minnie attracted to this being?

Charlotte nodded her head, pressing a hand to her chest. "You are so kind. I'm so pleased to see not all the rumors about you are true." She nodded to the duke, who winked in return, then she walked the length of the room, closing the distance between herself and St. Bridgeman and the baroness, and offered a more formal curtsy.

St. Bridgeman sneered and bowed slightly. "I hope you find the evening enlightening."

"Do you? I'd hate to make a liar of you."

He inclined his head, his eyes flashing.

Cosmo immediately strode over to her, pulling her away from the mother and son as well as the other party members. "Make a liar of him? Will you tell me what you're about?" His voice was hushed.

"Cross my heart." Charlotte pressed against the wall, fully taking in the people in the room for the first time.

Several influential members of Parliament mingled together, and the smell of humans in close quarters interlaced with the acrid tang of tobacco. Baroness St. Bridgeman sat in her ornate armchair, back straight as a rod, her eyes crackling with intelligence as she conversed with the duke.

"There's something odd here," Cosmo whispered.

Charlotte snorted. "Besides the imposing decor and over-fascination with sea plants? Or was it the obsession with power—"

"It's not that," he hissed.

Something in his tone pulled her eyes to him. The muscles in his neck were taut, and he looked as if a stake were pressed against his heart. "Cos, what is it?"

He shifted on his heels. "I am not entirely certain. There's a curious feeling coming from this house, and it's intensifying. It's familiar, almost like I've returned home only to find everything a mirror image of itself—like stepping through a looking glass."

Charlotte knit her eyebrows together. "You were here before, need I remind you?" She lowered her voice. "Breaking and entering?"

"That was only for a few minutes; hardly enough to take in the atmosphere."

She leaned forward. "Did it feel familiar then?"

"No. At least, not that I noticed. I was somewhat preoccupied with not getting caught."

Their conversation was cut short as St. Bridgeman moved closer, deep in talk with Lord Kimball. Charlotte and Cosmo would have to continue their discussion later. She shifted, straining to hear the baron's and Lord Kimball's conversation. St. Bridgeman mentioned that dinner would be announced shortly.

It was now or never. She had to intercept St. Bridgeman.

She pulled away from Cosmo, but he tugged on her arm, pulling her back. "Where are you going?" His brow twisted.

"To find enlightenment."

As Charlotte strode over to St. Bridgeman, the goggles and vial within her reticule thumped a marching cadence against her silk trousers. She forced herself to wait for a pause in St. Bridgeman and Lord Kimball's conversation before she said, "Good evening, Lord Kimball. St. Bridgeman."

He frowned at her.

Lord Kimball coughed and left to join another group.

"I wouldn't call it 'good,'" St. Bridgeman said. "Mingling with supernaturals is necessary for tonight's purposes, but in a war there are many unpleasant things one must do."

"Are we at war?"

"Of course. I'm surprised you, of all people, don't see it that way. You've staked and shot your share of vampires and werefolk."

She bit back her instinctive retort. "I prefer to see it as stopping citizens of England who are breaking the law. And I believe that in this so-called war—since you insist on such a brutal paradigm— you and I are on the same side. We both want a calm and peaceful society."

St. Bridgeman paused before nodding slowly.

Charlotte forced her mouth to curl up and plowed on. "In that interest, I would like to share information. What do you know of the soul-eater?"

He stiffened, some of the color draining from his face. "It is a vile and despicable beast."

"During my last encounter, we wounded it, and it fled in the direction of your house."

His nostrils flared, but otherwise he maintained an impressive composure. "Are you accusing me of harboring such a creature?"

"No, my lord." That was somewhat of a lie. She was technically accusing him of working with or possibly *being* the creature. "I was simply hoping we could work together—"

"An accusation is exactly what you are insinuating." His fingers hooked around the stem of his glass. "But I can assure you I would never harbor that monster and would tear this home apart brick by brick if it meant capturing and destroying it. Good evening." He left.

*Hateful man.* She only hoped Minnie would come to her senses before too long.

Cosmo appeared at her side. "That went well. You might also want to unclench your fists."

The corners of her mouth turned up in an almost-smile. Of course Cosmo had eavesdropped. "Unsurprisingly, diplomacy is not something St. Bridgeman has accepted. Society may not be at war, but he and I are. Which means I'll have to execute the second part of my plan to extract information from him."

"Won't you please tell me what it is?

"And spoil the surprise?" She paused. "Are you still feeling like Alice through the looking glass?"

He grimaced. "My instincts insist that I've been here before. That I've...*lived* here before."

Charlotte's gaze flicked to the other guests. The duke chatted with someone who, judging by the wiry beard sprouting from his chin, was either a phooka or simply a grizzled human. Their surface behavior seemed normal, but was West more mechanical in his movements? Did the others sense whatever Cosmo was sensing?

West turned and upon seeing Charlotte quickly excused himself from his conversation. "A word," he said to her.

Cosmo's face darkened, but Charlotte gave a quick nod and moved leisurely with West toward the fireplace.

When they were out of most of the party-goer's earshot, he murmured, "The soul eater's scent is here."

Her stomach twisted on itself. "Here?"

West nodded. "Very faint. The smells of dinner and the rain have dampened it, but I detect traces." He smoothed his jacket sleeves, then rolled his shoulders as if trying to scratch an itch.

"What is it?"

The duke scowled. "There's also a...something. Not a smell, but a feeling. I find I quite dislike this evening and what it portends." He nodded towards the group.

Her insides squirmed. Both Cosmo and the duke were mentioning a strange sense of familiarity. But what was here, at the St. Bridgeman estate, that could be affecting the supernaturals so?

*More.* Her logic screamed like the desert for rain. *I need more information, more truth.* Her palms tingled, and she rubbed her fingers together. It took all her self-control to root her feet in place when every impulse roared at her to ransack the estate for clues.

Charlotte rested her hand on West's arm. "Would you mind terribly if I used your impressive stature to it's full advantage?"

A bemused smile lit up the duke's face, the candlelight glowing across his dark skin.

Charlotte maneuvered the man in front of her until he was angled just so. Now she had a protected view of the room—for the next few moments, at least.

She quickly rummaged in her reticule and pulled out the goggles, and held them up to her eyes for a quick glance. Her vision lit up with colors.

"What do you see?" the duke asked.

Lavender and maroon lines crisscrossed and bled into each other making the entire room looked like an incompetent Impressionist's painting. Blast. There were just too many supernaturals gathered in one place.

"Nothing," she said, replacing the goggles. Her fingers curled and dug into her palms.

West turned back to her and offered his arm and they moved slowly towards the door. "I find that diner always helps."

She inhaled, her brain registering the aroma of roasted meat. She was in the middle of a dinner party. She *could* investigate further, but when? During dessert? No, after dessert.

She nodded and took the duke's arm.

The butler stood discreetly in the doorway, a signal that dinner would soon be announced, and St. Bridgeman helped his mother to her feet. The baroness stood, then grimaced—rheumatism, perhaps—before a calm mask slid over her face.

A deep furrow settled over Charlotte's brow.

"Lady Astley?" West was staring at her intently. "Are you well?"

Charlotte opened her mouth to respond, but a droning voice cut her off.

"Dinner is served," the footman stated.

"I am well," she said, waving West on. It was simply that she had more questions than when she'd arrived.

He gave a quick nod, then excused himself to escort the baroness as was proper. As an unexpected guest, and most likely in retaliation for her social faux pas, Charlotte was shuffled to the back of the line next to the linen-eating phooka. The timid man barely squeaked a greeting before the guests began to move into the dining room.

Entering the dining room last was a slight to be sure, but at least she hadn't been thrown out.

West and the baroness led the way into the dining room where another, larger Tesla chandelier cast its amber glow over the elaborately set table. The decor all paled when held against her burning questions.

The weight of Charlotte's reticule pulled at her arm. She glared at the back of St. Bridgeman's head, willing her gaze to burn off his bushy sideburns. She'd been direct. Civil. But none of that had worked and now she'd have to endure an entire meal with him. As she sat, she tucked her reticule in her lap. It gave a tiny clink, promising that if she didn't get answers at dinner, she would get them afterwards.

Charlotte bit down a sigh as she pulled her chair closer to the table. Dessert. She just had to last until dessert. Then propriety's concerns would be satisfied, and she could concentrate on satiating hers.

217

# Chapter 14

Fabric rustled as Charlotte shifted in her chair. The first four courses had passed—consisting of soup, various meats, bland conversation—and she was dying of boredom. The political intrigue was as dry as the turkey. The baroness had placed West and Cosmo next to her own seat near the end, leaving Charlotte to converse with Mr. Hayman, the phooka. St. Bridgeman was seated across the table from her, but he'd proven tight-lipped about most topics to the point of surliness. Charlotte fought against two urges: the first was to rest her head upon an elbow and listlessly push her food around her plate; and the second was to overturn the table, hold St. Bridgeman at fork-point, and demand answers.

Charlotte pressed her lips into a tight line and glared at her food, stabbing as though it might transfer to St. Bridgeman. Could her luck be any worse? She delighted in witty exchanges, but most phookas she'd spoken to tended to have limited conversation topics. There was only so long Charlotte could pretend to be interested in vegetation varieties and their taste.

She stifled a sigh. How did she manage to get placed between the phooka and her uncooperative worst enemy?

"Dessert is served," the butler said.

Mr. Hayman stopped his droning and Charlotte sat up straighter. Finally, something worthwhile.

After clearing the table of dinner, the staff set up an elaborate Grecian centerpiece surrounded by tiny jellied fruit, sugared grapes, and Victorian sponge cakes. Dessert plates came and went amid relative silence. St. Bridgeman largely ignored her, most people were enjoying their dessert too much to hold steady conversation, and Mr. Hayman seemed content to keep to himself.

Somewhere between the sponge cake and a particularly sour lemon tart, St. Bridgeman spoke to her, as though continuing their previous conversation. "Surely, with the soul-eater running amok, you have to see that supernaturals are dangerous things to leave unchecked."

She scowled. This was hardly a dinner-worthy subject. "Only those intent on breaking the law. By your logic, any humans running amok should also be checked by the law and prison, since humans have the capacity to be as dangerous as supernaturals." She shoved the last bit of tart in her mouth, the citric acid tinging her tongue.

St. Bridgeman scoffed. "Humans are—"

She plowed ahead. "Most supernaturals, such as Mr. Hayman here are law-abiding citizens merely seeking to have the best life possible. So unless someone like Mr. Hayman here suddenly goes on a rampage, I have no jurisdiction whatsoever to hunt."

Hayman colored all the way to his ears. "I don't rampage." Charlotte's heart warmed at the timid man's blush. The entire evening he'd hardly said more than ten words together and appeared in awe of the supernatural predators in the room. West in particular seemed to make him nervous.

Charlotte smiled. "Perhaps a goat in the canning factories would be considered a rampage."

Hayman grinned and murmured, "Me on a rampage." It might have been her imagination, but he appeared to sit a little taller.

St. Bridgeman's eyes narrowed to slits. "Lady Astley, I understand your parents were killed in the Origination."

Charlotte's fingers itched for her wooden hairpins. Though St. Bridgeman had never shown any evidence of being a monster, she wondered if a stake where his heart should have been would do anything at all. Fortunately for him, though, Charlotte was extremely well bred…when she chose to be.

She dabbed at her mouth with the corner of her napkin. "Everyone has someone who perished, was transformed, or was affected in one way or another during the Origination."

"Mostly by their insane families or friends who killed without thought." St. Bridgeman's strident tones easily carried over the others' discourse.

Charlotte ignored the other guests' looks, however the weight of their collective stare raised the hair on the back of her hand. "My parents died a year later, in the Upheavals."

"Yet you would protect their murderers? Didn't you care for your family at all?"

All conversation the table crashed like a rusty autocab.

"Trevor!" The baroness's shock echoed across the table.

The room had fallen silent and all waited for Charlotte's response. The baroness shot a dark look at her son. A chair creaked and Charlotte was keenly aware she held the attention of the room. Surely most of the guests would be used to St. Bridgeman's view on super-naturals, but this personal attack was a new low.

Charlotte took a drink to drown her anxiety, but the cloying wine lodged the panic in her throat. *Don't let him win,* her mind whispered even as her ribs pressed into her lungs.

Speaking of the Origination, especially such a personal part of it, was one of the most extreme faux pas. Society was happy to sweep the ugliest bits of the Origination and Upheavals under the rug. Cosmo had once remarked that if society hadn't moved forward so quickly, England might have collapsed beneath the collective trauma of it all.

That, Charlotte could understand.

Her eyes darted the length of the table. She needed something. An anchor. She spared a glance at Cosmo. Sympathy filled his eyes, and a sudden soothing calm caressed her. The mental support Cosmo sent her braced her against the past's torrential flood. Tears pricked behind her eyes, but she ordered them to retreat.

Charlotte waved her hand at the baroness. "Thank you, baroness, but my answer will explain my stance on your son's bill—something I've already explained to him, but it seems it bears repeating."

She turned again to St. Bridgeman, making sure her voice carried the length of the room. "My parents were killed by a blood-frenzied vampire, then they were dragged to Hyde Park and scavenged by werewolves. I was thirteen. I hid in my wardrobe for two days. On the morning of the second day, I opened the door. A man in tattered clothes was curled asleep on the floor in front of me. He woke. His face and hands were covered in dried blood, but the haunted look in his eyes was unmistakable. When he saw me, he started to sob. He apologized over and over, saying 'I didn't hurt you, did I?'"

Someone's dinnerware clinked. Charlotte sipped at her water, the cool liquid doing nothing to soothe her barely in-check emotions.

"That poor werewolf, Mr. Burton, cleaned himself up and together he and I ate whatever food was left in the house. He—" She swallowed. "He removed the bodies of the staff who hadn't survived. He was kind and just as scared of himself and the Origination as I was. Perhaps even more so."

Another wave of support washed over Charlotte. *Cosmo.* He knew what was coming.

"That evening, a second werewolf came. At that time, if you'll recall, there was no alpha to dictate transformation time. This wolf had already transformed. It attacked me. Mr. Burton immediately took on his wolf form and saved me."

Charlotte wrung her fingers around her napkin. "Several days passed. There were riots of so-called monster hunters roving the streets killing anyone who seemed 'wolfish.' Someone had seen my parents being taken to Hyde Park. One evening, a group of these hunters came to my house and broke down the door. They checked us both for bite marks. A man recognized me and separated me from Mr. Burton. Then, despite his and my protests, they dragged Mr. Burton into the street and shot him."

No one seemed to breathe.

She pushed back another wave of threatening tears and fixed a steady gaze on St. Bridgeman. Her voice was strong as she spoke. "And that is why I protect all of London's citizens supernatural or not."

West shifted in his chair and nodded. His tone was firm, but calm. "The Upheavals were dark times. It was chaos. We are fortunate that once the Pack and Coven were established, civility and order were brought to bear. Society, though altered, pieced itself back together."

"Yes, we all know the effects of the Origination were earth shattering," St. Bridgeman said, waving his hand as if to push the past aside.

"Peers of the realm had been bitten, the gentry and aristocracy were affected." He sounded almost bored.

"Perhaps you mean, 'infected,'" West growled. "No one knows why or where the first vampire or werewolf originated."

"Perhaps they are dead," St. Bridgeman said.

"We can all agree the origins of supernaturals are still a mystery," Charlotte said, hoping to stave off any argument before it occurred. "But my point is that while everyone was affected, both humans and supernaturals committed acts of cowardice and valor. The loss of my parents led to a life-altering decision for me. I will never willingly allow another family to be destroyed as mine was. But I do not protect murderers. I protect citizens of England from those who deem themselves as above or outside of the law. Rogue supernaturals. I am more like a supernatural law-enforcement specialist." Her ribcage relaxed and her breathing steadied.

"And a very lovely one indeed," Mr. Hayman said.

Charlotte smiled, dipping her head towards the phooka.

The clink of silverware ensued, the table resuming some of its normal activity. She took a sip of her nearly cold custard, suppressing a shudder. Her left hand squeezed her napkin and trembled in her lap, but she forced herself to breathe evenly. She had done it—explained everything calmly and rationally. How could St. Bridgeman not see her side?

St. Bridgeman leaned in. "Wouldn't you agree that there would be fewer rogue supernaturals, as you say, if they were registered, tabled, and kept track of?"

Her fingertips pressed into the silverware. This man was worse than a dog worrying a bone. "Seems like being placed in a very large cage. And why should humans not be tagged and tracked?"

St. Bridgeman sneered. "You want all potential victims of vamps, hags, and werefolk to be placed in a single list? A convenient index for anyone bent on murder."

Plates clinked as the servants began clearing the table.

"You misunderstand, Your Lordship," Charlotte said. "According to your logic, all potentially dangerous humans should be recorded. From your viewpoint, that wouldn't be an index for murder—it would be a warning of whom to avoid. So if we put potentially dangerous supernaturals on a list, why should it not be done to potentially dangerous humans as well? Specifically, all humans, since all humans are potential killers and thieves and traitors." She sipped her water again. "On the other hand, as you have already suggested, a list of supernaturals would be convenient for anyone with personal vendettas or prejudices. An index for people bent on murder, as you say." And your new acquaintance Minnie would be on that list, she wanted to add, but she kept herself in check. After this soul-eater business was over, keeping Minnie safe from this man would be moved to the top of her list.

St. Bridgeman didn't respond. Without a word, he simply wiped his mouth with his napkin and stood.

Charlotte knew that she had won the argument for now, but her righteous fury and triumph died inside at a realization: no matter what she said, there was no way she was ever going to change St. Bridgeman's mind.

And whether he was the soul-eater or not, his bill was going to give the creature a much easier way to kill people and get away with it.

The guests retired to the drawing room. Charlotte made her way toward the balcony. The chilled air splashed welcomely on her face. She ran her fingers along the stone balustrade as she descended the stairs. The tips of her fingers were rubbed slightly raw as she dragged them along the cool, grainy stone railing. She stepped onto the grass. Impressive hydrangea bushes nestled beneath the balcony.

*Curse that man.* She kicked at the grass and glared at the flowers. If she couldn't take her anger out on St. Bridgeman then at least his shrubbery would suffer her wrath.

Voices from the party grew louder and floated down from the balcony. Several people had stepped outside as well and moved near the railing above her.

She pressed herself against the bushes, their bulbous blooms enveloping her. Her ears pricked as she recognized the voices.

Cosmo and St. Bridgeman. She craned her neck slightly to see their outlines. *How thoughtful of St. Bridgeman to provide after-dinner entertainment.* It was impossible not to overhear the man's asinine comments.

"You're the predator," St. Bridgeman said. "You have no idea what life is like living as the prey. We don't even know exactly how dangerous vampires are."

St. Bridgeman paused as another set of shoes shuffled along the stone above her. At least one more guest had joined them. She shifted her weight to the side, but only St. Bridgman and Cosmo remained visible.

"How do you know," St. Bridgeman continued, "that your saliva isn't part of the transformation? Or even venomous? How do you know it requires measured exsanguination for someone to become 'undead?'"

That last word sounded like fingernails on a chalkboard to Charlotte's ears, but Cosmo merely smiled at the mudslinging that the baron had descended to. "Firstly, if saliva were the sole factor, how would you explain that the blood-harlots at the docks are still alive and still human? I can also name several human-vampire marriages that have remained intact."

St. Bridgeman visibly shuddered, disgust dripping from his frame. Charlotte shook her head and curled her fingers into a fist.

"And secondly,"—Cosmo held up a finger—"I know because I do. How do you know you prefer lemon ices to raspberry, or that carrots are a truly abhorrent vegetable—"

"I like them," a thin voice cried from next to Cosmo. Mr. Hayman. Charlotte pressed her lips together to stop any laugh from escaping.

Cosmo nodded to the side, probably at the phooka, then continued. "How do I know? How does a snake know it is venomous. It is in its nature to know."

"So we are simply to trust you?" St. Bridgeman ground the last two words out of his mouth.

"What other choice do you have?"

"Eve trusted a snake once. And look where it got her." St. Bridgeman's heavy footfalls stormed away. Apparently, he was the type who ran away when he could not win an argument against a more intelligent foe.

Charlotte turned her gaze to the view from the balcony, wanting to throttle every last flower around her. The leaves rustled as she exited the bushes and stopped near the base of the stairs. She crossed her arms, fingers tapping against her sleeves. The arrogance with which St. Bridgeman was conducting himself blasted away the remaining wisps of reservation from her conscience. She was going to get answers from him—whether he wanted to give them or not.

Someone moved beside Charlotte, and a scent as familiar as her own home surrounded her. Her anxiousness about her plan retreated, replaced by a fluttering of her heart. "How is your patience this evening, Cosmo?"

"That thickheaded clod, asking about your parents over dessert. I ought to toss him off his own balcony."

"If you did that, you'd miss the part where I force St. Bridgeman to tell us everything."

A grin spread across Cosmo's face, revealing his canines. "Wouldn't miss it for the world."

"Perfect. Would you please lead His Lordship into the library? I'll join you shortly."

Cosmo took his leave and practically pounced on St. Bridgeman. Talking animatedly about a sudden interest in seeing the estate's books, Cosmo guided the spluttering man back inside.

Charlotte slipped to a corner of the balcony, shielding herself from any onlookers, and opened her reticule. She transferred several drops of serum onto her handkerchief. Then she balled it in her fist and followed Cosmo into the library.

As she entered, she spied her friend next to St. Bridgeman, peering over a well-worn book, the lay of its pages indicating hours of being open to that exact spot.

"Is this Burke's peerage opened to your ancestry?" Cosmo lifted the book, checking the cover.

The baron sniffed.

Cosmo's shoulders shifted as his finger traced the page. "Is Hyacinth really your mother's middle name?"

Charlotte rolled her eyes. Of course a member of the St. Bridgeman family would be named after a poisonous bulb flower.

"Lord Wilmott, what did you wish to speak to me about?" St. Bridgeman's voice was a mix of revulsion and annoyance.

Charlotte entered the library and strode to St. Bridgeman. Her heart pounded with each step. If she failed, she'd most definitely be thrown into jail for assaulting a peer of the realm—that he was a mis-guided politician more focused on the end than the means would have no bearing on her outcome whatsoever.

"What do you want?" he asked when he saw Charlotte.

She rolled her eyes. St. Bridgeman was determined to be the most detestable person in England.

Cosmo tapped the baron on the shoulder, who flinched away. "A word of warning: it is unwise to anger Lady Astley."

Charlotte slipped behind St. Bridgeman while he was distracted, then pressed the handkerchief directly into his face. The fabric released a sharp petrol-like odor.

St. Bridgeman collapsed immediately.

"Mind his head!" Charlotte moved to catch him, but was unable to support his weight.

Cosmo jumped forward and could easily have caught St. Bridgeman. As it was, Cosmo merely pushed St. Bridgeman's body away from the table allowing the man to thud on the floor, his head narrowly missing the furniture. Charlotte winced. St. Bridgeman must have annoyed Cosmo more than Charlotte had thought.

Cosmo nudged St. Bridgeman with his toe. "Did you just kill him?"

Charlotte shrugged, then bent and took the handkerchief, replacing it in her reticule. "Only a little."

"What did you use on him?"

"It's new, so I haven't really named it yet. I'm open to suggestions. And no, I'm not naming this one 'Cosmo's Revenge.'"

Cosmo's mouth clamped shut and his shoulders slumped in disappointment.

"I refined the solution from an extract I bought off a bodysna—"

"No, no. Don't tell me. I don't want to know." He shuddered.

"In short, it's simply a truth potion with amnesiac properties."

"And this is simply a poisoned peer of the realm."

"Pish. Now do you see why I didn't want you involved? Stop fussing. We don't have much time."

Cosmo harrumphed at Charlotte, then reached down and dragged St. Bridgeman over to a foot rest, propping him against it.

St. Bridgeman groaned and half-opened his eyes.

Charlotte crouched down in front of him. "What do you know about the soul-eater?"

"It…eats…souls," he muttered.

Cosmo pulled his hand down his face. "We'll get nowhere at this rate."

"Be patient, this is the first field test."

"You're working with a prototype?"

"Control yourself, Cos. Besides, serums can't be 'prototyped.' They are merely labeled—serum one or something similar."

"So which one is this?"

"Serum two."

Cos bared his teeth, the vampire equivalent of sticking out one's tongue. She turned back to St. Bridgeman. "How many known attacks of the soul-eater have there been?"

"Officially, ten."

Charlotte knit her brows. *Officially?* "How many attacks to you believe there to be?"

"Sixteen."

Cosmo hissed.

That was much more than what the police had known of.

Charlotte leaned closer. "Where?"

"Gressenhall." He drawled his words, hanging on the consonants.

"But that's a workhouse," Cosmo said.

St. Bridgeman continued in his monotone cadence. "Almshouse. Prisongate."

"Workhouses and the prison?" Her knees protested the wooden floor, but she ignored them. "So the soul-eater started with the poor. What happened after that?"

St. Bridgeman continued. "It moved on to the supernatural population. Since that time, no humans have fallen victim to its hunger. All the better."

*Ugh, he's spiteful even when he's drugged.* Charlotte and Cosmo shared an exasperated look, then focused once again on St. Bridgeman. "Why attack supernaturals now?" she asked. "Is a supernatural soul somehow superior to a human one? Does it offer different benefits for the soul-eater?"

He shrugged, his head lolling to one side. "I've suspected as much."

Charlotte rubbed the palm of a hand across her chin, adding his words to her growing mental file on the creature.

"Have you seen the soul-eater?"

"No."

"Have you ever seen anything strange around your house recently?"

"Yes."

Charlotte's heart pounded. "Explain."

"Two nights ago," St. Bridgeman swallowed, his eyes open but seeing nothing. "Coming from Brooks's and saw a smoky thing circling our house."

"Where?"

"St. James's Street."

Charlotte shook her head so violently, tendrils of hair loosened. "No, where was the smoky thing? Where did it go?"

St. Bridgeman raised his eyebrows a fraction. "It disappeared when I came around the drive." He fell into a coughing fit, his chest heaving.

Charlotte stood. "Let's go."

Cosmo clapped his hands. "Why? We are jutht now getting to the bleeding heart of the matter."

Blazing suns. A fang lisp? She couldn't take him anywhere. Hooking her arm around his, she dragged him to the library door. "Because it's about to wear off. Coughing is the first sign. And you're lisping. Let's go."

Cosmo heaved a dramatic sigh. "Pity."

They left the study and entered the hall.

"There had to have been other witnesses placing the soul-eater at the St. Bridgeman estate." Charlotte thumped her fist into her palm. "I'll have to talk to the staff."

Once they entered the drawing room, Cos beelined for the *vin de sang* and Charlotte stood at the entry way, searching momentarily. Then she strode over and latched herself to the arm of the duke. He tensed at the sudden contact, then relaxed when he saw who it was.

"What have you two been up to?" He raised his thick eyebrows and inclined his chin towards Cosmo, then inhaled deeply. "You smell like chloroform and mischief."

Charlotte smiled. "One of my staff commented on my smell only this morning. Why is it I never hear of a werewolf chef?"

West chuckled. "Probably because most humans prefer their meat cooked."

Now it was Charlotte's turn to sigh dramatically. "Pity."

St. Bridgeman stumbled into the room a few moments later, blinking furiously but looking none the worse for wear. He pressed a hand to his forehead and his eyes focused on Charlotte.

"Oh dear," she said as St. Bridgeman staggered toward her and the duke. "I'll need to increase the amnesiac effects of that serum."

West turned to Charlotte, his eyebrows scrunched together.

"If you'll excuse me," Charlotte said, unhooking her arm and dipping a quick curtsy, "I believe it is time I left."

Before the duke could respond, she unhooked her arm and moved toward the door, away from St. Bridgeman. Luckily the drug made him as unsteady as a newborn deer.

Cosmo caught her eye and took a minuscule step toward her. Charlotte shook her head, striding toward the exit. *Almost there.*

She nearly jumped out of her skin when the baroness glided up behind her. Did she know what happened in the study? It was possible she'd heard, but Charlotte doubted a baroness would be so impassive about a drugged son. If the baroness knew, it would be a short trip to the cooler.

Charlotte itched to run. She didn't fancy living behind bars.

"Baroness," she said, inclining her head. *High noon, take the St. Bridgemans and their propensity for obstructing my goals!*

The woman's steely gaze bored through Charlotte's bones, and Charlotte's insides churned. There was no hint of the friendly overtures the baroness had shown Charlotte on the *Asteria*. Charlotte's eyes darted to the door. It was right there.

"I trust you enjoyed your meal," the baroness said.

Charlotte nodded. Where was St. Bridgeman?

"I saw you were able to speak with my son." The baroness turned toward the study almost imperceptibly, but her meaning was clear. *Blazing suns. She knows* something *happened.* The baroness's eyes narrowed a fraction and she folded her arms.

"Trevor's bill will be very important for some of the people of London."

Charlotte nodded again, rocking slightly on the balls of her feet. She glanced over the baroness's shoulder at St. Bridgeman. He still held a hand against his head. She wasn't sure which 'people' the baroness had meant by her last statement, but Charlotte hadn't the time to tease out conversational intricacies.

"It was a very enlightening conversation," Charlotte said. "And thank you for your hospitality." She hoped she didn't sound too ungrateful.

The baroness's aggressive smile rooted Charlotte to the spot. A sudden spike of fear sliced at her heart and she suppressed a shudder. An instinctual dislike for all the St. Bridgeman's reared his head deep within Charlotte. Perhaps Charlotte needed to worry about both Minnie and Aunt Hespa's associations.

The baroness stepped closer and raised her chin, peering down her angular nose. "I trust that you have enjoyed your evening and that you will enjoy the rest somewhere else. Unless, of course, you'd rather be arrested for trespassing." The baroness's voice glided over her teeth like a snake over dry leaves.

Charlotte barely kept from gasping. Had she heard her correctly? Was the baroness threatening her? Had she completely misunderstood their meeting on the airship?

"I will leave." At least the baroness was letting her go. Even so, tiny waves of fear lapped at her racing heart.

Baroness St. Bridgeman turned back toward the party, the hem of her rust-colored gown undulating across the carpet.

Charlotte beat a hasty retreat towards the entryway, trying to calm her pulse. *This is only a temporary setback. There is something going on here and it must be connected to the soul-eater. It has to.*

Doubt, however, niggled at the back of her mind. She shoved it away.

As she rushed past, the less-than-Tiller butler sprang belatedly to life. "Lady Astley, may I send for your cab?" he asked chasing after her.

"That won't be necessary," she called over her shoulder. She stormed onto the top of the landing, her eyes raking the estate. *Aha! There it is.* Her sudden retreat and rejection of help was sure to add a layer of wounded pride sufficient to deter the butler from following her.

Charlotte's heels clicked against the stone steps, then crunched on the gravel as she proceeded toward the carriage house and auto-cabs waiting for their owners. When she reached her cab, she turned to the house and seeing the butler gone, gave a curt nod. She pulled open her reticule, extracted the goggles, and flipped the spectral lens to cover the frames. Her fingernail flipped a tiny lever and with a snick, the lens was locked into place.

The St. Bridgeman estate was submerged in a Prussian blue light. The black sky lightened to cobalt, the stars to shining pricks of baby blue. Now she simply had to find a glowing spectral signature.

Threaten her with trespassing? Charlotte smoothed her gloves, then set her jaw. Might as well make the crime fit the bill.

# Chapter 15

The greenhouse was a rectangular addition to the St. Bridgeman house, jutting out as an afterthought onto the lawn. As Charlotte walked from the pebbled drive, the gravel gave way to a carpet of grass, and two small stone steps led the way up to a glass door spanning from ground to roof. She darted across the lawn, then reached for the elaborately carved brass doorknob bearing the initials STB. Charlotte rolled her eyes. Of course even the conservatory door's handle would be ostentatious.

*Please be unlocked.* Her breath released as the hand turned easily. She swallowed and stepped inside.

The painted tiled floor could have contained a host of colors. Their brilliance was lost to Charlotte's lenses eyes. The damp air tasted of jasmine and secrets. Several tables laden with all manner of foliage filled the corners of the room. Terra-cotta pots and metal pitchers littered the areas beneath. An entire table was dedicated to what looked like hyacinths, their small clustered flowers filling the air with a gentle fragrance. Charlotte's boots scraped loudly against the tiles, catching minuscule bits of dirt and debris left behind by the staff. She darted across the room, ignoring the plants, then passed through an adjoining hallway and found herself back in the dining room.

St. Bridgeman's dinner conversation grumbled in her mind like her stomach did as she remembered that abysmal excuse for turtle soup. "'Didn't you care for your family at all?'"

Charlotte curled her lip, glaring at the chair he had occupied. *Bad form, St. Bridgeman, bad form. But I will have the last laugh once I discover what you've been up to.*

From the dining room she could easily access the study, provided the guests were still occupied in the parlour. She poked her head out of the dining room into the ludicrous great hall. The muted voices and laughter floating from the parlour assured her that the port was still underway. She examined the floor that led to the study, then glanced at her feet. They made no noise on the rug, but they would clatter over the nauseatingly marbled entrance.

Suddenly, across from the hall in the direction of the study, Charlotte detected a faint pale blue glow. She chewed her lower lip. She had to get there. Hopefully the staff, including the un-Tiller butler, was otherwise occupied and had more important things to do than sit in the foyer.

Charlotte took a tentative step into the great hall, careful to tread on her toes and then roll back onto her heels. Her heeled boots clicked softly on the marble anyway. She winced and held her breath, listening.

Nothing.

Laughter burst from the parlour then died down again.

Perhaps the staff was busy with the guests.

Step, click. Step, click.

The glow from the study beckoned like the call of a siren. Finding its source would be the linchpin to everything. It had to be.

Her muscles relaxed. This was much easier than expected and certainly easier than her pre-pre-engagement party with Mr. Hollands—or teatime with Aunt Hespa, for that matter.

She had just rounded the first pillar when a maid bustled in from the left, then stopped.

Charlotte ducked back behind the pillar, her heart racing. Had she been seen? *Blazing suns.* If she was caught, she'd be jailed for certain.

Fabric rustled as the maid moved about. What was she doing?

Blast. Blast. Blast.

Heels clicked on the marble in rapid succession, and Charlotte's heartbeat matched pace.

Then silence.

Charlotte peered around the pillar. The maid was gone. Hopefully, she had merely forgotten something and gone to retrieve the item and not the host or hostess. The muscles in Charlotte's shoulders tightened. Better be quick, all the same.

She bent down and yanked at her boot's laces. The smooth marble chilled her toes, but at least her stockinged feet made no sound. Scooping her boots in her arms, Charlotte darted across the great hall and didn't stop until she'd reached the study and the beckoning glow.

She quietly shut the door of the study and released a breath. First task, complete. Now to find St. Bridgeman's glowing secret.

After quickly replacing her shoes, Charlotte stood. A large globe stood on the right side of the room. Bookcases lined the left side and an immense desk squatted beneath a window. With the goggles, the study was cooled by the pale cerulean light. The blue and turquoise light exactly matched the color from the Piccadilly attack.

Her muscles drew tight. The soul-eater wasn't here, floating in a corner and waiting to spring, was it? She quickly inspected the room until she was satisfied that she was alone. But what was causing the glow? It was most certainly the soul-eater's signature.

St. Bridgeman *was* in league with the soul-eater. That had to be it, despite his professed disgust and objections about supernaturals. She'd been right. Now she just had to prove it.

She followed the muted sea-green glow emanating from the bookcase then smiled. No, not from the bookcase. *Behind* it.

She stepped closer, and the glow intensified like light through a magnifying glass. A thick leather-bound tome titled *The Wildflowers of the Cotswolds* radiated the soul-eater's signature color. *Odd reading for such a creature,* Charlotte thought. Her fingers hooked over the tip of the cracked spine and pulled the book out. Perhaps it was hollow and something of the soul-eater was glowing from within.

The book tilted back, then was yanked out of her grasp, perched on the bottom of its spine as if it hadn't yet decided whether to fall or not. Charlotte frowned, then gasped as a tiny mechanism clicked and the bookcase swung forward a few centimeters on cleverly concealed hinges.

A secret compartment.

Charlotte tamped down a very unladylike squeal of excitement by pressing her hands to her lips. This was just like *The Mysteries of London,* the penny dreadful with the mad scientist.

A large chalkboard leaned up against one wall of the compartment. Remnants of chalk dust filled her nostrils and covered the ledge of the board. The door of the secret compartment had small shelves on it full of glass vials and miniature models of octopi. She reached up and pulled a tiny ampoule from the topmost ledge. It radiated the same sea-green as the soul-eater. Inside, a minuscule, but distinct, cloud of smoke billowed and collapsed in on itself.

St. Bridgeman had a bit of the soul-eater.

Her fingers tightened around the vial. Here was proof that at the very least, he was in league with the creature. Her blood boiled as snippets of her conversation with St. Bridgeman in the alley resurfaced. The pompous, hypocritical clod.

She tucked the vial into her bodice. Satisfied that this was all the proof she needed, she turned her attention back to the compartment. A map of London dominated the main portion of the chalkboard, nearly reaching the edges of the small chamber. Her heart skipped a beat and she moved the goggles to the top of her head so she could see better. *St. Bridgeman can keep his notebook. Here's the map.*

From what she knew of St. Bridgeman's notebook, this map was far more extensive. Her eyes greedily darted from one item to the next. Large *x*'s were scratched all over the city, making it look as if an angry jackdaw had clawed London for worms. Sixteen *x*'s in all peppered London from Westminster to Regent's Park, but most of them were clustered in the West End, near the docks. St. Bridgeman had placed small *x*'s in Hanbury street, Dorset Street, and Bethnal Green. A few even dipped into Spitalfields. The *x* in Whitechapel was the darkest as it was more recently placed than the others. Next to it, like the date on a tombstone, was the date "Aug 1891."

That was the vampire she'd found in the alley. These were victims. She hissed. There were far more than she'd thought, some dates reaching nearly all the way back to the Origination.

"Why are they all in the slums?" she breathed, then shook her head. The answer was clear: what better way to hide murders than in a press of humanity? Plus, the soul-eater could mist like a vampire and could camouflage. That must be how it was getting in and out of the slums to feed without being detected. Instinctively, she reached for her telescriber, frowning when she realized it wasn't there. It would have been very hard to explain her "accidental" presence at the St. Bridgeman party in her full investigative gear.

Music sounded from the parlour and her heart raced. Blast, they were already into the musical portion. She'd have to be quick. If guests started leaving soon, the staff would see that her autocab hadn't actually left the premises and that just wouldn't do.

Her eyes flew across the remaining items. Pages of notes written in a tiny hand adorned the left side of the board. "Open doorway completely" and "supernatural reign" flashed across her vision.

She had no idea what doorway St. Bridgeman was talking about, but "supernatural reign" did not bode well.

Newspaper clippings fluttered as Charlotte pulled the doors wider, revealing the edges of the chalkboard. Her gaze raced over the titles. "Mysterious Murders in Poorhouses" and "White-eyed Bodies Found in Slums" screamed for her attention.

Several of Charles Darwin's books were propped against the chalkboard's ledge, bearing austere titles such as *On the Origin of Species* and *From so Simple a Beginning.*

She squinted and stepping closer, bent to examine them.

Echoes of fading music sounded.

*Hurry, old girl. Just a bit longer.* She pressed her fingers against her cheeks. There was just so much information.

Diagrams of more octopi and squid. Political notes on St. Bridgeman's bill.

*There has to be something else in here. There just has to be.*

Applause sounded.

Her brain itched to read everything she could, but common sense told her it was better to not be arrested.

She scanned the books again. *Look for the differences,* she thought. Then she saw it.

An unassuming notebook lay nestled among the others. It had no title and was bound in thick black leather. A journal. Could this be the journal she had seen St. Bridgeman scribbling in at the crime scene of the dead vampire?

She picked it up. The well-worn spine creaked softly open. *Hmm.* The notebook's contents must be important enough for St. Bridgeman to have read through it multiple times. She began rifling through its pages."Incredible discovery of a portal...'" She licked her lips. This was a scientific journal.

She began reading the tightly looped handwriting from an entry dated nine years ago.

*Only when the first vampire and werewolf attacks in London occurred did we realize they must have come through the portal. We rushed to close it, but something charged. Robert closed the gateway, but was wounded. The gateway closed around the monster's tentacle, slicing it in two...*

First attacks? Was this referring to the Origination? Charlotte frowned, her eyes flying over the unsteady handwriting. And what portal where they referring to?

*Blood sprayed in my mouth. It burned through me. I am frightened... and so very hungry.*

Cold fear washed through Charlotte. She flipped to a later entry. *Charlotte, you fool.* It's never been St. Bridgeman. Well, not only St. Bridgeman.

The handwriting changed; the pen had left deep gouges in the paper, gouges which had been filled by the pooling ink.

*Because of this doorway, we have successfully, if accidentally, introduced not only vampires and werewolves, but all manner of creatures into this world…*

Her heart stopped.

*There are more supernatural species within the portal. I can usher in a new era and create a new society—supernatural and better—than the human-based one we have now. All the good that will come—it will atone for the mistakes of the first one. I have only to throw open the door and let them in.*

Her mind reeled.

According to this journal, the Origination was caused by a human opening a doorway. A portal. But a portal to where?

*More information. I need more.* Charlotte's eyes flew to the notes, her breathing quick.

*I must open the doorway completely.*

It couldn't be. If the Origination had begun here, with this portal, opening that doorway again would be catastrophic.

Charlotte pressed her lips into a hard line. Had St. Bridgeman caused the Origination? Impossible. He was a few years senior to Charlotte but had still only been a youth during the Origination.

Her eyes flew across entries, ripping words from the pages. *'Power over fear…human souls consumed…supernatural diet leads to increase in power.'*

Charlotte's fingers clenched the journal. That was why the monster now attacked only supernaturals—why it had gone for the werewolf pups.

Johnathan's howls of misery echoed in her mind igniting a cold anger deep in her core.

The journal then broke off, the writing changing to something else that wasn't even English. To Charlotte, it looked like a mix of Egyptian hieroglyphs and ancient runes. The deep scrawls filled the entire page. Was this a code or another language entirely? Charlotte flipped through the rest of the pages, her frustration building as she saw that the remainder of the book was filled with this strange writing.

St. Bridgeman. He must be controlling the soul-eater. He was working with his mother. Perhaps he had even used it in earlier years to target people in the slums as he trained the soul-eater to follow his commands. Killing a few humans from the working class rarely meant much to arrogant ratbags like St. Bridgeman. Plus, it would only bolster his political stance once he presented his findings of a dangerous unknown supernatural that had been assaulting humans. With the soul-eater attacking, arguably the strongest species of supernaturals, St. Bridgeman would have little difficulty convincing Parliament that identifying and registering the supernatural population would prevent unknown creatures like the soul-eater from running rampant through the streets and would keep the ones that were known in line. St. Bridgeman's bill would pass as easily as clouds over the face of the moon.

Noises sounded from the parlour and grew louder.

Blazing suns. She stepped backwards pressing the compartment shut.

A small scrap of paper fluttered to the floor.

Charlotte cursed, then bent, and scooped the paper in her hand. She threw herself behind the desk, her mind spinning.

A woman cleared her throat outside the door, then spoke. "Tonight's dinner party was an excuse to gather you here tonight. I have something to show you."

The soft thudding of boots on carpet felt like pounding on her heart as the party entered the study. What in the blazes was everyone doing here?

She needed to get to Cosmo. Together they could apprehend St. Bridgeman and take him to the police; and Charlotte was certain of the duke's support in capturing a murderer like St. Bridgeman. She pressed a hand against her bodice, feeling the vial press back. She had proof. St. Bridgeman wouldn't be able to win this time.

"The rest of our evening's entertainment is here." The baroness's soft voice filled the room.

Two sets of feet detached themselves from the group. Charlotte easily recognized Cosmo's polished Congress shoes with the flashy button spats. The second pair of boots were no less cared for and even more expensive. West.

Charlotte risked a peek. She could just make out their faces from her angle. Should she signal them? She dismissed the idea as quickly as it had come. Too risky.

A collective murmur of surprise went through the group. What had happened?

Several feet moved forward to the left of the secret compartment, towards the bookcases.

Cosmo started to do the same, but West pulled him back. "St. Bridgeman is nervous," he muttered. "He's as in the dark about his mother's surprise as the rest of us."

Cosmo's brow furrowed. He looked uneasy. "How can you tell?" he said.

The duke tapped the side of his nose.

The muscles in Cosmo's jaw stood out as if he were clenching his teeth. He nodded, and they moved to join the rest of the group in the corner.

What were they doing? She needed to get to Cosmo and West so they could stop St. Bridgeman before another attack happened.

Her back started to ache as she curled further inward, remaining concealed from the group. How long would this take?

She didn't have to wait much longer.

From her vantage point, she could see various sets of shoes shuffling around, all facing the bookcase. Charlotte shifted and peeked around the desk. Baroness St. Bridgeman stood in front of one bookcase and pulled on the only unlit sconce in the room. The entire bookcase swung open, revealing a rough-hewn stone staircase leading beneath the estate. A cool draft wafted up, from the bottom smelling of damp and rock. It pooled along the floor and wrapped itself around Charlotte's wrists.

"If you'll follow me," the baroness said.

The sound of boots scraping along rock grated on Charlotte's ears. *Rock?*

As the noises faded, Charlotte uncurled herself from behind the desk. Only then did she realize she still clutched the scrap of paper from the compartment. It crinkled as she unfolded it and her eyes darted across the large, bold print.

*Complete Origination.*

# Chapter 16

Charlotte's throat shriveled and she struggled to swallow. Screams and memories from the first swirled around her, snarling at her mind. What did it mean by "complete Origination?" The Origination was done, finished. It was over long ago. Wasn't it?

No, no, whatever this paper meant, it couldn't be less than devastating. No one might would survive this time. Charlotte thought back to the notes and entries she had just read in the journal.

*No* human *would survive, that is.*

A steady breeze from behind her tugged at the loose strands of her hair.

Impulsively, she followed the downdraft to the open bookcase and dashed across the room. Her fingers pressed into the smooth leather-bound books, steadying herself as she looked down the passageway. Noises echoed against the stone as the baroness and her guests descended below the estate.

West had said that St. Bridgeman was nervous.

She tapped her fingers against the wall, peering after the baroness, waiting to follow at a safe distance. She couldn't think too much about what she'd just read—she had to act and keep breathing steadily. If she allowed her thoughts to linger, she was going to panic.

Shadows from the party danced on the wall as they descended the stairs. Tesla lamps hummed, their warm glow doing little to ease Charlotte's piercing worry.

She had to reach Cosmo and apprehend St. Bridgeman and his mother as soon as possible, before anyone else got hurt. That would be the easy part. Her fingers tightened into fists. Once she had her hands on St. Bridgeman and his mother, come high noon or blue moon, she'd get them to talk. And nothing would do but the truth. It was obvious they were either working with the soul-eater or one of them *was* the soul-eater. Combined with the journal, how else could the soul-eater's signature be here, blazing like the sun?

Despite the evidence, she still hoped her suspicions about the pair were wrong.

She pulled the goggles from her brow and pushed them tight against the bridge of her nose. A trail of sea-green particles hung like an oily London fog descending the stairs, too bright to be anything but recent. The question was going to be if Charlotte could rescue whoever was with the St. Bridgemans before the soul-eater arrived. or revealed itself. But what did the St. Bridgemans gain by controlling the soul-eater? Especially with their political views differing? She swallowed as she placed her foot on the first step and pressed her fingers against the jagged rock walls.

*This is not at all sinister,* Charlotte thought, grimacing. *It's just a secret passageway in the home of your enemy. This is perfectly natural.* It all felt uncomfortably familiar to *The Barber of Fleet Street*. But she hoped it wouldn't end in the way that book had. She rather preferred not being baked into a pie.

The stairs curved slightly, so Charlotte was able to follow the group at a distance without the risk of being seen. The breeze tugged at her ankles as air was pulled from the house, down the stairs, and into the next area. The party reached the bottom of the stairs and turned left. Charlotte waited for a moment, pressing herself against the rock wall. Tiny jabs of uneven rock pricked through her blouse. Once the last boot was out of sight, Charlotte slipped down the remaining steps and peered around the corner, trying to see through the sea-green haze that filled the room. Shelves lined the wall nearest her. If she wedged herself between the cases and the rock, she might be able to remain unseen.

Loose strands of hair whipped and stung her skin as they flew in the rushing air, and she chewed on her lip in anticipation. If the blue-green glow was this prominent, the soul-eater had to be near. She was going to catch the St. Bridgemans in the act.

She darted across the opening and pressed herself against the shelves. She peeked around them, hoping to see the room at large, but the blue glow was now too intense. She squinted but was unable to discern anything through the goggles beyond the glowing particles. She grimaced, then pried the specs from her face and tucked them in the front of her bodice.

Her mouth dropped open as she further took in her surroundings.

The ceilings were extremely high, the walls lined with bookshelves. Jars of unknown liquids and strange instruments, meticulously labelled and organized, crowded the upper portion of one bookcase. Several welding masks sat on the shelves as well. A large ornate mirror and hatstand stood at the base of the stairs. Two aprons hung from the stand.

*Cozy,* she thought sarcastically. *Home, sweet home.* Tables and chemistry equipment were pushed against the wall, creating a sort of amphitheater for something large covered by a sheet in the center of the room. A faint breeze refreshed the room, and Charlotte turned to see the immense opening of the cavern. In the distance, the lights of London twinkled.

The natural formation of such a spacious cave so close to London was impressive, but what really caught Charlotte's attention was the object in the center of the room. It stood three meters tall, its circumference easily four times that, dwarfing the small party. Charlotte's instincts lit up like an overheated Tesla coil. The hairs on the back of her neck stood straight up. Her hands itched to throw something. Or shoot something.

She tried to pick Cosmo and St. Bridgeman out of the group, which had moved closer to the center, next to the giant object draped with heavy cloth. After a moment, Charlotte was able to distinguish West, Cosmo, St. Bridgeman, and Mr. Hayman from each other. The rest of the dinner party must either have left or still be upstairs in the parlour.

Even from a distance, Charlotte could see Cosmo's hands growing more and more restless, first smoothing his hair, then knotting together, then drumming a rhythm on his vest's buttons. West fared no better, his lips curled in an almost snarl as his head tilted from side to side, swiveling to look around the room. St. Bridgeman stood like carved alabaster marble and was just as pale, his face frozen in astonishment.

Something didn't add up. If St. Bridgeman's gaping mouth and wringing hands meant anything, he clearly hadn't been to this cavern before.

Charlotte was on high alert, scanning the cave for the soul-eater, but there was too much residual signature for Charlotte to be sure of anything. If the St. Bridgemans were controlling it, the soul-eater could be contained in a similar glass crate, though Charlotte doubted that the soul-eater, as intelligent as it appeared to be, could be captured. But the alternative just seemed to fantastical to be true.

*Logic, Charlotte.*

She eyed the guests again. Should she go in guns blazing or wait? She knew what she'd have preferred, but there were still so many questions. And without knowing for certain who, what, or where the soul-eater was, she'd have to let events play out before she could be sure of what action to take.

The group clustered around the center, blocking her line of vision to whatever was under the giant cloth. The longer she looked at it, the more it appeared to be some kind of machine.

The sweat on Charlotte's face chilled as a gust swirled across her face, then circled the room. The scent of the room was…old. Very old. Besides the damp, earthy smell, a metallic tang laced the air.

Charlotte put a hand over her mouth to stifle a gasp. This had to be where the portal experiments had taken place. The Origination had started here. A primitive instinct to run exploded in her chest, but she collected herself and remained in place. Barely.

The baroness stiffened, frozen to her spot. Was she…sniffing.

Charlotte's heart sank even has her muscles tensed. She'd seen that posture before, on rogue werewolves who had picked up her scent.

Without turning, the baroness spoke, her words undulating through the cavern. "Stop skulking in the corners, Lady Astley. You reek of curiosity."

Charlotte stepped gingerly from behind the bookcase, feeling much less bold than usual. Nervous energy electrified every muscle in her body. The floor of the cave crunched as she joined the group, filling the space next to Cosmo.

The baroness, still not even deigning to look at her, strode over to the covered machine.

"That familiar feeling is even stronger here," Cosmo whispered.

Charlotte eyed West and Hayman. They, too, looked extremely unsettled. West cocked his ear as if listening to an invisible tune. What was going on here?

The baroness basked in the pale-green light, her skin seemingly smoothed of its age. Her smile was predatory. She walked from the machine to a dais, then turned and addressed the group. "You are all leaders in your respective supernatural spheres. I've brought you here to garner your support as I usher in a new development in our history."

Charlotte's heart leapt into her throat. The baroness *was* the soul-eater—that was the only answer as she hadn't spotted the creature hiding in any corners through the goggles. She simply hadn't expected the baroness's words to sound so much like the journal. *'Usher in a new era and create a new society—supernatural and better.'*

She weighed her options. She could attack the baroness now, or she could wait, and watch, and learn. *Let this play out, Charlotte. You need to have complete truth.* It would also wouldn't do to attack an old woman in front of such important people without iron clad proof.

St. Bridgeman deflated at the baroness's words. "Don't you mean 'we,' Mother?"

Charlotte raised her eyebrows, surprised at how little he knew of what was going on.

"What makes you think that the Alpha of the London Pack would ever consider supporting that ludicrous supernatural registration bill?" The duke's voice rang against the cavern walls.

The baroness's nose wrinkled. "My son's bill is progressive in its goal but shallow in its depth."

St. Bridgeman's shoulders drooped, and Charlotte coughed to cover a smile, but the rejection on his face wiped the smile from hers. *If this wasn't about St. Bridgeman's bill, then why were they all here? And why only invite supernatural leaders?*

The baroness interrupted any further thoughts. "I brought you all here as a professional courtesy. I have plans for the world, and you are a part of them. I'd prefer willing…associates." For a moment Charlotte half-expected her to say "victims." The baroness's hard eyes skewered Cosmo, the duke, and even Hayman, who, if possible, looked paler than he had at dinner. Charlotte suppressed the urge to reach out and shield the poor man, though from what danger she wasn't yet sure.

"There is already an alliance," Cosmo said, stepping towards the sheeted thing.

The baroness shrugged. "The Treaty of Greenwich is a paltry thing when compared to this."

With that, she yanked the sheet from the bulky object. The fabric hissed over metal, revealing the goliath machine. The contraption was unlike anything Charlotte had ever seen before. Two stacked Tesla coils—merged with a grayish lump suspended in liquid—hummed with power and pulsed an ethereal green. A control panel adorned with knobs and dials was joined to the machine. The apparatus looked like something that could raise the dead.

*Blazing suns, we really are in a penny dreadful.*

The baroness glided to the dials, and soon the device crackled with electricity. On a raised dais, an oblong wire frame stood. With the machine on, lightning sparked from the tip of the coils, arcing from the wire frame, then in and through the pulsing core.

Charlotte's stomach tightened. Blazing suns.

She suddenly felt terribly underdressed sporting only a few weapons. She needed one of those new steam-powered Smith and Wesson double-barreled revolvers. She eyed the baroness and Cosmo's still uneasy face. Two revolvers and some bayonets. And maybe some Chinese grenades.

"What is this?" Charlotte's vocal cords felt as if they'd snap. Her mind was fitting the pieces together, but she had to keep the baroness talking until she had a plan.

"A door." The baroness glided to the conductor, her fingers caressing the metal.

"A door. To where?"

The baroness gave a hungry smile. "The aether."

Awe and terror struck Charlotte like physical blows. That was supposed to be a myth. The others in her group seemed equally dumbstruck. If this really was a gateway to the aether, it was a discovery for the ages. The aether was supposedly the in-between place, brimming with magic and energy. Some Origination theorists believed it was the birthplace of all supernaturals. In some aetherial theories, the aether was both a realm and a changeable, malicious power.

They might actually be right.

"H-how?" she cracked. Charlotte cautiously reached for her ray gun.

"My late husband was an exceptionally strong medium. Together, we worked on creating a window into the aetherial realm." The baroness looked absolutely delighted. "Imagine our shock when an overcharged Tesla coil created a door."

Hayman let out a squawk and fabric rustled. Poor man was probably chewing his cravat.

With the grace of a snake, the baroness slid to the console and flipped the power switch. Instantly the air was charged with energy. Brilliant blue electricity crackled from the coils to the conductor, turning into one immense green bolt. The center of the oval conductor glowed with translucent green power. The lightning pulled at the chartreuse core as if it were ripping a hole in front of her. A thin opaque layer, similar to a layer of glass, shimmered across the growing oval. As the shape grew, the opacity dimmed. Instinctively, Charlotte knew that the door wasn't completely open, that she was looking at a something more like a window. For now.

The sight of the glowing green core and the blue lightning struck Charlotte so hard, she nearly stumbled. Memories from the *Asteria* surged forward. The strange storm and this portal. They were the same. That meant that the *Asteria* had narrowly avoided being pulled into another realm.

Fear froze Charlotte's bones, and icy wings fluttered in her stomach. Her mouth was tingling at the scientific possibilities a machine like this could offer, but she couldn't afford to focus on that right now. She knew the soul-eater's residual energy might be too great to make anything out through the goggles, but she had to try. She fumbled with the frames, nearly dropping the blasted things in the process.

After two attempts, she rammed the goggles on her face and squinted through the light's intensity, then gasped. The green energy was merely an outline. The center of the oval burned with a turquoise light, bleeding outward until it filled the shape entirely. Charlotte recoiled, her hand pressing against her throat. *That color.*

Charlotte whipped around to face a frightened-looking Cosmo and flipped the lenses to purple. The vampire still radiated his lavender light. And, there! The filament-thin layer of turquoise framed his silhouette. She did the same for West, who was yelling something at the baroness, and Hayman, whose eyes were wild as he chewed on his own shirt. They each had a turquoise layer identical to that of the portal.

A passage from the journal she'd found came to her mind.

*'We have successfully, if accidentally, introduced not only vampires and werewolves, but all manner of creatures into this world...'*

Charlotte turned her gaze to the baroness though she already knew what she would find. The baroness was wreathed in the same aura as the soul-eater—the same as the other supernaturals, and as the portal itself.

The dinner in her stomach roiled as she removed the goggles, blinking away the spots. She pressed the heel of her hand against her temple.

This woman had dabbled in tremendous power that until this point, was supposedly a myth. Horrific fantasies burst into her mind. The baroness had written, "Complete Origination." After years of slaughters and murders and devastation, what was missing?

What was waiting on the other side of that portal?

"With this door, we can control and access the aether," the baroness was saying.

Charlotte barely heard her. The green glow from the aether was mesmerizing, almost hypnotic.

Cosmo, the duke, and Hayman all took involuntary steps forward. The machine pulsed brighter. Cosmo raised his arm, as if to touch the light.

"Cosmo!"

Something large and tentacled passed near the opening, swiping at him. Charlotte wrenched Cosmo back, and the tentacle missed. The group gasped, retreating, the spell broken for a moment. Cosmo paled and gripped Charlotte's arm. His fangs had extended, and his fingertips looked sharper than they had a minute before. *Good. At least he's thinking now.*

"Mother," St. Bridgeman said, stepping towards the baroness. He looked completely flummoxed. "What does this door do?"

She turned to her son, practically baring her teeth.

"The same thing any door does. It allows passageway. And I can control what comes out of the portal." The baroness circled the control panel, her fingers caressing the controls. It set Charlotte's teeth on edge.

It all felt like a trap.

"Liar," Charlotte hissed, stepping between Cosmo and the baroness, her chest tight. "The first vampire and werewolf came from the aether—from this very doorway."

"Very good, Lady Astley," the baroness muttered. She steepled her fingers and nodded in West's direction. "It might even feel familiar to you," she crooned. "Like coming home."

"I don't understand," St. Bridgeman said, his brow furrowing.

Now Charlotte was angry again, at everything. She whirled and grabbed St. Bridgeman by the collar, forcing him to meet her eyes. "Your parents started the Origination, *Your Lordship*," she spat. She remembered what the journal had said. "Your father died in the process."

Charlotte glanced at the men's faces around her. They clearly were still processing, but Charlotte needed their heads clear in case the baroness tried anything.

Something moved the baroness's skirts, like a wind gusting from behind. *Was* it the wind? There was a tiny breeze from the outside blowing into the cave, but it was only enough to tickle Charlotte's face, not blow fabric.

At the movement of the baroness's dress, a flash of memory whisked through Charlotte's mind. The soul-eater had billowed and then collapsed on itself—almost identical to the hem of the baroness's skirts.

Charlotte took the vial of soul-eater smoke from her bodice. The men around her all wore expressions of bewilderment, horror, and confusion. She herself didn't need any more confirmation of who or what the baroness was, but she knew seeing was believing. She held up the vial, the men's attention turning to the object. "This is a bit of the soul-eater." She threw it on the floor as she drew her ray gun. The vial shattered, and the tiny storm inside it escaped, joining with the baroness.

There was no way this woman was human, not anymore.

St. Bridgeman took a step back, betrayal etched all over his face. "No, it can't be." Normally, Charlotte's heart might have softened, but he was too angry, too scared, to worry about St. Bridgeman and his feelings.

The baroness turned a knob on the console. The machine hummed. A familiar smell, like burnt toast, filled the room.

The image inside the oval conductor sharpened and the opaque center turned translucent. The baroness's lips pressed into a hard line.

The smell of charred food intensified.

The baroness licked her lips. She'd hardly touched her dinner. There was a look in her eyes that chilled Charlotte's bones.

A faint whisper of sadness laced through Charlotte's thoughts. This woman must be brilliant to discover and harness the aether.

The baroness's skirts undulated and rippled in an unnatural way, going against the breeze from the cave's opening.

Charlotte pressed her lips together. However, no scientific discovery was worth being transformed into a monster.

The real baroness—the woman she'd been before she'd ingested aetherial blood—was most definitely gone.

Only one thing remained: the soul-eater.

And it looked hungry.

# Chapter 17

Charlotte leveled her blaster at the baroness, but St. Bridgeman was in her line of fire.

She clicked the safety off. "St. Bridgeman, step away from the soul-eater."

The baron's wide eyes whipped back and forth between his mother and Charlotte. He tried to speak, but the only sound that came out was a strangled cry.

Just then, whatever creature was on the other side of the portal moved its grotesque tentacles. One pressed against the now-translucent green glass of the gate, probing. At each touch, the blue electricity surrounding the portal flared and sparked. It could break through at any moment. That scared Charlotte almost as much as the baroness's hungry features.

Charlotte pushed her thoughts toward Cosmo. *I'll distract her. Turn off that machine.*

She glanced at her friend to make sure he'd been listening. His body stiffened and he nodded imperceptibly.

*Keep her talking, Charlotte,* she told herself.

St. Bridgeman made another pathetic sound and moved towards his mother.

"Baroness St. Bridgeman," Charlotte said. "You will answer for your crimes against the crown."

She tried to step around St. Bridgeman, moving to the right, so that Cosmo would be out of the baroness's line of sight, but the baroness shifted, keeping her son between herself and the ray gun.

"I won't shoot you if you come quietly," Charlotte said. The damp caustic tang of the soul-eater filled her nostrils.

Cosmo advanced to the left, now ten feet away from the machine, but stopped when the tentacled creature began to press its immense body against the opening and the blue lightning crackled. Small arcs of electricity shot from the device, scorching the floor. He crouched lower, his eyes wide with fear. Everyone but the baroness took a step backward at the sight. If anything, the baroness moved closer, drawn in by the monster and the ghostly green light.

The creature stopped, then moved away from the portal, as if unsure about how to get past the barrier.

West shifted beside Charlotte, his knees bent as if preparing to spring. He had clearly seen Cosmo moving toward the machine. In a few moments, Cosmo would be at the base of the device. They had to keep the baroness talking.

West's voice rose above the growing whine of the engine. "If you help science understand your discoveries, the crown may be lenient for your crimes."

Charlotte nodded. "Let us end this peacefully."

The baroness snarled. "I've done nothing wrong. Supernaturals will see this." She was a good liar. Or did she actually believe it?

Cosmo took a step on the dais. Now he just had to get to the control panel. Once he was close enough, perhaps he could mist to the controls.

"You should be thanking me, Your Grace," the baroness said in a cloying voice that snaked around the room.

"You're the cause of hundreds of deaths," West continued, his anger flaring. All pretense of calm disappeared. He hovered on the boundary between man and wolf, much like he had in Johnathan's home. "Thousands if you include everyone transformed and ripped away from humanity. The Origination was a massacre!" His voice rumbled, threatening as thunder. His face elongated, and his pointed ears slid to the top of his skull. His dark skin took on a silver sheen as fur prepared to grow. "Brothers and sisters murdered their families. Wives and husbands devoured each other. I killed my brother because of you! My life has been forever changed," he growled around elongating teeth.

"For the better," the baroness said. "Can you deny you don't relish the hunt? That you don't shiver each time moonlight caresses your skin?" Her ravenous gaze tore into the duke. "Do you deny your own evolution?"

*Evolution? This woman is insane.*

Cosmo's outline began to blur, when the baroness whipped around to face him and he froze.

"And you, Lord Wilmott," the baroness smiled. "Your undead heart soars every time you take to the skies. I've given you a new life, given you gifts no mortal could have even dreamed of."

The baroness advanced toward Cosmo.

Blast.

Charlotte's grip tightened on her ray gun, ready to fire.

"And you," the baroness snarled, turning to face Charlotte once again. "Let us open the portal and see what kind of evolution befalls the bold Lady Astley."

Charlotte's blood froze, and Cosmo made a choking noise from behind the baroness. This maniac woman wanted to use whatever came out of the portal to turn *her*? She had specific plans to remain human, thank you very much.

A tentacle thudded against the barrier, sending green sparks flying, and everyone recoiled from the machine. The device's hum jumped an octave. The pulsating increased, and more lightning zapped from the portal. The creature behind the portal struck again then hung back, like a shark circling the waters.

The baroness cackled, madness creeping into her eyes.

Charlotte still held her ray gun at the baroness, but with the portal, the monster, and the baroness to contend with, along with protecting West, Hayman, Cosmo, and St. Bridgeman, she felt thoroughly out of her league. What sort of weapon did one use to fight aetherials? Her rapiers, throwing knives, and other weapons suddenly felt inadequate.

The portal flashed again as another tentacle crashed into the barrier and Charlotte called for Cosmo. If the creature broke free, she wanted Cosmo close.

A grim truth hit Charlotte. If that portal opened completely, the only humans in England would be dead ones.

"Baroness, this is your last chance. Close the portal or I will shoot. Normally Charlotte liked to give rogue supernaturals every opportunity to come quietly, but this was well past the boundaries.

"About time," Cosmo said, his elongated fingers curving wickedly.

Charlotte took aim, but someone grabbed her weapon, trying to lower it.

"But you can't," St. Bridgeman said, finally finding his voice. "What if there is a cure for supernaturals?"

"A cure?" Charlotte stared at him, thunderstruck, but everything quickly made logical sense. If anyone could discover a panacea, it would be the baroness. If she'd cooperate.

Suddenly the inside of the portal exploded. The monster smashed through the barrier, huge ropy tentacles reaching into the room.

Then Charlotte watched as the baroness transformed. The woman's eyes whitened, engulfing her brilliant green irises. From beneath her dress, smoky tendrils formed, snaking about her. For a brief moment, the baroness's form was human, fused with the writhing tentacles of an octopus for legs, and then she was wreathed in shadow.

"Don't let anything happen to my mother," St. Bridgeman shouted.

"That's not your mother anymore," Charlotte returned.

Hayman bellowed and in a flash of pink transformed into a goat. He fled towards the stairs. The cavern shook with energy and two bookcases toppled, blocking the door and the goat's escape. He promptly fainted, his four stiff legs impaling the air.

Charlotte grabbed her sack of salt from her neck and hurled it at the baroness. The salt sprayed into the air, but the baroness flew right through it with no reaction at all.

Cosmo shouted and leapt into the air, but the baroness slithered to the side, her smokey tentacles propelling her faster than any human legs could. West, now fully transformed, snapped at her with his jaws but missed.

"Keep her distracted. I'll go for the machine," Charlotte yelled, already moving towards the device. Perhaps she could still cut off the power and close the portal. "Her body is hiding in the smoke," she called over her shoulder. "She can also manipulate fear and can fly."

The immense wolf snarled then lunged after the baroness.

Charlotte ran toward the machine. She spared a backward glance and saw Cosmo in mist form flying above the baroness trying to force her to the ground, where the duke was leaping upward, his enormous jaws snapping shut with every jump.

In the midst of all of this, Charlotte saw the black aetherial monster press ropy tentacles against the unopened portal.

*Blast.*

She turned her attention back to the machine. There were dials and levers everywhere. She saw now what formed the heart of the contraption. *Blazing suns, is that a brain?* The brain pulsed faster with each burst of lightning. With her close proximity, her hair stood on end.

The lightning snapped and sparked, fueling the portal. The intensity of the electricity increased. The air smelled like burnt hair. *Please, don't be mine!* Blazing suns, where was that lever?

Aha! She wrapped her hand around a silver lever and pushed down. The lever was stiff, but it reluctantly complied.

Suddenly, something barreled into Charlotte from behind. The lever jabbed into her hip. A hissing and snarling mass behind her clawed at her hair. Smoke-covered tentacles twisted around her shoulders.

All Charlotte's willpower abruptly left. Colors bled from her vision, leaving only grey. *She's eating my soul,* she realized. Happiness was being siphoned from her very bones.

There was a second impact, and Charlotte was knocked to the floor, released from the soul-eater's grasp. West and the soul-eater wrestled each other, then Cosmo joined, trying to help West.

Charlotte pulled herself up to the machine on wobbly legs, took a deep breath, and felt her strength returning. When her vision normalized, and she stared at the device. The power lever had been jammed to the highest level, then wrenched off, and she couldn't see where it had landed. *Now what?*

Lightning flared and the machine roared. Stray bolts rocketed around the cavern. The black monster's tentacles pulled against the barrier, widening the opening. The ground shook again.

Charlotte snapped into action. Water would fry the machine's circuits. She needed water. She ran across the room toward the shelves, dodging the fight, which Cosmo and West actually seemed to be winning. No, wait. The three flipped, and now the soul-eater had dominance.

St. Bridgeman stood in the middle of the floor, staring.

She shoved him, both to get him out of the way and to wake him up. "Don't just stand there! Help me!"

He managed to come to himself and fell in behind her.

Together they grabbed armfuls of the jars of liquid, some strangely bioluminescent. St. Bridgeman, loaded with five large jars, turned and ran back to the machine. He looked over his shoulder. "What are you waiting for, you git!"

Charlotte had frozen in her tracks.

Four large tentacles snaked through the fully open portal, completely filling the entrance to the aether. One tentacle wrapped itself around a large globe and pulled the it back into the aether, then another tentacle snaked out to replace the first one.

Charlotte swallowed, her heartbeat thrashing in her ears. There was no way to make it across to the machine with the tentacles snapping up everything in their paths.

A tentacle reached for the apparatus and Charlotte's hopes rose. Maybe this creature would do the hard work for her. It wrapped around one of the supports, but then a bolt of lightning zapped it, and the tentacle disappeared back onto the void. A resulting stray blast of lightning bounced off the mirror by the door.

Charlotte hurled two of the jars at the machine, hoping to short-circuit it, but tentacles were whipping around. One jar was swatted away and the second was knocked off course, crashing to the floor. St. Bridgeman copied Charlotte's action with surprising accuracy. He had better luck, and one jar sailed through a gap in the tentacles. It thudded against the machine, but instead of breaking, it simply crashed to the floor.

"Follow me." Charlotte tore around the room, leaping over groping tentacles, and around swiping claws and teeth.

*Where was West?* Ah, there. The alpha werewolf clamped his teeth onto a tentacle from the portal creature, thrashing his head. But where was Cosmo? And the soul-eater?

Charlotte watched in alarm as another tentacle snaked around West. He snarled and tried to claw his way out of its grasp, but it was dragging him towards the portal.

She and St. Bridgeman reached the base of the stairs. "Grab the mirror," she said, pointing. "We'll redirect the lightning." He nodded, and they hefted the large mirror.

Charlotte spared another glance at the room. A tentacle was creeping towards the fainted Hayman. West snarled at a second tentacle trying to trap his jaws. Charlotte looked again for Cosmo and the soul-eater. Nothing in the air. That worried Charlotte more than anything.

Her heart dropped onto the floor when she finally spotted them in the corner. The soul-eater was looming over Cosmo.

He looked like death. His skin was icy white, his hair drained of color, his jaw slack. As Charlotte watched in frozen horror, a gauzy white substance flowed from Cosmo to the soul-eater.

*No!*

Charlotte adjusted the angle of the mirror so it faced the open portal and the mass of tentacles. "When I say now, you use the mirror to intercept the beam."

"And do what?"

"Aim for the beast," she said, pointing to the creature pulling a now-still West towards the portal.

St. Bridgeman nodded.

Without waiting for a reply, Charlotte ran into the center of the room. She lost her balance and had to drop onto her knees to dodge a lightning bolt. In one fluid motion she drew her throwing knives from underneath her sleeves, aimed, and released them both. A shrill scream from the soul-eater told Charlotte that at least one of them had found its mark.

Charlotte stood and faced the immense tentacles. She spotted West and aimed another knife from her corset at the tentacle wrapped around his midsection. For a moment, the monster moved and West was in the way, but the monster pulled back just enough that the knife could sink deep into the tentacle. The creature recoiled and dropped the werewolf, who fell with a sickening thud and didn't move.

Charlotte pulled the last knife from her corset, then screamed a war cry and charged the soul-eater.

The soul-eater thrashed, trying to reach for the throwing knife that still protruded from what looked to be its shoulder. It took a few steps away from Cosmo. Charlotte raced into the gap, her dagger resting comfortably in her hands.

The soul-eater dislodged the blade—which clanged to the floor—hissed, baring its teeth through the black mist.

Charlotte fell into a crouch, waiting. Two of the baroness's tentacles lunged for her. She dodged one and spun around the next, taking a step closer. She slashed back and down, using her momentum from the spin. Her knife cut through the soul-eater's smoke shield. But she'd over-reached, and only the blade's hilt connected, ramming against solid flesh.

The soul-eater roared in anger. Another of its tentacles raced for Charlotte's neck. Charlotte dropped and at the same time lunged forward with her dagger. A few inches into the smoke, her knife sank into the soul-eater's body. The creature gasped and staggered backward. Still holding onto the hilt of her dagger, Charlotte pressed the soul-eater towards the portal. *A little farther.*

A thick black tentacle wrapped itself around the baroness.

"Now!" Charlotte screamed.

St. Bridgeman angled the mirror into the beam. Lightning bounced from the surface and hit the monster in the portal. With an otherworldly screech, the creature retreated into the aether, dragging the screaming soul-eater along with it. For a moment, the portal opening was completely empty. Then tentacles charged through the portal again.

"Destroy it!" Charlotte pointed to the machine.

St. Bridgeman stepped into the beam with the mirror as a shield. The lightning bounced and struck the machine, which exploded in a shower of green sparks.

The aetherial barrier lost its transparency, became opaque, then snapped shut. Most of the tentacles were able to pull back in time, except one, which twisted and coiled on the floor. *Revolting.* Whether it was from the soul-eater or the other monster, Charlotte couldn't say.

Ash and electric green particles rained down, dusting the floor. St. Bridgeman stumbled towards the smoking remains of the machine. It pulsed twice, then grew dark. He raised a hand, catching some of the electric dust. He held it close, examining it. Even in the now-dim light, Charlotte could see him struggling against tears.

"Probably best not to come in too much contact with the stuff," Charlotte warned, though gently. "Don't know what effect it might have."

St. Bridgeman turned away from the machine, wet streaks silently running down his face, but he wiped his hands on his trousers.

Mr. Hayman, having recovered at some point during the altercation and dusted in the green specks, tried to swipe the glittery motes off himself.

West's wolf form twitched and began to blur. "See to the duke," Charlotte said to St. Bridgeman.

St. Bridgeman managed to pull himself together enough to rush over, but the duke was able to finish his transformation and stood. West held the heel of his hand against his forehead and waved St. Bridgeman off. "I'm all right."

With a jolt, Charlotte whirled towards Cosmo, her heart in her throat. It didn't look like he was moving. The world went silent as she rushed to him, dropped to the floor, and scanned him for injuries. His breathing was shallow. His skin was tinged blue.

*No!* She gripped her head in alarm. How was she supposed to treat soul-sucking? Her thoughts swirled in growing panic. "Don't you dare die!" she growled, her voice choking at the end.

A surge of logic snapped to the front of her mind.

She whirled on St. Bridgeman. "He needs blood. Do you have any *vin de sang*?"

St. Bridgeman shook his head, his features numb. "Just what we purchased for dinner."

"Blazing suns!" Her chest tightened. Her mind raced. Cosmo's breathing was slowing, his fangs retracting. She had only moments.

"Get me something sharp."

West's features twisted, telling Charlotte he had little hope for Cosmo.

Panic squeezed her heart. Cosmo was dying. His chest was deflating. She had to do something.

Charlotte ripped off her bracer and slashed her wrist against his almost-dull fangs before they disappeared completely. "No, no, no," she whispered, holding her hand over his face. A thin line of blood dripped from the jagged tear on her wrist and into his mouth. "Come on!" Tears spilled down her face. "I'm not going to let you go. Not like this."

Cosmo's color returned, and she froze. He gave a small groan, then coughed. It was the most beautiful sound in the universe.

"Yes," she breathed. "That's it."

Suddenly his fangs sharpened and elongated, then they pierced her skin. She gasped but didn't pull away.

Cosmo's eyes snapped open, wild and intense. His cheeks were flushed. His hand flew up and grabbed Charlotte's wrist, pressing it against his mouth. He pulled, drinking deeply. An intoxicating heat spread from his lips, and her heartbeat thrummed in her ear. Reason shrank to a dim memory. Her eyes widened and she bit her lips. What was this feeling? She'd never experienced anything like this before. This went far beyond Cosmo's usual vamping mischief.

Her body ached for him.

"Wilmott." West's voice was a distant echo, but it carried a warning note.

Charlotte knew she should be worried, but the thought washed away in the torrent of heat filling her body.

"More," she croaked, her eyes unfocused with heady anticipation. She lifted her chin, elongating her neck, and sighed, deep and throaty. Every muscle simultaneously constricted and relaxed in waves of wanting. She blinked, realizing that darkness was creeping into the edges of her vision. She was growing weaker, and the room began to spiral. *He's taking too much blood, but...I don't think I care.*

Someone was shouting from very far away.

"Cosmo!"

Was that...the duke?

It didn't matter, nothing else mattered, except how Cosmo was making her feel. She needed to make sure it never stopped.

Someone tugged at her arm, and the warmth from her wrist dulled, pulling away.

"No," she tried to croak, but no words left her throat.

Everything stopped, the heat and desire retreated, and she was left feeling hollow. Cosmo had let go of her wrist. Every muscle in her body went limp, empty with exhaustion.

She reeled backward and someone—West?—caught her. The room kept spinning. *Why is it spinning?* She felt strangely detached from her body.

Someone bound her wrist—staunching the blood, she instinctively knew. Slowly the room steadied, and a modicum of warmth spread back into her limbs. Coldness from the stone floor pressed against her back. When her breathing steadied, she pressed her fingers against her forehead.

Cosmo's face filled her vision, his brow twisted with pain. But she'd saved him, hadn't she? Was he still in danger?

His strained voice choked on a sharp whisper. "I almost killed you."

Relief surged through her veins. Cosmo was alive. He was safe. She gave a weak smile. "I would have killed *you* if you'd died."

Both his hands raked through his hair as he looked heavenward and barked a laugh. Then he leaned forward, his eyes skipping over her features as though they didn't believe what they were seeing.

Charlotte raised her hand, and Cosmo enveloped it in his. His touch reassured her more than anything. He was out of harm's way.

Her throat constricted, and tears pierced through her mental armor. She'd come so close to losing her dearest friend.

Soft fingers brushed her hair away, almost to her complete undoing. She inhaled deeply, biting down on the wave of emotions. He kissed her forehead. "My life is yours." His lips brushed her ear, sending delicious shivers across her skin once more. "But I suspect you already knew that."

A cough behind Cosmo caught her attention, and Charlotte's face warmed for more than one reason. Somehow, her blush took the last of her energy, and her eyelids fluttered. She shook her head and tried to rally her strength. Her brain wanted rest, and her heart wanted to envelop itself in nothing but Cosmo.

She opened her eyes and looked deeply into his eyes and nearly lost herself again. The memory of his near-death sent her heart skittering even faster inside her chest. She was mildly embarrassed. She should have known she'd feel the full effects of a bite and should have prepared for it, but experiencing the headiness firsthand…well, that was something else entirely.

Now that she was in full control of her mental acuities, she knew it was something she wasn't ready to face. So, for now, she took refuge in science.

She sat up, pointing to the duke, St. Bridgeman, and Hayman, who had recovered sometime while Charlotte was…saving Cosmo. They stood around her, staring.

"Make sure…all the green particles are gathered." The room spun again. "And, Lord Wilmott, see that the tentacle is collected as a specimen." *Phew. Even breathing is exhausting.*

Cosmo scooped her in his arms and pulled her close. She really was so very tired. "Saving the world is exhausting and you work too hard. You need to rest." He was humoring her, of course—mentioning what had just happened would be gauche.

The duke bowed deeply. Charlotte blinked hard only just noticing his ruined state of dress. His clothes were a mess, and blood was visible from several scrapes on his face and neck. Cosmo, Hayman, and St. Bridgeman looked no better.

"You have my eternal gratitude," West said, straightening from his bow.

"We finished it," she whispered, the weight of everything that had just happened beginning to sink in. A second wave of exhaustion hit, and her head bobbed. She narrowed her eyes at Cos. "None of your"—she yawned—"nonsense."

"None of yours," Cosmo whispered, pulling her closer. She drifted in and out, catching snippets of conversation.

"Sorry about your mother…"

"…members of the coven to help you, St. Bridgeman…"

"…report to the crown…"

"…all need a rest."
Charlotte heaved a sigh, then fell asleep.

# Chapter 18

When Charlotte's eyes fluttered open, green thistly wallpaper greeted her from every side, and the sight of her delicate lace drapes assured her she was at home in her bedroom.

Flitting movements above her head caught her eye. Colorful macaws and peach-faced lovebirds fluttered around the ceiling of her room. She blinked. *Those are native to Africa…what are they doing in my room? And what is that blazing smell?*

She turned to the side to investigate and was met with the gaudiest bouquet of flowers she'd ever seen. There were no less than thirteen white stargazer lilies, with smaller pink and yellow variations nestled among the massive blooms. Sympathy, devotion, and friendship, she noted. Next to them was a smaller bouquet of hyacinths. *Who could have sent these?* She tried to breathe in through her mouth, but the pungent scent jumped down her throat, and she coughed.

"Charlotte." Cosmo practically leapt from the chair near her bed and was instantly by her side. "How are you feeling?"

"I am feeling a headache coming on." The flowers' aroma burned through her nostrils and set her head pounding. "Those lilies positively reek. Get rid of them."

Cosmo shook his head. "Gifts from a duke cannot simply be tossed into the bin."

Charlotte's eyes widened. "These are from West? How thoughtful."

Cosmo snorted and muttered something under his breath.

A mischievous idea sparked inside, and she held her arms out for the arrangement. Cosmo woodenly complied and moved them towards her until the blooms filled her vision. She peeked over the flowers, delighted to see Cosmo wrestling with jealous annoyance.

She took a shallow breath. The heavy fragrance slammed against her brain. She coughed again, waving a hand to clear the air. "But they still stink."

Charlotte moved to sit up, but she cried out when her wrist buckled painfully under the pressure. Cosmo put the flowers down, then darted forward, wrapping one arm behind her back, and reaching around her waist. His face stopped inches from hers. She held her breath, not daring to break the silence. Warmth from his body radiated against her skin.

He eased her back down onto the pillows, the creaking of the brass bed frame the only sound in the room. He lingered a moment, his searching eyes full of concern and…was there something else there too? Charlotte searched his eyes, hoping to tease out his feelings, but instead lost herself in their jade-green depths. She blinked rapidly and glanced away.

"Th-thank you, Cos." She swallowed dryly.

He cleared his throat and straightened, removing his hand from under her back.

Her headache intensified until locomotive pistons pounded in her brain. She eased herself into the pillows and pressed her fingers to her temples.

"I'll see to these." Cosmo took the offending bouquet out of the room and returned to open the window, setting the draperies fluttering and clearing away the remaining aroma.

She closed her eyes inhaling deeply, the cool night air filling her lungs. "Thank you."

For a moment, she lay with her eyes closed and tried to relax, but her mind was whirring. Her brows furrowed. She could *hear* the whirring.

The birds on her ceiling still fluttered noiselessly above her head. Something was off. Why hadn't they flown out the open window? She must have been hit on the head during the fight with the soul-eater. She didn't remember that, though. She did remember Cosmo. She stared at him sidelong, heat flaring along her collarbones and rising to her cheeks.

She lifted a hand to point to the remaining flowers, the bouquet of hyacinths, and was momentarily surprised to see a gauze bandage wrapped around her wrist. "These then,"—she pointed to the flowers—"must be your offering."

His eyes darted to her wrist then up to her face and he rubbed the back of his head. "No, actually, I provided the birds." He pointed to a squat rectangular device that she recognized immediately—his kinetoscope. *Of course.* Once again, a soft clicking noise emanated from marvelous machine. She looked up again at her tiny African aviary. They were lovely.

She tilted her head to stare at the small stalks of pink and purple flowers. "So who are these from, then?"

Cosmo glared at the flowers, and Charlotte raised her eyebrows at his reaction. "Those are from Trevor."

She wrinkled her nose. "Trevor who?"

"Trevor St. Bridgeman," he huffed.

She blinked. "St. Bridgeman sent me flowers?"

"Yes. As I've mentioned before, he's actually not so bad—and I expect he'll be a little more open-minded after the incident with his mother and the portal. Still, he's a bit of an acquired taste, and we can only hope that his sudden change is permanent."

Charlotte's brow tilted. Odd that the hyacinths were coming from St. Bridgeman. Not necessarily the flower. She had seen hundreds in the conservatory when she was sneaking about. But the hyacinth was the flower for an apology.

Cosmo sniffed at the blooms and murmured something about the bouquet lacking originality.

*St. Bridgeman, open-minded? Change? Apology?* Maybe she *had* hit her head.

She processed Cosmo's words and absently took the glass he offered her, the liquid swirling like the thoughts in her head. "What change? You and he are…friends? How long was I unconscious?"

"Two days, a bit less. Your blood loss was fairly severe"—he blushed at this—"and you did need rest. Trevor wanted to see to your health personally, but I didn't think it would be wise, all things considered, so I went to keep him company—"

"Keep him company? I'm convalescing for two days, and you both are suddenly best mates?"

"More like amicable acquaintances…" Cosmo chuckled, then his shoulders slumped. He raked his hands through his hair. "He is grieving and lost. Poor fellow had some…latent abilities awaken shortly after the aetherial encounter."

Charlotte's mind spun that information around for a moment, then it clicked into place like the gears of a pocket watch. "He's a s-supernatural?" The irony of the situation burst out of her mouth in extremely unladylike guffaws.

Cosmo's voice rose to talk over her laughter. "And he's having a very difficult time. Adjusting to supernatural life is a trial."

She shook with laughter, making the bed frame quiver.

"Although he has more support than many others had had," Cosmo continued. "The Pack have been downright gracious, and even the Coven have offered help. They're very sympathetic toward new supernaturals."

She doubled over, clutching a stitch in her side with her uninjured hand.

"He hasn't told Minnie yet, but that's no surprise. It's only been two days, and there is no understanding between them. But that may only be a matter of time."

Charlotte reached for her glass, sobering slightly. Minnie and St. Bridgeman. And now he was a supernatural. "I'm not worried about Minnie. There is still time to guide her towards more…sensible suitors."

Cosmo rolled his eyes. "By any means, and after all that has happened, I hope that he eases up on the bill. High noon take him if he doesn't."

Silence descended but only for a moment. A strangled laugh caught in Charlotte's throat. "St. Bridgeman is a supernatural." Her voice wobbled, and she barely managed to keep a straight face.

He leaned back in his chair and folded his arms, waiting for Charlotte to regain her composure. "Are you done?"

"What kind?"

"A variety of medium. Primarily emotion-based," he said, raising an eyebrow and waiting for Charlotte's reaction.

"It's nice to know that he is capable of"—she barely held back a snigger—"emotions."

Cosmo narrowed his eyes at her, so she sealed her lips together, her cheeks reddening from her bottled mirth.

He leaned forward, closing much of the space between them. His voice dropped to a near-whisper. "He's a very sensitive soul, my dear."

Now a heated silence filled the room. *My dear.* Her fingers fiddled with the edge of her bandage, fraying the hem, trying to hide how much her heart was expanding and pressing against her chest.

Was this residual from Cosmo's bite? Did this happen with all vampire bites or just his? Heat pushed through her torso.

As if he could read her mind, Cosmo reached forward and pulled her uninjured hand away from the fabric. He brought her fingers to his lips, then kissed them gently. Charlotte shivered, a slow burning heat spreading from her fingers to her waist. Echoes of the yearning she'd felt when he'd bitten her thrummed in her memory.

He gestured to her bandaged wrist. "I am so sorry, *mon petite soliel*," he said, his voice soft. "Allow me to kiss it better?"

His attention moved from her fingers to her palm and the new sensation set her feelings roiling inside. Would things be different between them if she opened her heart to him? How would she even begin? Fear and anticipation flipped over each other tightening her throat.

He leaned over her bed, his hair falling around his face like a dark halo. He brushed his fingers against her cheek. His thumb traced her jawline, sending shivers skipping along her spine.

She swallowed. A small furnace burned in her chest. This went beyond the bounds of propriety for tending to the sick. If Cosmo actually closed the distance and kissed her, she wasn't sure what she'd do. Slap him? Kiss him back? Maybe she'd simply explode. All of these possibilities seemed highly likely, and all of them terrified her.

*Charlotte, you are convalescing!* But her body seemed to act of it's own accord, and she raised herself toward him. Her eyes darted to Cosmo's mouth and her lips parted.

Suddenly the door burst open and Charlotte nearly shot out of her skin. Cosmo jerked back and flickered into mist in surprise.

A shrill voice filled the room, each word jabbing like a spear. "What. Are. You. Doing?"

Aunt Hespa strode into the room, glaring at the vampiric mist now reforming in the corner, well away from the bed. When Cosmo solidified, his posture was ramrod straight, a slight flush across his cheeks. Aunt Hespa walked over to Charlotte's bedside and turned back to Cosmo, watching him like the Queen's Guard watched suspicious persons approaching the royal residence.

"Aunt Hespa." Charlotte smiled. Relief at seeing her wonderfully demanding and bossy aunt washed through her. Her thoughts lingered on Cosmo's touch, but she quickly buried her feelings and… whatever she'd been about to do with him. She exhaled, and the last of the tension from Cosmo dissipated. At least her aunt hadn't seen the events in the cavern. At this thought, a raging blush charged across her features once more.

The floorboards near the door creaked again as Minnie entered the room. She smiled as she moved to the corner opposite Cosmo, a thin rectangular package tucked under her arm. She glanced between the room's three inhabitants, knowing she'd just missed something important.

"Charlotte, you are ill, but you must still think of propriety," her aunt said. "What would Mr. Hollands think?" Aunt Hespa glared at Cosmo. The vampire swallowed, his Adam's apple bobbing.

"Yes," Charlotte blurted out. "Mr. Hollands. We must think of him." She inwardly cringed as the words left her mouth.

Her aunt began to fuss over her, rearranging the side table. Charlotte glanced over the older woman's shoulder at Cosmo. A small wave of guilt washed over her when she saw him lower his brows, an irritated and wounded look in his eyes. She glanced away, promising herself she'd make it up to him later.

Minnie settled into a wicker chair in the corner, careful not to catch her ruffled yellow sleeves on the plaited straw.

"Charlotte," Aunt Hespa said, "are you sure that Lord Wilmott isn't bothering you?" The older woman shot the vampire a pointed glare. "I'm sure he wouldn't want to tire you."

Cosmo gave a nervous chuckle and then reached into his jacket pocket. He removed a dark leather-bound journal and awkwardly shoved it into Charlotte's hands.

"The baroness's notebook!" Charlotte eagerly took it. Her scientific curiosity piqued, she fingered its edges. The encounter with the baroness had left so many questions unanswered. If she could transcribe these strange markings, then science could find out everything that the baroness had known about the aether. From a scientific standpoint, it was a shame the woman turned out to be a murderous villain.

Of course, Aunt Hespa was still probably unaware of all this. "Lord Wilmott, have a care! Detective work is the last thing Charlotte needs." Aunt Hespa reached for the book, practically shoving Cosmo out of the way to get at it.

Charlotte quickly tucked it behind her back and crammed it under her pillows.

An awkward silence pressed down on them.

Cosmo rocked back on his heels.

Minnie coughed.

Aunt Hespa glared so fiercely Charlotte was afraid the woman's eyes would begin to spark.

The kinetographic birds on the ceiling froze, and the steady ticking of the device whirred to a stop.

"I should be going," Cosmo finally said. He quickly gathered the machine into his arms. He bid farewell to Minnie and Aunt Hespa. Minnie returned the sentiment, though Aunt Hespa merely sniffed.

He moved to the open window, his form blurring at the edges.

Before he could fully mist, Charlotte spoke. "Thank you for the birds, Lord Wilmott."

"*Mon soliel,*" he said, flashing Charlotte a broad smile, his sharpened canines on full display.

Charlotte's eyes dropped to his mouth, focusing on his fangs, and heat exploded over her face. She knew she'd have very different feelings about that particular feature of his from now on.

Velvety blackness swirled around him until only his jade-green eyes were visible. He gave a quick wink to Charlotte—which sent her pulse skittering once more—before the mist enveloped him completely, and he swept out the window and into the night.

Aunt Hespa muttered something about flashy vampires and closed the window. Charlotte was glad for it, as it gave her time to recover from his heat-inducing presence.

Her aunt turned and leaned toward Charlotte, studying her. "You look feverish."

Charlotte nodded, unsure of how else to explain the blush that had stolen across her face.

"Should I ask Beth for some tea?" Minnie asked, the braided tassels on her skirt swinging as she moved to stand.

The older woman held up a hand and Minnie sat back in her chair. "I will. Charlotte's staff needs a firm hand." Aunt Hespa fussed over a few pillows. Charlotte quickly saw through the ruse. With her injured hand, she pushed the journal further under her until she was practically sitting on it.

Aunt Hespa gave a huff and stood straight before moving to the door, when something green and white on her aunt's clothing caught Charlotte's eye. The small item had blended in with the gold-dotted red-tulle collar her aunt was wearing

"Aunt Hespa," Charlotte asked.

The older woman turned back at the doorway.

"That pin." Charlotte pointed to a small lapel pin on her aunt's collar. "Where did you get that pin?" The pin was a cheap green-petaled flower brooch with a white center, very unlike the jewelry her aunt usually wore.

The woman's hand rested along her neck, and a look of sadness crossed her face. "This? Mathilda gave it to me on the *Asteria*. It's just a paste pin. And even though Mathilda was using it as a sort of symbol for her supernatural charity"—the older woman's voice broke, and she swallowed—"I'm wearing it because it reminds me of her."

Charlotte's eyes went wide. Though it was smaller than the broken pin they'd seen at the inquest, there was no mistaking that it was the complete version of Mr. Draper's. She glanced at Minnie, but her friend didn't seem aware of the pin's significance.

Aunt Hespa cleared her throat. "I'll go get us that tea." The door closed behind her.

"She's taken the baroness's passing with great difficultly," Minnie said, a note of sadness in her own voice.

Charlotte blinked. So either the police or St. Bridgeman were keeping quiet about this whole affair. *At least for now.*

The journal poked into her backside. This book had to be examined and the baroness's knowledge on the aether had to be explored. The Originologists would kill for definitive evidence about the Origination. Even though it would mean not giving a complete report of the incident to Chief Inspector Dawson, perhaps omitting the baroness's full involvement in everything was prudent.

Minnie stood from the chair and smoothed her pleated skirt. "Those were very interesting birds Lord Wilmott brought," she said, moving to the end of Charlotte's bed.

Charlotte nodded grateful for the change in topic. "They were. This last case…he's been so helpful and incredibly thoughtful." She thought of his concern over her lack of sleep. Of him creating the goggles to help with her cases. Memories of the endless tests that she and Cosmo had run with the goggles pushed through her mind. Cosmo glowing lavender. His allurement charm. And the way his shoulders filled out his suit when he used his vampiric glamour. She bit her lip.

Minnie cleared her throat and Charlotte blinked. "Did something happen between you and Lord Wilmott?" Minnie asked.

"No, of course not," Charlotte said, a little too quickly. "We are friends."

Minnie hummed in the back of her throat, her dark eyes flashing."I think it's time I played detective," she said, removing her lavender gloves. She placed a hand on the side table, where Cosmo had been standing.

"No, Minnie—" Charlotte moved to stop her, but pain lanced through her wrist and set her head pounding again. With a groan she leaned back in her bed and watched her friend. It was only a small consolation to Charlotte to know that Minnie would be unable to see Cosmo reflected in the room. But at that moment, Charlotte still wanted to cover herself with the bedsheets and never come out.

Minnie's eyes went slightly unfocused as she focused on her powers, and Charlotte watched with mortification as reactions flitted across her friend's face. At one point, Minnie's round lips formed the perfect O, and a small blush crept over *her* cheeks.

"It seems you and Lord Wilmott are *very* close friends," Minnie said finally, replacing her gloves.

Charlotte opened her mouth to retort, but the door opened and Aunt Hespa returned with a harassed-looking Beth in tow. Beth set the tea service on the dresser and dipped a quick curtsey, then scurried away, seemingly anxious to leave Aunt Hespa's company.

"Charlotte, you should really attend to your staff. Their training is atrocious…" Aunt Hespa began pouring the tea, all the while pointing out ways in which Charlotte's staff was inferior.

Charlotte glared at Minnie. Using nothing but glances and small gestures, the two friends had a conversation behind the older woman's back.

*You had better not tell her anything,* Charlotte glared.

*How can you think I would do such a thing?* Minnie's brow arched.

*You'd better not.* Charlotte's eyes narrowed.

*Ugh, you are infuriating.* Minnie rolled her eyes and moved to retrieve the rectangular package from the table, making as if to bring it to Charlotte.

"…if you need references for new staff members I would be happy to provide them," Aunt Hespa finished, handing Charlotte a steaming cup of tea.

Minnie grabbed the package from the table and turned it over in her hands, addressing Hespa. "I know you cautioned me against bringing Charlotte the social pages, but perhaps you were correct, Lady Hespa." Minnie turned to Charlotte an obvious false pout on her face.

Charlotte eyed her friend, then scrutinized the size and shape of the package. It was thin and book-shaped and seemed flexible. Her eyebrows shot up. The penny dreadfuls Aunt Hespa had confiscated!

"No, I'm feeling much better," Charlotte said, snatching the parcel out of her friend's hand before she could move away. It set her head pounding again, but it was worth it.

Minnie gave a satisfied smirk before pouring some tea for herself and returning to her chair.

Aunt Hespa's eyes narrowed. Clearly more concessions were needed. Charlotte bowed her head. "And perhaps I will take your suggestions for new staff."

Her aunt's gaze softened, and Minnie rolled her eyes again.

Charlotte accepted the tea from Hespa and took a sip, then closed her eyes and sighed leaning back in her chair. For a moment, the trio sat in a comfortable silence and Charlotte felt that all was right with the world.

Then Aunt Hespa cleared her throat and fixed a pointed stare at Charlotte. "My dear niece, I confess I am glad to see you so much recovered and thinking favorably of Mr. Hollands."

Charlotte nearly choked on her tea. "Mr. Hollands?" she croaked, regretting invoking his name as an excuse to distance herself from Cosmo.

Minnie scooted her plump frame to the edge of the chair, her eyes merrily taking in Charlotte's discomfort.

"Yes, I—" Aunt Hespa started, but a series of ticking sounds interrupted her.

The telescriber on Charlotte's table clicked away, and a small strip of paper emerged. Charlotte leaned over the edge of her bed and pulled the paper away from the device.

Aunt Hespa was beside Charlotte in an instant, her cheeks pinched tight. "I forbid it," she said, reaching over Charlotte's shoulder.

"I am of age," Charlotte protested holding the paper out of her aunt's reach.

The older woman stood, some of her grey hair frizzing out from its chignon. "I still forbid it."

A ridiculous rebellion rose in Charlotte. "And I forbid you to forbid me."

Minnie coughed.

Aunt Hespa gave a loud sigh and gestured wildly. "Charlotte, you must understand. You are a lone woman in a man's world, with murderers and vagrants and criminals."

"I—"

"No, you must listen!" Aunt Hespa placed her hands on her hips. "Surely you must see the impropriety of…well, all of your choices."

Charlotte was cowed into silence, but a small niggling idea was sewn into her mind. *Lone woman. Lone woman.* "'A lone woman?'"

Aunt Hespa sighed again, this time in relief and she sat on the edge of Charlotte's bed, taking Charlotte's hand. "Yes. I'm glad you are finally listening to me."

"I am alone."

"Indeed." Her aunt nodded.

"And being alone is more difficult than having support. Having someone to help."

"Yes," Aunt Hespa hissed the word, looking heavenward as if all her prayers were being answered at once.

Charlotte's mind spun. *Help, hmm.* Her mind raced to the confrontation between the baroness soul-eater and how nicely she, Cosmo, and the duke had worked together. *Even St. Bridgeman,* she reluctantly conceded. Then she glanced to her friend in the chair. Minnie had been helpful earlier, too, with Mr. Draper's possessions. Perhaps…

Charlotte sat up as straight as she could. "You are correct, Aunt Hespa."

"Of course I am." The older woman smiled. "Which is why you need a—"

"Team," Charlotte said.

"Husband," Aunt Hespa said. Then she blinked. "Team?"

Charlotte grabbed her telescriber and pulled it into her lap, ignoring the pain in her wrist. She quickly typed a response to Mr. Singh. *Debrief tomorrow STOP*

And to Chief Inspector Dawson she wrote: *Have proposal for SPN dept STOP See you tomorrow STOP*

Aunt Hespa closed her eyes and sank into her chair.

Minnie sipped her tea loudly, then nibbled on a biscuit. Her face was passive, but Charlotte suspected she was thoroughly enjoying the show.

Charlotte sat up straight again and took a bit of one of cook's famous raspberry scones. She smiled as the delightful crusted glaze crunched between her teeth, giving way to tart raspberries and buttery crumb.

*Yes*, she said to herself. *A team will do very nicely.*

# Epilogue

Stares from uniformed policemen followed Charlotte as she strode through the police station late the next afternoon, her heels clicking on the linoleum. As uncommon as it was for a woman to walk through the police station, it was even more so when the woman was titled.

Charlotte held her head high, inhaling the herbaceous and woody aroma of the men's tobacco smoke filling the interior. A few faces looked familiar—they had assisted on a few cases—but she was still so new to her monster hunting appointment that she was still learning everyone's names. Although Charlotte and these police officers all sought to stop criminals and bring them to justice, many on the force were still unsure of how a woman could adequately hunt monsters.

*Chin up, old girl. Give them a few more solid cases and they'll come around.* She broke her aloof air and allowed herself a quick scan of the room. Policeman Singh was nowhere to be seen. Charlotte steeled herself as she wound her way through the room, continuing to the chief's office.

As she neared the hallway leading to his office, several men muttered darkly under their breaths. A few words were loud enough that Charlotte was forced to ignore them, though insults like "traitor" and "leech lover" never failed to rankle.

Just before she'd reached the door, a man stood up, blocking her way. His prominent jaw and salt-and-pepper hair combined into hard features. Charlotte eyed the man, raking her memory for his name. Ah, there it was.

"Lieutenant Howe," she said.

The man pursed his lips and shifted his weight. Everything about his stance was a challenge.

Charlotte peered around his shoulder. The chief's door was right there.

Ugh.

Lieutenant Howe gave a cocky smile and spoke, his voice loud enough for half the men in the room to hear. "I heard you met the Duke of Keighley. Is that correct, Miss Astley?"

Conversations quieted as the police officers turned their attention to what was clearly going to be a show. Charlotte inwardly cringed at the blatant drop of her title, but she chose to ignore it, instead pasting a smile on her face. "Yes, that is correct, Mr. Howe." She clenched her teeth, knowing full well this wasn't anything but a test.

Mr. Howe leaned forward but maintained his volume so all could hear. "Tell me. Does he know any tricks?"

Several men snorted and a few gave low chuckles.

"Does he know how to sit and stay?" the lieutenant pressed on and more officers joined, their raucous laughter growing. "Is His

Grace sweet like a Scottish westie pup?" Lieutenant Howe threw his head back, his hooked nose reddening. His and the other officers' guffaws ricocheted through the building.

Charlotte turned to face the rest of the room. Men were leaning against their desks, some wiping tears from their eyes. As she took in their derision directed at her and the supernaturals, Lieutenant Howe stepped close behind and whispered in her ear. "Do tell, what's it like being a wagtail for the weres? "

All the color drained from Charlotte's face at the depraved suggestion. She reacted instinctively, swinging her elbow behind her, aiming it for the lieutenant's voice. It smashed into his nose, and the sickening crack snapped through the officers' laughter.

The lieutenant yelped and Charlotte wheeled around to face him, following through with a right cross square to the eye. The man doubled over, groaning.

Silence fell over the rest of the room.

A door in the hallway opened. Chief Inspector Dawson emerged from his office and took in the frozen policemen and the bloodied face of the lieutenant.

Charlotte avoided the chief's eye as she smoothed her dove-grey pelisse, satisfied no blood had stained the fabric. Then with an air of mock surprise, raised her gaze. "Oh, Chief Inspector. I was just about to knock on your door."

Lieutenant Howe stood and held his hand against his nose, blood already seeping around his fingers. "She hit me," he whined, pointing at Charlotte.

The chief trained his sharp blue eyes onto Charlotte. "Lady Astley?"

She lifted her chin. "The lieutenant and I were discussing my working relationship with the Pack, one that I felt needed clarification. Words were insufficient."

The chief's face remained neutral, but Charlotte saw the corners of his eyes wrinkle in a suppressed smile. "It seems that Lady Astley as made a strong point. One that you," he said to the lieutenant, "were unable to contest." The chief addressed the room at large. "And I imagine there will be no more 'discussions' on this matter?"

The man glared at Charlotte out of the corner of his eye but shook his head at the chief.

"Dismissed," the chief said to the lieutenant. To Charlotte, he gestured down the hall. "Lady Astley, this way."

Charlotte stepped towards the office. The dark wood and deep-blue paint she could see inside were already offering her the remaining bit of calm she needed to completely settle her nerves.

She heard the chief stop walking. Charlotte turned in time to see him facing the lieutenant and officer's room. "Oh, and Mr. Howe? Clean yourself up. You're a mess." The chief pointed derisively at the blood spatters staining the man's collar.

Lieutenant Howe nodded, and Charlotte entered the chief's office without a backward glance.

Charlotte settled herself into the wood-and-leather chair. The studs fastening the leather to the frame were shiny from use. With the exceptions of a map of London, some file cabinets, and some personal effects of the chief's, the office decor was somewhat scant, but the austere colors and spartan atmosphere were soothing.

The chief inspector closed the door and sighed, running a hand over his bald head, then came to sit at his desk. "Did you have to break his nose, lass?" His familiar Scottish burr rolled through the room.

Charlotte shrugged. "He deserved it."

Dawson pulled open a drawer and poured himself a whiskey. "That he may. But it's you who'll pay for it later."

Charlotte folded her arms and now it was her turn to sigh. It was true. She'd taken Howe down more than one peg *and* in front of his fellow officers. It was a debt she'd have to pay tenfold.

She held her hand out for a drink. He hesitated and then handed his glass to her. She took a quick swig, the smokey liquid washing down her throat. Because of Dawson's seniority and authority over the monster hunter position and Charlotte's gender and class, they'd both struggled to maintain a delicate balance between the familiar relationship he and her father had had and the professional relationship he now had with her.

The chief leaned back in his chair reminding Charlotte of when he and her father would spend many late hours discussing Dawson's cases and her father's supernatural research.

Before Dawson could speak, a knock sounded at the door. Policeman Singh entered, carrying a large file under his arm. "The soul-eater file, sir," he said, placing the folder on the chief's desk and then backing up to stand at attention. He turned and quickly bowed to Charlotte. "And Lady Astley, if I may," he said, a smile crossing his face. "S'nice to see you feeling well."

"Thank you," she replied, grateful she knew at least one friendly face within Scotland Yard.

Chief Inspector Dawson opened the file, lifted a pen, and gestured for Charlotte to speak, his demeanor once again that of chief of police. "Begin. And start with Mr. Draper, if you please."

Charlotte clasped her fingers together and leaned forward. She told Dawson everything that had happened since Mr. Draper's body had been found until the events at the St. Bridgemans', finally ending with the portal. She ended by placing the baroness's worn notebook on the desk.

Dawson scowled at the journal, clearly allowing everything to sink in.

"I believe the baroness was using her charity as a cover to find and…consume supernaturals."

The chief paled, the lines of scars on his face turning pink. "I see," he said, rubbing his chin. "And what about the words the victims were whispering? 'Holy,' 'ink,' 'cloud,' and"—the chief paused to consult his file—"'brolly.' What the devil do those all mean?"

"I've been giving this a great deal of thought, and the words, I believe, were imprints, vague concepts the soul-eater was leaving on its victims."

The chief scowled.

"Impressions that the baroness left on her victims and that they were forced to repeat until they died," she explained. "'Ink' was because the baroness in her soul-eater form greatly resembled an octopus. 'Cloud' could refer to this as well, or due to the fact that she could fly."

The chief raised his eyebrows.

Charlotte nodded then continued. "'Holy' was probably due to the 'saint' in St. Bridgeman."

The chief nodded slowly, then jabbed at the file with his finger. "It's this 'brolly' that I just don't understand."

"This has puzzled me as well, and I believe it was because the victim was so young and his grasp of the world was so limited."

The chief opened his mouth to speak, but Charlotte plowed on anticipating his question. "The 'brolly' was most likely referring to the shape an octopus makes when its tentacles and web are completely open." Charlotte splayed her fingers as a visual example. "Which, to a young child, would resemble an umbrella."

"But why mutilate the bodies?" The chief stood and paced behind his desk.

"I'm not entirely sure. We do know that supernatural souls provided her with more sustenance, so perhaps mutilating the bodies did so even more. Or she could have just been trying to destroy evidence. Many killers increase in violence with each victim." Memories of Liza and Johnathan and their young babes flooded her mind, and she tried to shut them out.

The chief fell still, and the room was silent for a moment. "Nasty business," the chief murmured, then he took a drink from his glass.

Charlotte nodded. "I have kept quiet about the true nature of the soul-eater, counting on your desire for discretion, sir."

"Yes, a wise idea, Lady Astley." Dawson finished his drink and returned to his desk. "I'll be glad to officially close this case." He gathered the baroness's notebook and moved to place it in the file with the other papers.

Charlotte raised her hand to stop him.

"Sir, I was hoping I could keep her journal. I believe there is more about the aether and her other experiments, and I'd like to have a crack at translating it." She felt her features twist as she voiced one of her concerns that had been sprouting in the back of her mind, growing since she'd woken up after the soul-eater attack. "I also believe the strange storm that threatened the *Asteria* was another portal."

The chief cursed and Charlotte heard Mr. Singh suck in a breath, reminding her that he was still in the room.

"Are you certain?" Dawson asked.

"Yes, sir. The storm and the portal were nearly identical."

"But why did it appear in the sky? You said the baroness was with you at the time."

Charlotte nodded and began pacing. "The portal in the cavern didn't appear very stable. If the aetherial opening truly is so unstable, it's possible that more than one portal was opened. These portals could have appeared indiscriminately at different time and in different parts of London. Possibly even when the baroness's machine was powered down and not in use."

The implications were clear. Such unstable portals would not limit themselves to appearing in deep caverns and an almost isolated sky—they could materialize in alleys or palaces, in kitchens or courtyards in London and beyond.

Chief Dawson sighed at Charlotte's words, then he pulled out the notebook and handed it to her. "Tell me of your findings."

"Of course, sir," Charlotte said, tucking the notebook in her reticule.

"Mr. Singh." Dawson stood and held the file toward the policeman, who stepped forward.

"Yes, sir?"

"Take this down to records and see that it's filed properly. I know I can also count on you to remain silent as to what we've discussed in here today."

Mr. Singh nodded and turned to leave.

"Oh, and Mr. Singh. Lady Astley here telescribed earlier and mentioned you'd been of special help on this case."

"Sir, it was my pleasure." Mr. Singh executed another precise bow, then closed the door behind him.

Chief Dawson fixed a firm stare at Charlotte. "I'm glad you're on the mend. Good work, Charlotte." He nodded his satisfaction at her work, then sat back down at his desk and immediately fell into some paperwork. She had clearly been dismissed.

She leaned toward the desk and cleared her throat, suddenly a little nervous. What if he said no?

"Sir, about the proposal I mentioned in my message."

The chief raised his eyes from his desk warily. Dawson was an old enough friend of her father's to have witnessed her antics as a curious young girl. He had seen her petition her father for a chemistry set, for fencing and shooting lessons. He'd also seen Charlotte indulged in exploring several other unladylike pursuits—like monster hunting. "Yes, what is it?"

"Actually, this is inspiration from my aunt," she said, her confidence growing with each word.

At this, Dawson heaved an enormous sigh and rubbed at his bald head again. "What does Hespa have to do with any of this?" Having attended a handful of Aunt Hespa's dinner parties, he had witnessed first hand the sometimes sometimes strained relationship of the two women.

A mischievous glint sparked in Charlotte's eye. Aunt Hespa's words from last night echoed in her mind. *You are a lone woman.* Her aunt would, of course, be livid about Charlotte's interpretation of her words, but there was nothing the woman could do about it. She herself had given Charlotte the idea.

"Out with it, lass." Chief Inspector Dawson leaned back in his chair and clapped his hands behind his head, looking at the ceiling. "Hurry, before I change my mind."

Charlotte smiled, her own mind in high gear, anticipating possible arguments and counterarguments. She leaned over the desk, resting her weight on her fingers. "Sir, how would you feel about putting together a monster hunter team?"

Chief Dawson closed his eyes, then he stood and strode to the door. He grabbed a junior officer, his deep baritone filling both the office and the hallway.

"You, grab Mr. Singh and bring him back here. Tell him to come prepared to take notes."

Charlotte shifted happily in her seat as the officer scurried off to follow orders.

The desk chair creaked as the chief settled into it once more and poured himself another whiskey. He downed it in one gulp, then picked up a pencil and tapped it against the desk.

"All right, Charlotte. Tell me about this team."

# Acknowledgments

Hello, dear reader! Thank you so much for reading and thank you for reading this far! I used to think that reading and writing was a solitary affair, but I can assure you, it takes a village. In no particular order, I'd like to introduce you to and thank my village.

Thanks to my husband and children who have cheered and pushed me through and who I hope see that the pursuit of dreams is hard and worthwhile. My dear kiddies, never give up. Hubby, thanks for believing in me and getting behind me each step of the way.

Thanks to Ruth for suggesting I write a short story for a portal contest in the first place. Thank you for all the writing sessions and more.

Thanks to my writing gals of DWENT (Christene Houston, Marleen Gunnerson, Amelia Kynaston, Garaghty Bayne, Jenny Esplin, Veeda Bybee, Soquel Baumgardner, Meslissa Buckely, and

Bonnie Hopkinson). I'm latching onto your collective wagon and am amazed at the view among the stars. Thank you, DWENT-ers, who have cheered me from afar and are close to my heart. I count you as some of my dearest friends.

Thanks to Soquel Baumgardner who is a diamond and read almost as much of Charlotte as I have. For alpha, beta, anytime reads and of course, for all the emotional support and dear friendship. For all the tears and topics covered and shared—moving, parents, families, pets, kids—you know, life. The universe. Everything. Thank you.

Thanks to Kayla, Emma, and Suzanne—who took Charlotte and her madcap adventures in hand and worked with me to finesse the novella and a big thank you to Suzanne who helped watch it turn into a novel. Thank you so much.

Ashely Olsen deserves a special thanks for my last minute begging to help search for bad writing. And for helping me realize that imposter syndrome can strike anytime anywhere, but it simply means one cares deeply for their work.

And thanks to Stu whose D and D experience and killer training protocol led to some fascinating conversation and brainstorming sessions. You were key in creating the baroness and her dastardly deeds. I believe we've proven that stronger muscles make for stronger stories.

A special thanks to anyone I may have forgotten. Please forgive me. It was not intentional.

# About the Author

Rebecca Gage writes to cope with the horrors of not being a vampire, werewolf, or other supernatural being. She escaped her mundane non-magical roots and managed to get an education with lots of writing credentials behind her. She even placed first in a writing contest—she may or may not have been its only contestant. She resides in Colorado with her husband and a gaggle of children, and she is plotting how to secretly raise chickens without getting caught by her HOA.